EXCELLER
SELECT

TOP PICKS

The Winged One

The Winged One

A Collection of Short Stories

Binod Ghosal

Translated by
Dr. Chandrajyoti Sen Majumder

EXCELLER BOOKS®
A GLOBAL PRESS

The Winged One
A Collection of Short Stories

Cover by Exceller Books

ISBN: 978-93-48892-58-4

First published in India in 2025 by Exceller Books,
An imprint of GE Group
Address: G1, Dream Apartment, Degree College Road, Belgharia,
Kolkata, 700056, India
www.excellerbooks.com

EXCELLER BOOKS®
A GLOBAL PRESS

To Baba

Author's Note

At our home, my father had a personal cupboard, locked away from everyone's sight, with keys tied to his sacred thread. Sometimes, he would open it in private, while my mother, elder sister, and I were forbidden to peek inside. From childhood, I had an intense desire to know what was in it, but I never had the chance. On the day of his funeral, I took the key from the sacred thread hanging from his lifeless body and finally unlocked the cupboard. I must admit I shuddered with fear, worried that my deceased father might be angry with me for opening it. But I opened it anyway. I could smell my father's scent everywhere inside. There were old copper coins, photographs of gods and goddesses, keys to lost locks, a few hundred currencies, and a diary that my father used to write in. One by one, I pulled out these items, and then… a bundle of torn papers, pages from notebooks and diaries, clipped together, came into my hands.

Those were pages I had discarded over time during my book writing process—pages I had discarded without a second thought. But I'm not sure when my father had gathered them behind my back and collected them in the secret corner of his favorite cupboard. I believe that's why he used to advise me: even if you don't find something useful, never discard it, because someday it might be of use. Perhaps that's why I don't discard any of my write-ups completely; instead, I keep them separately somewhere else. While authoring the foreword to my book, I don't know why this memory came back to me. What else I could write now?

I loved acting in amateur drama and later in group theaters during my younger days. I also used to paint. But as I grew older, I left painting and turned to writing poetry. However, my poetry always stayed inside my diaries and never saw the light of day. After graduating from college, my group of friends and I used to hang out at the local rickshaw stand, smoking bidis. Once, a friend's mother passed away, and I saw the face of a beautiful person horribly distorted after death. The thought kept coming back to me, and the sound of my soul pushed me to express something. A few days later, the feelings erupted into writing. I wrote a story, and it made me feel lighter inside. The story stayed in oblivion until a senior from my locality invited me to read one of my write-ups at a literary meet.

While searching for something suitable to read, I suddenly remembered this story. I took it to the meet and read it aloud. People praised me and insisted that I send it to *Desh* magazine. I followed. In a few months' time, it was published. That was my first story, *Ekti Jibaner Barnana* (A Description of a Piece of Life). The day I received the letter of appreciation from Desh magazine for the story, my father was the happiest person. He kept the letter with him, kept reading it and didn't want to part with it. That was just the beginning, in the year 2003.

I have asked myself many times: What do I want to write? What content do I love to write the most? I could never find a suitable answer, only silence. So, I stopped asking. I understood that I am as helpless as anyone else. The more I try to mask the pain of my helplessness, the more I expose it to myself. I try to express this pain. I'm not claiming to have succeeded, but I try.

I will always be grateful to my readers, who have, at least once, picked up my book, flipped through its pages, and read its words. I thank them, as well as those who have not done so.

Table of Contents

A Description of a Piece of Life

I

While the lifeless body of Maa was being stretchered away to the gate, ready to be placed on the cargo bed of the waiting mini truck, Romit momentarily noticed the face of the girl. Amidst the weeping crowd of relatives, she wore a different expression—dejected but different.

Bubai intervened, asking, "Are you carrying the death certificate?"

Romit gestured in the direction his uncle had gone, "He might have it."

"Where's uncle? I will make some extra copies of it quickly." Bubai hurried off to search for Romit's uncle.

Romit ascended the truck. His brother-in-law gently advised, "Go and sit by Maa's head. Make sure to keep your hand on her."

People seemed to be treating Romit with unusually high affection today. Why were they suddenly treating him like a celebrity just because he had lost a parent? Would they start asking for his autograph next? By daybreak, these dollops of extra care were beginning to make him uncomfortable. It was sinking in, though, with the passing hours. Such tender care from loved ones during this time of excruciating pain felt like a balm, and Romit couldn't agree more. After all, a man in his thirties who couldn't manage a proper nine-to-five job—apart from a handful of tuitions—shouldn't expect such care. Romit knows that. And he doesn't. A couple of outdoor sales jobs are all he could manage so far in life. The first one was selling nylon brooms and floor cleaners for a meagre ₹1,200 a month. After a month of hard work and earning more swear words than money from potential customers, he realised the pay wasn't worth the humiliation. His next job paid slightly better—₹1,800 a month—and involved selling water purifiers, claiming to purify gutter water into drinking water. But after just five days of walking Kolkata's streets under the blazing mid-summer sun, he ended up with jaundice and fifty days of suffering; he gave up.

"How is your father doing in all of this?" Dipu asked Romit.

"He is doing well. My sister is staying with him. My younger uncle's there too."

He answered, but Romit knew well that it was hard to assess his father's feelings. Last year, his father suffered a heart stroke and slipped on the staircase at the bank while going to withdraw his monthly pension. The accident left him completely paralysed. He can't speak a word since. Now, lying on his back, he keeps dumb sighting the walls. The two open eyes are blank, almost like a dead fish. Who can say what he's feeling now? He probably understands everything but fails to express it. Is he in sorrow? Does he cry deep inside? It might even help if he could cry. A person like him should …

Meanwhile, the familiar face of the girl appeared again; Romit was merely sitting, touching her mother's lifeless body. The girl put on a glance and went aboard the blue van standing nearby to ferry relatives to the funeral. It means the girl is a part of today's funeral party. Romit felt good. But why is he feeling good? It surprises him. The car belongs to his elder uncle. It means the girl must be known to him. Romit tried hard to remember if he had seen her face in the past. He failed. It made him feel uneasy, puzzled. He argued inside that he was probably mistaken. She might not be a known one but rather an acquaintance. After all, people usually come closer to each other during hardship—for example, Romit's brother-in-law. The kind of person he is, he won't even romance his wife without a proper cause, but now he is serving the family voluntarily. Romit's sister, after a marriage to an affluent family, has also turned into a showpiece. Seemingly beautiful but without any effectiveness. She came today clad in a soft pink saree and blouse. Why so? Because light-coloured clothing suits a funeral home? No more can he think of all these. A fly sat on Maa's lips. Romit shooed it off. The bright, glaring sunrays have fallen on her face. An umbrella would have been of help. Meanwhile, the mini truck's engine started. Friends who are supposed to accompany quickly boarded. The trailing blue van completed the little convoy of the funeral party. Maa probably didn't know the meaning of convoy. She would have been glad to learn. There are a bunch of incense sticks burning by the stretcher. Thick smoke is burning the eyes. Romit eyed the van in the following. The girl can't be seen inside. Can the girl see him?

"Oh, forgot to take auntie's footmarks on a piece of paper," Ayan lamented.

Romit frowned, "Umm Hmm, not required."

His brother-in-law chipped in with support, saying, "Oh no, those were old-dated practices." He would have added more had his phone not rung up in the middle from his chest pocket. He quickly took the call –"Hello... Hmm... AT 7... Okay". And he put it off.

Romit could make it now that his brother-in-law would be signing off from the funeral at around seven. Maybe some office meeting has cropped up. He is an executive, after all. A busy man like him may even have to attend a meeting after expiring. The word *expiry* brought Romit back to the present, and instantly, the girl's face came to his mind. But he tried to distract himself immediately and looked around. Sujoy is throwing popped rice on the way. Popped rice and paisa. A few minutes earlier, a handful of children had been sprinting behind the vehicle, lured by those. They collected a few paisas. But now they have withdrawn. After all, how long can little children keep pace with running cars? In a roadside shop, the sound of a cheering crowd alerted everyone. The funeral party convoy had to stop by as the traffic signal turned red. A sudden "O-U-T" shout explained why the crowd was cheering and people were dancing. Today, the India-Australia cricket match was scheduled. Someone in the Australian team must have been struck out. The roads are adorned in the colour of the Indian national flag on both sides. The pomp has crossed the extent of even India's Independence Day celebration. Friends at the funeral party tried their best to catch a glimpse of the television to get an update on the burst of joy and happiness.

Poor fellows had to sacrifice their enjoyment to accompany Romit. It is such an injustice when people die on match days.

As the cars rolled into the funeral centre at Nimtala, the sight scenes changed in a whisker. The peculiarity of the spot is sheerly unexplained. The residents here are all too tired of watching funerals and counting deaths. They are too blunt to express sensitivity towards a family recently experiencing a loss. Nobody seemed to look at them even after their two cars arrived at the venue. A small group of people had laid a towel and were playing cards. They kept playing. Someone was laughing loudly at the crack of a joke. Dark-tanned street children were fooling around. Nobody seemed disturbed at their sight. Romit's brother-in-law said in a hastened voice, "Bubai, follow me to the funeral office clerk with all the necessary documents. Others may please bring down the body from the car."

Body! Just the day before tomorrow, he came to ask, "How are you doing, Maa?" While hastily climbing down the truck, his brother-in-law slipped slightly. He bit his lips. Probably, the slip hurt him in the legs. His eyes seemingly shrivelled in pain, and he started hobbling like a lame while walking towards the office. While everyone was bringing down Maa's stretcher, Romit looked at the blue van behind from the corner of his eyes. The rest of the uncles and aunts got out of the car. Where's the girl? Hadn't she come? But she boarded alright. Oh. There she is. Alighting at the end. Maa is being laid in front of the funeral office room. His Brother-in-law, meanwhile, has finished the official work. He returned to Romit and informed him, "All works are done, you see. Now we only have to arrange the puja items and your white dress." Completing his words, he turned to Sujoy, "Sujoy, go to the funeral priest, make a list of items required and buy them. No more hastening is required. We have ample time in hand now. There's already a body inside the furnace. We will have our turn only after that. Keep the money." He handed two hundred rupees notes. Sujoy went off along with Ayan and Dipu.

Next, his brother-in-law left Romit alone and went off for a quick smoke. Romit, too, was eager to smoke a cigarette, but then who would keep company with Maa in her last few moments?

Suddenly, Romit's elder uncle and his family arrived. The mysterious girl, too, is accompanying them.

"What are you doing by yourself? Where are the rest of your companions?" Auntie asked.

"They got chores to complete."

The girl is standing barely four feet away. Romit could now see her—middle height, slim, wearing a yellow salwar kameez, complete with a white dupatta. A pretty fair complexion and brownish hair; Romit thought those must be smeared with henna. The hot weather has shot blood on her face. The weather is too harsh today. The shape of her face is so much like... Romit was once again trying to gather himself amidst his wild thoughts. Maa covers too much of his mind, making him think like this. Romit does not wish to remember this pale white face of Maa with eyes covered by basil leaves and cotton balls pushed into nostrils. Instead, he would remember how, in his childhood, Maa used to pull him onto her soft, cosy lap and cuddle him, but neither did he want to get carried away in the thoughts. Romit falls back to the present. He won't think of the past. What if tears start to roll out of emotion? The girl always notices him with quick stares and then promptly looks away. Why is she stealing a look? Who's she? He can ask nobody. The whole family of uncles and aunts behave as if she's not even present here. What if she's not a reality? Oh, Romit thought he was going crazy. He needs some fresh air.

"Uncle, can you stay back with Maa for some moments? I will come back soon." Romit made a quick glance at the girl and took a walk towards the furnace. It has a shivering, cold atmosphere. But there's a noticeable warmth, too. Romit moves away from the place. There is a flight of steps on the bank of the Ganga River, and at the corner of the first step, two persons are sitting, immersed in a very philosophical conversation. Romit overhears, "Hey, mark my words, this burning of the dead in their last journey of life is an unnecessary ritual because the whole life, one can only avoid burning in his own karma." The listener nodded calmly. Possibly, someone among his parents is inside the furnace, but he does not look upset. People who lose parents at a mature age like this don't appear to be disturbed. The man is bald and, therefore, is not even required to tonsure his head as per the funeral ritual. Romit looked away. The vista of the Ganga seems so dull, so quiet, much like the lack of lustre in the glasses of a poor old man. Romit couldn't enjoy his sight anymore. He moved back where Maa had been laid.

His brother-in-law and friends had returned by then. Another corpse has arrived in the queue—another woman. The two bodies are lying side by side. They appeared identical. A lady is weeping monotonously beside the other *body*. There are no tears, though. Probably, they dried up.

His brother-in-law retorted, "Hold the cot tight; it's our turn now." *Our turn*—the phrase sounded very harsh. But who would tell him that. He now hastily pulls up one corner of the dead's cot on his shoulder. He always acts in excess whenever uncle and auntie are around. Romit too has to join in holding one corner of the cot but a hollowness is spreading inside him. His heart is going numb at the thought that Maa is set on her final journey now. She will never return. The body which is dead will be lost forever. No one can meet her ever again when one has the strongest urge to meet. Maa has got rid of all her flowers and garland adorning. She is laid before the furnace, shifted on a scaffolding of a cot made of bamboo lath. The bamboo laths are too sharpened in places. The priest made Romit sit beside him to do the ablution ritual, and then gave him a handful of rice and black sesame in an earthen pot. "Mix them with this banana," he instructed.

All in the funeral stood in a circle around Romit and his Maa. Romit's hands shuddered. The girl is standing by him really close.

"Now roll the mixture in balls. Take one of those between your thumb and the forefinger like this and repeat after me…"

The priest was carrying on with his instructions, but those hardly went in his ears; Romit could only think that Maa had gone forever. Completely gone. None of her part will be staying back. Now, who remains in this world to be described as close to Romit… The Norwester locked inside for this long under the numbness of his heart and now stumbled inside his whole body. The veins, arteries and every little fibre inside are getting shattered, the skull is grinding, the bones are breaking, even the rib cage...

but still what amazed Romit is the fact that he's still not crying, absolutely no tears! And then a drop of water fell on his hand. What is this? He thought. Is it tear? Is that girl crying his share of cry? Let her, then. Let her cry till her last breadth. Till her death. But Romit didn't look back. He wouldn't dare. What if she's not crying? What if the drop is no tear? Then..?

Tears or no tears, rice-sesame-banana mixed blobs are adorning Maa's neck. Tears or no tears, dollops of ghee are oozing from Maa's limbs and mouth. Over and above, there's nothing but a white shroud on Maa's body. Someone has untied the amulet fixed on a red thread on Maa's waist. After circling her with the burning jute sticks, Romit managed a look at her face. The face is looking so distorted. So scary. Barely recognisable. Before touching those burning sticks to her mouth, Romit shuddered and closed his eyes. And after that... There was nothing more after that. The iron trolley rolled, Maa riding it, inside the opening of the burning furnace. Romit, for the last time, once and for all, looked on and looked away from the sight. The white shroud caught fire almost immediately after it entered. The furnace door dropped with a bang. The numbness again caught hold of Romit. He started feeling all the tiredness of the world. His legs keep shivering. His brother-in-law and friends quickly grabbed him and took him away from the place. They got to the bank of Ganga. "Sit here. Are you feeling sick? Will you have a cup of tea?" his brother-in-law asked.

Romit gathered himself, "I am alright. I won't have anything now. Rather if you can arrange something for my friends, that will be good. They have been working on empty stomachs since the morning."

Sujoy and Ayan promptly denied, "You don't have to think about us now."

But Romit's brother-in-law keeps insisting, "How can that be? You all have been working hard since morning. It's such a shame that I haven't cared about that. I will make it up now. I'm very sorry, fellas. Can you find a good restaurant around here for me?"

Dipu answered, "Please don't be busy with these thoughts now. None of us will eat now. It will take hardly an hour more."

But unable to restrict the excessive eagerness of the brother-in-law, they finally agreed to have tea.

Meanwhile, the phrase *hardly an hour more* buzzed inside Romit's head. He kept getting disturbed by the thought of how the fifty-six years long life could end in "hardly an hour more."

Ayan said, "You people go. I will be staying by Romit."

Romit protests, "You too, go with them. I'm fine. I will be by myself."

"Okay, but don't go far now," his brother-in-law agrees, leading the little pack of friends to a nearby tea shop. Close by, Romit's uncles and aunties are sitting in light conversation. Their topic centres around sublime stories of Maa, her good deeds, her greatness etc. All could be seen as being in pretty good moods. The Ganga, too, is seemingly now flowing with a revived vigour. Romit's eyes searched for those two gentlemen chatting at the steps a while ago. Perhaps their philosophic statement at the moment could have been, "Take it from me, brother, death never calls in grief. Actually, the atmosphere does so." It is pretty clear that expressing grief over the news of someone's death is more of a show of courtesy, a sociable practice everyone picks up as a liability. Ending the liability ushers, in a sense, a relief among all humans and even others... But where's the girl? Romit now realises that, since Maa entered the furnace, there hasn't been a glimpse of the girl. Surprising! Then, is it what he's thinking... Nah! Oh, there she is, standing by herself by the flight of steps on the river bank, standing and eyeing Romit. The wind blowing from the river has tightened her dress around her curves. Romit quickly tried to look away from her. He doesn't want to think this way now. The girl at least could have come to him to comfort. She could have said a word or two of solace... No, he would think no more of the girl. It's far better to recoup by himself. But how? In what way can he do so by himself? He falls short of ideas. He looks back the way. Uff, there's no sign of the girl again.

Meanwhile, the group of his friends and brother-in-law returned after the short tea break. They're even carrying tea for those who have stayed back. His uncles and aunts got tea cups. Bubai holds a teacup to him, "Have it; you will feel better. Need a biscuit?" Romit nodded in denial mode for the biscuit. He silently took the teacup, though. The tea has already released its heat.

After quickly finishing the cup in two long sips, he restrained himself from throwing the empty cup into the river. Looking around, he finds this old banyan tree. Under it are the ramshackled remains of a statue of the planet King Shani. He put the cup down there in a stilly manner. Bubai looked into his watch and announced, "It's almost time to wrap. You stay here. Let me get the news," and he went off.

Some more time flew away in the wind. And then brother-in-law's voice could be heard, "Romit, come along. It's done."

Romit rises. There's still smoke trickling from the heated furnace. They alighted down by the side of it to collect the remains of the navel in an earthen urn. When water is poured over the fiery reddened umbilicus, a lump of smoke clouded out of the urn, almost taking Romit's breath away. Everyone poured water by turn. Then, without looking back, Romit smacked the urn behind him as the ritual says, and thereafter, collecting Maa's last remains pressed inside Ganga clay, he climbed up with an earthenware. The mortal remains are the navel of a human body. The connection of life has been so strong that even a heat storm at six thousand degrees Celsius couldn't burn it down. If the navel part can be immortal, why can't the whole human stay back forever?

While immersing the last remains in the earthenware, a feeling crept inside Romit's mind: how millions and billions of human remains are doing with one another under the riverbed, how they will meet Romit's Maa today. Possibly, Maa will usher a new marine life deep under their community. There's no name for their relationships. But only recognition.

"Do not go deeper. Take three dips and come up," Auntie shouted. Romit doesn't have the habit of diving. As he struggled to dive, the water buoyed him up. Closing the pores of his ears, he made some crude efforts what roughly looked like diving and slowly made his way back to dry land. His skin is well visible under the wet white clothing. He noticed it and quickly wrapped the towel around the waist. While taking out the new set of white cloth from the packet, brother-in-law advised, "Pat dry your head, and hair. Otherwise, this untimely bath might cause a cough or cold."

Romit calmly answered, "Okay. Let me dress first."

Tying a dhoti correctly is a challenging art which Romit couldn't manage, and he finally had to seek the help of his uncle. Meanwhile, Romit tried looking around. All but the girl were present. He felt relieved that he didn't have to dress before an unknown girl. Two children came along. They asked for the abandoned wet cloth, "Uncle, can we have this?" they eagerly extended their hands. While his brother-in-law was about to scold them, Romit's uncle acted kindly, "Let them take it. After all, those are of no use to us now."

The children gleefully accepted the alms and ran off. Romit, dressed in white, his brother-in-law, declared, "Let's go back home then."

Romit started shivering even on this hot summer afternoon. Maybe his hair was still wet from the late bath. Maybe there is still water dripping from his hair. The mini truck, which carried his Maa's body to this place, now feels so empty. All except the cot is in place. Romit looked towards the blue van in the trail. The girl must have boarded as well. But he is feeling a headache, perhaps because of the blowing wind.

His Brother-in-law reminded him, "Choose a good single photograph of Maa in the night after returning home. Tomorrow we will take it to frame."

Returning to the house, friends from the funeral party followed the ritual of biting neem leaves and touching an iron knife. They then had a rosogolla each, and they left for the day. The house, though, swarmed with relatives and visitors. Romit went straight to his father's room. His Baba is still lying on his back as he always does. He went closer to his face to check if he could discover drops of tears in the corners of those expressionless glaring eyes. After ending the search, he retires to his room for the night.

II

The clock struck and went past eleven in the night. The tired lot in the house had retired to sleep after a strenuous day. Nobody switched off the light tonight. Why? In fear? The funeral priest repeated the word "Spirit" several times while chanting the mantra. It was hurting Romit every time. He would have indeed protested, had he been younger – "My Maa is not some spirit."… But since the return, Romit hasn't noticed the girl yet. Why? It's not something that he can ask his aunties. They may mock, "Really, amid such trauma, how can you even ask about some girl?" But the more surprising thing is how they did not mention the girl even once. Why? – Uggh! Meaningless thinking is eating his sleep away! Ohh, amidst all the business, he missed taking out a good photograph of Maa. Tomorrow it will be taken to be framed. There's an album in Baba's room. Romit walked into his father's room. The man was sleeping like a baby. Romit took the album from his shelf and sat on the floor. Most of the photographs are from his sister's marriage ceremony, and there is no single photo of Maa. All are group photos. The rest were clicked during their Nainital trip. There's a single photo among those, but the click by a poor camera resulted in such a small image that it does not suit the purpose. After all, Maa's dead, and one only requires the face part of a dead one, which can be remembered easily. The other parts are quickly forgotten.

Oh, but isn't there another album on the shelf too? Where's that? He looked around the shelf among Maa's sarees and Baba's clothing, carefully inspecting every part. Lastly, he could rescue the prized possession from the locker of the safe. An album in the safe, how priceless it is!

It's a thick, black album book. The whole book smells of the old days. Romit couldn't even remember the last time he saw it. Possibly, that happened during his forgotten childhood. Romit concentrates on turning the pages. Black-and-white old-dated photographs. Even those whites are smeared in sepia tone. There are marriage photographs of Maa-Baba, page after page. Many unknown faces crowded those. While frisking through those pages containing their honeymoon pictures in Puri, a photo on the left leaf suddenly hit him hard inside his head. Romit is startled at the sight. He panics. Who's this? Is this... Is this the girl whom he had been spotting the whole day long? Standing in front with the sea in the back. Possibly, Romit's father had clicked the picture. The violent sea breeze had made the yellow dress tighten around her chest, much like the girl standing by the river this afternoon watching Romit—the same look. Romit started shivering. Slowly, he took out the photograph from the album page. As he touches the surface of the picture, his hands shuddered. There's something scribbled behind. Romit read it. "Tapu, my sweetheart." It's Baba's hand written praises. Just below it, someone has written in very untidy handwriting, "Issh, all your praises are false." No, Maa's handwriting was never good. Even her spellings are wrong. Romit looked up to his father. This is the man—the white hairs flowing under the swirling fan blades. The skin has wrinkled around the corners of his eyes. Saliva dried up beside his lips. This is the bed where Baba Maa had playfully written these words on some old nights like today. He returned the photograph to where it belonged and looked to the next page. There's one photograph of Romit, which must have been taken during his infancy. Kohl smeared eyes, tied long hairs, moving forward, raising both hands. Maa and his photographs are fixed face to face. As he was closing the book, Romit watched with awe how the mysterious girl was getting in between those raised hands of the infant. The baby inside him.

Blank Space

Bijan felt a bone-chilling thrill as soon as he woke up in the morning. He was about to leave the bed but couldn't rest his feet on the floor. At first, Bijan thought he was perhaps unmindful and still in his imagination. He blinked both eyes and then coughed loudly to check if he was still in his slumber. But the sound of his phlegm-stricken cough assured his ears that he was jolly well awakened. He tried again to put those feet on the ground, but Alas! He missed again.

He pressed harder to touch those feet to the ground. He still couldn't. Repeated efforts yield nothing. The feet could never reach where they intended. They stopped a couple of inches above ground in the air every time. He tried a foot one at a time, but luck didn't change. Then he noticed that his body was not quite touching the bed either. Nay, he's not feeling perturbed out of fear; rather, a stronger feeling crept into his mind—this must be the hangover from last night's booze party. The one Anik threw at the Trinca's restaurant. Anik is an Income Tax Officer. The month he earns more in bribes and sops, he treats his close friends at famous bars and clubs in the city. But then, on second thought, even that seemed to be a far-flung imagination because, as far as Bijan could remember, he hadn't taken more than four pegs. And four pegs of spirit hardly worry his stomach.

"What the fu**" grunted, Bijan finally stood up on his feet. But they were not on the ground but in the blank void a couple of inches above. This made his head spin. And he sat back in panic. What's all this about, he thought, which he failed to understand. Then he found the television in the room still on but mute. He understood it must have been running since last night, as he sure had fallen asleep while still watching TV, lying in the bed. Quickly, he took the TV remote in hand from beside his pillow to switch it off, but then, on second thought, he casually started surfing the channels. Suddenly, his fingers stopped at a Regional News channel broadcasting the unsettling chaos that had gripped the city. On-screen, the entire population was shown floating above the ground—as if humanity had collectively lost the earth beneath their feet. Bijan turned up the volume, and the television blared with a live telecast featuring a bewildered journalist narrating the events:

"...This is seemingly a situation that's unheard of ever. The earth's gravitational force has unnaturally reduced worldwide for unknown reasons. It remains unchanged, though, for the rest of all matters and substance, organisms and objects, birds and animals on the earth, but for the humans. It seems Earth no longer attracts man. Till now, no one understands the real reason behind this ..."

Bijan couldn't take this anymore and turned off the TV. At first, he started laughing at the situation, but then anger replaced the laugh. He started having a feeling that today's plan is going to get jeopardised. It felt dreary. "You swine, son of a bit... Couldn't you get a better day to show your tricks," Bijan tried in vain to kick the ground under his feet, but instead, he got a kickback from the blank space down under. He sprained his groin. Confused and shattered, he sat back on the bed. Or, rather, he tried something like that to think over what he should do next.

Actually, after months of efforts, his target had finally agreed to take the bait today. So today, Saturday, he made an elaborate plan to go on a pleasure trip to Gadiara with Rosy Patra. Bijan Karmakar is a senior sales manager at a reputed multinational company. He is thirty-four and lives in a twelve hundred square feet apartment on his own. He was not really alone, though, as he got his chef-cum-butler Rabi and chauffer Alam staying by him there. The woman, Rosy Patra, is a sales executive who joined the company six months ago. Her interviewer was Bijan himself. Though she's twenty-six by age, she looks at least a couple of years younger. Starting from her figure, complexion, and facial edifice to her very feminine torso, arms, and even underarms are just perfect. But it took Bijan significantly more effort to persuade her to agree. This was unexpected, as the previous ones had been relatively easy hunts. None of the ladies took more than a couple of months to give in to Bijan's proposal. While sleeping, Bijan always finds girls the same, but for each of them, he has to make completely different efforts, thus discovering himself as a different person every time tackling them. This thing somewhere defeats Bijan's male ego and adds unease to his poise so that he can't enjoy all of them being the same person he actually is. The uneasiness hurts him so much that he once even planned to visit a psychiatrist for some therapeutic relief. That hasn't happened yet, though. Meanwhile, Rosy Patra finally relented much in the line of her predecessors. But she refused to visit Bijan's house, citing the reason that one of her relatives lives nearby. However, she won't have a problem if they meet somewhere else. As per the plan, so now Bijan has to drive down to Rabindra Sadan at eight in the morning to pick her up, and from there on, both will drive to their destination. Bijan switched his mobile on. The two digital hands touched each other on the welcome screen. Before dialling, Bijan tried changing the TV channel. In one English Channel, there was a debate going on between two experts. One black man, Dr. Robson by name and Environmental scientist by profession was vigorously swaying hands and explaining,

"It's pollution, only pollution that's to be blamed for the present situation. For years on end, we kept alerting everyone about this, but nobody's been listening to it. That for ages and generations, humans spread poison in water, air, earth and sky, and Mother Nature is taking revenge for that."

'Revenge', now that's a word that rings so much pleasure to his ears, Bijan doesn't know why.

The geologist present in the TV debate, whose name vanished from the screen even before Bijan could make out the spelling shown onscreen, asked,

"Why are you calling it a revenge? It can also be that, due to some unknown reasons, Earth accidentally lost some of its gravitational force."

"Well, if you think so, then how will you explain the fact that only humans are facing this issue while plants-animals-birds and none of the other objects are facing any less gravity."

"That may be what is happening due to some structural anomaly in human bodies..." mindless debates are going haywire and becoming unbearable, but Bijan noticed it and switched off the TV. In a flash, Rosy's figure came before his eyes. He promptly dialled her number. By her caller tune, Kishore Kumar sang "Rimjhim Girey sawan" and poured some honey in the ears for quite some time, and then the phone owner herself picked up and emptied all the sultry sweetness in the world,

"Good morning, Sir. How do you do?"

"Yes, morning. What's the news?"

"As same as all across the city. Couldn't understand what's happening around."

"Hmm, but will you go?"

"Sure sir. I don't have any problem; I mean, I already have managed it too at home for the day ..."

"Fine, there won't be a problem from my side either. Don't be late."

"I won't, Sir." Bijan was not sure, but did her parting words mix with deep breath? Bijan tried not to overthink and instead concentrated on getting ready for the day quickly. But it only turned out to be a futile battle in the loo and a waste of time until Bijan surrendered and moved under the shower with the toothbrush. Bijan loves to bath for longer times while preparing himself; it's his favourite part, and it gives him a beautiful feeling of cleansing and body purifying. Bijan was not sure even that's some kind of psychiatric incongruity or not. After spending a clear forty minutes under the shower, Bijan finally decided to pat dry, dress up and go to the breakfast table. There his butler Rabi was standing by the table, draping a fear all over the face, hanging a few inches above the ground. Bijan floated to his chair and amusingly asked,

"What's the matter, why are you panicking?"

"Isn't it God cursing upon us, sir? Afterall there are so many sins taking place around!"

"It's alright, everything will be okay soon. Don't be afraid."

Still looking dreaded and dejected, Rabi silently moved back to the kitchen, hovering in the void. Bijan quickly finished his sandwich and juice, put important few things inside a tiny kit bag and then quickly drove away in his hatchback Santro car towards Rabindra Sadan. He had relieved Alam for the day. It was an easy drive in the city today as streets have the least traffic. Even shops are mostly closed. Is this all out of a fright of the unknown? Bijan felt funny. He could notice a few passers-by. All were floating few inches above the ground. Some standing, some moving. Those who are moving are appearing in a peculiar motion, pushing the emptiness underneath. He even found a morning walker dredging both of his feet clumsily through the air while his pet canine was trotting normally on its all fours by the pavement sniffing the air. The man is holding his pet's chain and was literally dragged by it himself. Bijan thought people nowadays easily get frightened on surprising natural phenomena. Bijan put a brake before Rabindra Sadan. There is a lone loony sitting comfortably on the pavement. How could he? Isn't a loony a human too? Bijan was still lost in thought when Rosy finally arrived, slightly out of breath, just as the clock hands edged past nine in the morning. She wore a royal blue saree paired with a sleeveless blouse, radiating elegance. She's panting, "I'm extremely sorry Sir for being late. There's hardly any bus-taxi available today on the road."

Bijan quickly cut her short, "Come, let's go."

Rosy promptly opened the car door and took the seat beside him. Her known aroma quickly spread inside the closed vehicle. Bijan could see from the corner of his eyes, the folds of the fair skin of her exposed midriff. There are dollops of sweat and Bijan controls a strong feeling of drooling. "Let the feeling grow stronger", he thought. He started the car engine and suggested,

"We're late. So, let's not go as far as Gadiara. Rather we can go to Diamond Harbour. What do you say?"

Rosy silently nodded and that was so stiff that it appeared to Bijan as if he had asked the question to himself and then gave consent to it, himself. The car sped through the streets of a city eerily quiet, resembling a lockdown. Inside the car, two persons were seemingly sitting, barely touching the seats. A few people were moving on the roads, with hardly a dozen cars in sight. Suddenly, Bijan noticed something peculiar: the people floating in the void weren't all at the same level. Some were hovering farther from the ground than others. Like Rosy stayed inches closer to the ground than Bijan. Bijan couldn't understand the reason. But then the reason behind today's phenomenon is far beyond the understanding of mankind. He couldn't resist but remarked, "What a strange day's today, never even dreamed of such a day in life, ain't it?"

"True, never thought of anything like that ever, Sir." Rosy's response has a clear hidden reluctance.

"Don't say 'Sir', today we're partners... I mean friends. Is that alright?"

"Alright, Sir... I mean..." Rosy stopped and then smiled a little. She looks stiff; her gazes lacklustre. Her henna dyed untied long hairs, her buttery white shoulders, and her shinning smooth, undented arms all appeared very tired, morose and unmindful before Bijan's eyes. Rosy is looking outside the car.

"Rosy."

She didn't even notice Bijan calling.

"Hey-y"

"Ohh"

"What's the matter with you? Why are you so stiff? Relax, chill."

"Nah…No, I'm good."

"And how's your child… I forgot her name?"

"Shivangi."

"How many units of blood are required for her at a time?"

"Three to four units. We have a date next month. It's so rarely available that you often have to search the black market. Then there are expenses of Nursing Homes and medicines, and one has to only keep adding huge expenses... you fall short of ideas on how far you can continue with all these..." Rosy spoke non-stop, looking directly at Bijan.

Bijan smiled, "Bijan Karmakar forgets nothing, you bet. Your advance will be at your desk right on time. And you never know, that might be non-refundable even."

"Thank you, Sir; oh, sorry for the 'Sir'; thank you, though. So kind of you..."

Bijan was now forced to raise his hand to gesture her to stop. The word 'thank you' from the woman carries a bitter feeling; Bijan bites his tongue. He foolishly dragged an unwanted topic. Unwanted, maybe, but not so useless, because truly speaking, this is the reason why a timid and homely woman like Rosy has consented to escort Bijan to Diamond Harbour. Rosy's two year-old-girl-child has major thalassemia. She has to change her blood after every few months. Rosy's husband is an ordinary Accountant at a petty leather company. Bijan wonders how the man still won such a trophy wife like Rosy. It's an unbelievable thing! And it's not even a love marriage, as reported by Rosy. Bijan's not sure whether that's a bluff. But what he's sure of is that the man's earnings couldn't assure the right treatment of the child, and hence, the woman had to enter the job market. Now, a workplace naturally has its own professional hazards. Bijan still remembers that Rosy came with a reference from Mrinal. He is Bijan's friend and, at the same time, an acquaintance of Rosy's husband. He said,

"See to her, will you? Inexperienced, but then if she gets a chance, will definitely learn from you."

What Bijan is doing is simply obliging to that. Teaching her about work, about life. Once again, he felt a rage against Rosy's stupid husband. He wonders how, when either their pocket doesn't permit it or otherwise, two people living together get detached from each other. For example, the Bijan Karmakar, who happened to be the groom of Sonali, always earned handsomely. He could still have extras even after spending behind half a dozen such thalassemia patients. On the other hand, Sonali was a software engineer with an unnatural knack of growing ambitions. She had a job, one very highly sought after, that matched Bijan's.

Be it beauty or brains, they were both unmatched. Even after a couple of years of marriage, neither was ready to have children. Though Bijan was eager, Sonali still didn't agree,

"Now! Are you going nuts!"

"Then when? After age, catch up with us?"

"No. Let's only concentrate on our career now. The rest of the things can wait."

Bijan learned Sonali's life lesson that day, which is that her life and career flow in opposite directions. Sonali didn't want to have pills, so Bijan always had to use protection. There were piles of protection stored under the mattress of their bed. One day, accidentally, Bijan couldn't find one, as perhaps the stock was out. Helpless Bijan acted brilliantly that night of using one to deceive her. As a result, after a couple of months, she had to run for an abortion.

That day, a furious Sonali screamed at Bijan, "You cheat, liar, irresponsible brat, you knowingly did all these..! I can understand your intention well."

Bijan roared back, "No, you understand nothing beyond your own career."

"That's the most important thing in life."

"Yes, and one day, that will end your life, too."

Even after that, their bodies kept meeting on some nights. Even in such high moments, an alert Sonali used to check for Bijan's protective guard. Work, work and work – the woman knew nothing beyond. Sometimes, she would even stay back at the office. The result was inevitable; she was growing fast in her prosperous career. Then, one day out of the blue, she mentioned a proposal that had come to her,

"Listen, I got an offer from Google software."

"Nice. Where's the office?"

"California." The way she said it appeared as if she was talking about Shyambazar, not California.

"Oh, so what have you thought?" Bijan tried to hold his poise as far as possible.

"Hmm, still contemplating the offer... actually, they got branches here too, but then initially, one has to go abroad for a couple of years of training. You will blow your brain if you hear about the offer."

Sonali was gushing and talking, completely lost in her happiness. Though she talked about contemplation, she didn't, as it took her just a day more to convey her decision to Bijan. Years have gone by since then, and Bijan is not sure whether she has settled abroad. Since then, they are literally oceans apart. Bijan couldn't remember the names of the oceans which had now kept them apart. At first, there were telephonic conversations a couple of times a week, then once a fortnight, mostly courteous calls, and then once monthly. Bijan even suspects that she no longer lives there alone.

Bijan thought that Sonali and her partner, too, must have been facing today's situation wherever they were, losing ground under their feet and floating in the void! Bijan didn't want to think more.

But what else could he do? The person sitting beside him seems like a silent statue. Bijan desperately tried to break the silence. He switched on the FM Radio channel, which promptly started blaring, "Today nationwide schools, colleges, offices ..." another channel sang, "The night when my doors were broken and destroyed by the storm, little did I know that it was you who ..." Rubbish words all around, Bijan couldn't take all these. Let the world get destroyed; Bijan doesn't care about anything in the world. Today, rather, what he wants is only this new woman, Rosy Patra. Yes, he wants her badly. The car, meanwhile, has entered Diamond Harbour Road. Bijan contemplated where to board. It's the Rupashi Bangla Lodge. He had boarded there once before with a girl... Shweta used to pronounce her name in a funny way that Bijan still could remember. The lodge has good arrangements, and it's safe, too.

"Oh, I forgot to ask whether you had your breakfast."

"Oh, of course, yes."

"What you had?"

"A cup of tea and Biscuits."

"You consider that a breakfast! You should be hungry by now. Do you like to eat something?"

"Nah..."

"Drink some water, at least."

"Nah…"

Bijan suspects the girl is ignoring him and responding superficially. Is she thinking about someone else? Who could that be? Husband? Daughter?

"What you're thinking about?" Bijan reprimand.

"Nay, nothing serious," Rosy tried to smile. She has a bucktooth, which is revealed the moment she smiles. It makes her more attractive. "...Actually, since yesterday night, my daughter is not keeping well. She is having a fever."

"Oh..." Bijan frowned and looked away from her.

Rosy noticed her boss's annoyance and quickly tried to make it up, "But I think that's normal, as it always happens before it's time for her treatment. I don't worry much as her father remains by her side."

"Have you ever been to Diamond Harbour?"

"No, but I heard of it as a nice place."

"Let's go and find for yourself."

"You must have gone places in your life?"

Bijan felt a sense of pride in answering, "Now that's a part of my job. I keep swaying between hills and seas. How many times have you found me at my chamber so far? In future, you too may have to follow suit."

"Don't you think you are under much pressure, more than you required?"

"That's nothing. A lone person like me doesn't have many chores at home. So, the office is like my home."

Finishing the words, Bijan observed her reaction from the corner of his eyes; she tried to ask about something but ultimately resisted. There's a rickshaw stand on the way, but all the rickshaw pullers are absent. Clearly, who can pull a rickshaw in the air? Bijan knew Rosy stayed in the Paikpara locality. So, he asked,

"At what time you left home today?"

Rosy spoke out only after a noticeably long pause with a distinct dose of uncomfort in her voice,

"I... actually, I'm not directly coming from home today." Bijan was wearing a question mark, staring at her hearing the response, and she continues,

"Coming to work at such an early hour from home is like a bit awk... I stayed back at a friend's place yesterday at Bhawanipur. I'm coming now from there..."

Bijan could fairly understand her point. After all, coming out from home at odd hours often raises doubt; it attracts unwanted lying, too, and that's why she had planned a night out at a friend's place. Bijan rationalise the situation within himself—

It's true that she lied, but it's only for the sake of Bijan's friendship. After all, Bijan's also a friend of hers. Like a very cordial friend, he is lovingly giving her a joy ride. Her good-for-nothing husband could have never arranged for something like this. Like a responsible colleague, Bijan has already even thought of paying her back handsomely after everything so she can use that to treat her poor daughter. If she doesn't wish to take it on direct offer, he has a plan to offer it in the name of the company's business promotion expenditure. That way, it won't hurt her sentiment from taking the money.

"Hey, we've almost reached our destination," having said that, Bijan looked straight at her. He noticed that the girl had worn the end of her saree really tight around her breast. Useless! Bijan thought. Ultimately, when she would have to open up everything, it was sheer useless. In another quarter of an hour, Bijan parked the vehicle in the Rupashi Bangla lodge, standing on the bank of the boundless waves of the Ganga.

Rosy exclaimed, "I have never even imagined in my dreams that Ganga-river can be so wide, so extensive."

Bijan wished to cross-check to see if she was speaking for real. "Do you really like it?"

"Brilliant."

But Bijan was still sceptical about her expressions. He prayed hard that this girl would remain free, frank, fresh and fertile till everything ended happily. Bijan had a couple of previous experiences when his partners were so absent-minded that they had really annoyed him. He had even sacked one on a trivial pretext out of annoyance.

Getting out of the car, they kind of swum funnily in the blank space to scale the flight steps of the hotel. At first, there was no one at the hotel reception. But then, after some callings, someone came. The same funny way, swimming in the blank. Every man is swimming, sailing, floating. It's World Swimming Day for mankind, and the world is a pool of void left to swim. The receptionist silently stared at them for some time, perhaps out of disbelief that even on a traumatic day like today, how can one even chalk out such a trip? The hotel workers are trained enough to quickly understand the nature of relationships with their customers. Bijan didn't spend much time or words either and, after quickly filling the register with some odd names and an equally odd man-woman relationship, took the key of room number two hundred and five and went away.

As soon as closing the door of the hotel room, Bijan had this strong urge to jump at her, but then again, he restrained himself. He wants to rare his primitive lust some more, increase it more to enjoy it more. Till now, all the way, Bijan hasn't even shown the smallest of desire to even touch her fingers. Women and newspapers are the same; they get stale as soon as one touches them.

"You go first to the toilet and freshen up. Meanwhile, I'm ordering breakfast," Bijan looked at his watch, "otherwise we may have some light snacks since the day will quickly roll into noon in no time. So, we may have an early lunch instead. What do you say?"

Rosy's response was the same silent nod. She quickly unpacked a salwar kameez set out of her bag and hurriedly sneaked into the toilet. Bijan watched and doubted if the day, at all, would go well with such a kind of partner. He feared that her stiffness would surely jeopardise a big part of his elaborate planning. She appeared different in the office, though. But then a first time is always a nervous time, and Bijan can pretty well understand that. If that's the case, then Bijan thought it would be quite manageable for him. A couple of pegs of drinks then will change the girl. Bijan regained his confidence and lit up a cigarette, sitting on the white linen of the hotel bed. But his light body kept swimming in the void, and he couldn't touch or feel the softness and comfort of the mattress. "How high up is Sonali swimming? Is she swimming higher than Bijan?" No. Bijan won't think about that. She may swim, swim and sail away like a gas-filled balloon in the unknown space. After all, that's what she dreamt of. Sailing to the highest level. Bijan uttered the best swearing word he knew.

Then, taking up the TV remote from bedsides the table, unmindfully, he switched the television set on.

A regional daily soap was playing there where a girl was shown crying in a loud, melodramatic fashion, seemingly being driven out of her in-laws' place. Bijan couldn't bear it and changed the channel. The next is a news channel. And it's playing the same repeat story of today's awkward incidence –the same sop albeit dished out with somewhat new packaging – added story coverage and fresh live telecasted snippets. A porter of Burrabazar lamenting before the camera, "If the situation does not revive by tomorrow, we will die for want of a living; after all, how can one carry weights on the head if he can't put his feet on the ground." His tragic wail follows a commercial break all decked up with soap, toothpaste, and motorcycle ads. The channel gets changed by pressing a button, and now, seemingly, an assembly of people is shown. Bijan was about to change it too casually, but something sounded there that inspired his curiosity. Possibly an expert is giving a studio interview on the world's current situation. There, he's being asked if, when on the moon, the gravitation force, 'g' being one-sixth, people can at least rest their feet on the ground. But here, the whole of mankind is floating with the 'g' force drastically getting reduced, perhaps twenty times below normal. Okay, for the sake of argument, even if one accepts this as an anomaly of science, then what is sheer unacceptable and still unexplained is that humans can't even touch each other. When one attempts such, there's a repulsive jerk occurring, causing one to get knocked off from the other. The interviewer nervously inquired the expert. The expert, too, was already so puzzled that it took him a lot of twisting of lips and scratching of chin before responding with pounds and pounds of disbelief and awe in the voice,

"See, firstly, the phenomenon itself is so flabbergasting and out of the blue that no one can yet read it in full. I personally think there must be some scientific mistakes that occurred within the earth's crust, harming the normal earth's gravitational force. This must have deactivated man's normal attraction. There's no denying, after all, that our planet is everything to take call on attracting man to itself. I mean, the condition is such that even man's poop is not dropping on the ground. What an unbelievable situation!"

The expert felt fairly content after at least giving a tidy answer to the odd question.

"Okay, sir, your words are well taken. But why is there repulsion between humans attempting to touch each other? See the moment I try touching you what's happening!" with these words, the interviewer enacted a demonstration, and his hands repulsed inches away from the expert, as if out of an electric shock.

"Now, can you explain this?"

The program is being telecasted live. In between the talks, there's a phone call came there in the studio,

"Hello, I'm calling from Siuri..." but the voice got dubbed by some machine moaning.

"Can you mute your TV sound, please..."

It went on, but Bijan was already shuddering in an emotional outburst. He switched off the television. 'What the fu**.' he thought. The veins of his forehead swelled up with blood gushing in excitement. With some effort, he rose from the bed and rushed to the closed bathroom door.

"Rosy! Rosy!"

He started kicking the door in a mad rage. The tap water inside stopped.

"What is it?"

Rosy sounded inquisitive from the inside.

"Open the door, now. Fast. Will you?"

"Just a minute." The door opened as promised in a minute or so. There Rosy was standing, drenched and wrapped in a saree, draped hurriedly. Bijan jumped upon her without allowing her to understand what was going on. But Alas! He got knocked down a foot away from her. Both were stunned to observe this.

But Bijan felt outrageous and tried again and again to touch her body, and every time got knocked off at least an inch before a touch,

"What the heck is happening!"

Rosy, too, made some failed attempts when her hands slipped repeatedly. Bijan gnashed, fisted in anger. He was feeling bitter about defeat and failure. Saliva came out. He spitted, but the spit stayed floating before his face in the space.

"You bitch! You knew all of these. Ain't it?" Bijan roared in frustration.

"Believe me, please... I knew nothing of this..." Rosy broke down in tears.

"Urgh..." But that could hardly calm him; Bijan was dragged through the void to the hotel bed, all broken, shattered. He took out a pint-sized vodka bottle from his bag, gulped thrice, and roared again,

"What the heck..."

And then he threw the bottle on the floor. The bottle broke into pieces. Rosy stood before the toilet door, shivering in fear, when an angry Bijan sat silently for many hours. Then he looked up to her. The girl stared at him with a strange fear in her eyes, standing still in the damp saree. The fear gave Bijan at least some sense of comfort. But then he felt upset about his luck.

Bijan recollected himself, "Come by. Why are you standing there? Sir here. Come on. Sit."

Rosy silently came floating over those glass sherds of the broken bottle. She sat, keeping some distance. Her body was still convulsing, tears still rolling out of her eyes. Her breasts falling out of her drapes are pushing like pistons.

"Don't cry. For God's sake, please don't cry. Just tell me a single truth. Don't you know anything about this, really?"

Bijan bites his tongue while uttering. Rosy put her head down; only her breasts kept pistoning up and down.

"Speak out... why didn't you... did you think you would get rid of me easily in a day? You cheat. You liar." Bijan once again lost his composure and shouted. Suddenly, he thought that perhaps Sonali had shouted at him almost identically years ago. Rosy was startled by his sharp shout, but she managed to reply,

"Believe me, I didn't want to... I will come again... I will come whenever you want, wherever you take me to."

"Urgh... Shut up. Will you!"

Bijan took a glass sherd from the floor and threw it to the wall in front as hard as he could. Then, with long breaths, he tried to calm himself down, attempting a half-lying position on the bed.

"What's this!" Rosy's voice was loud and shrill.

"What?" Bijan frowned.

Rosy was shuddering with her big round eyes fixed on Bijan's hands. Bijan looked back at his own hands, which he had just used to throw the glass bottle. There was blood gushing out from some deep cuts caused by broken glasses. But he couldn't feel pain.

"O my God, now what will happen? What should I do?" Rosy continues crying like a mad woman.

"Don't be hyper; nothing serious has happened. Call the reception and ask them to bring some first aid here," Bijan felt irritated by her overacting. "Really, I don't feel any pain, so stop crying."

"No... No, it can't be! O my God, what will happen... there's so much waste of blood... what shall I do? How shall I stop the depleting blood?"

Rosy tried to hold Bijan's injured hand, but Bijan quickly moved away sternly, saying, "What's all this! I told you nothing happened. You better do what has been asked," but blood kept dripping from his injury, wetting the white bed sheet with fresh red gore.

She kept murmuring, "I... I..." and was not ready to listen to anyone, "Sir... please stop squandering... you don't understand... one won't get a single unit of this from anywhere except the black market..." she sounded delirious. And then she got the jug from the bedside, emptied it on the floor, put it under Bijan's injured hand and said, "Keep it here; otherwise, all are getting wasted, Issh... you have already wasted a lot." Bijan kept observing Rosy silently and in awe while she was impatiently running around the room from corner to corner. Unmindfully, the end of her saree was down from her shoulder, brushing the floor. Her bare chest, the one Bijan had fantasised so long about, was before his eyes, but now he didn't even care. Rosy raised the receiver of the phone and suddenly asked, "What's the reception number?" But even before getting an answer, she put it back and instead quickly emptied her side bag over the bed, searching for an unknown object. All the objects from her are bags spread around, some on the bed and resting on the floor. She tried looking at the floor. Meanwhile, Bijan was surprised when it appeared Rosy's feet were about to touch the ground in her madness.

Bijan reprimanded her, "What's all this madness about? Stop it!" The girl stopped hearing this. Bijan continues, "Come by and sit, arrange your saree. I will take care of my wound." He says this as he wraps his handkerchief on the cut and stands up.

Sitting amidst the gore red of the bedsheet, Rosy meanwhile started lamenting in mumbles, "What a waste... perhaps a unit or so..."

Bijan kept silently watching Rosy for a while. Then he stood up and, in a normal voice, said, "Don't be tense. The bleeding has stopped. See." Then, after a poise, he continued, "I'm feeling hungry; if we start immediately after lunch, possibly you could reach Paikpara before evening. I hope your husband could take care of your little daughter, Shivangi till that," saying, Bijan unknowingly tried to pat her, and what a surprise, his bleeding hand could easily touch her shoulders, so normally, so calmly, as if nothing has changed in the world.

"Go, get freshened up quickly, and we'll go."

While talking, Bijan could feel he was slowly getting down to the ground; the blank space under his feet was reducing till it melted completely.

View Change

'W.B. Goldsmith, 32/ 5′-4″, B.A., Own house at North Kolkata, family business, U-27 Boy seeks fair and beautiful girl, minimum H.S. qualification. No dowry. Box no…'

The newspaper circled with red ink can still be found at house No. 7 Debai Pukur Road in Hind Motor, but its meaning has faded, as Mita no longer lives there. For the last couple of weeks, she's been staying at her new address of 37/B Nivedita Lane, Bagbazar, in a two-storeyed building. Appearance-wise, this house looks like a haggard octogenarian man smiling with broken jaws showing off his catechu-stained dirty teeth.

As one enters the house through the heavy wooden doors, perpetually ajar, a wave of darkness seems to envelop everything. The steep staircase that follows leads upward through this unsettling gloom to the first floor. At the top, a dimly lit corridor provides some relief, but caution is still necessary; the loose mosaic tiles on the floor are loosely fitted and may topple balance. At the far end of the corridor, a small, Masonite-enclosed kitchen stands beside a tiny emergency toilet for nighttime use. The primary latrine, however, is downstairs, hidden in a pitch-dark corner that remains dim even during daylight hours. A feeble 25-watt bulb struggles to illuminate the space, revealing a rounded commode pan on the floor flanked by awkwardly high footrests. The rusted tin door barely hangs on its hinges, and the adjacent washing platform is perpetually damp, with an ever-dripping tap adding to the disrepair. Above, the cornices of the house are invaded by the roots of banyan trees, further amplifying the sense of decay. The discomfort escalates when one has to climb the wooden stairs to the terrace. The staircase resonates rhythmically all along while climbing, with the passing of trams and transport by the road in a risky fashion, giving a feel to break down. Even the floors of the first storey join the wooden steps in their trembling frenzy.

The day after their marriage, a concerned Mita asked her husband, "Aren't these vibrations going to harm the basement of the house?"

In reply, Sankar laughed out loud, "What the fuc... do you even expect there's a basement still alive in this ancient structure of a house?"

Mita was stunned, listening to a house standing without a base.

A couple of weeks passed, but Mita still couldn't accept this house as her own. The rites and moralities of this house are still quite offensive to her. The demise of her husband's father, her father-in-law, took place three years before her marriage. So, the only two other residents of this house except her are her husband, Shankar and her widowed mother-in-law, Niyati Karmakar, a woman with a terrifying appearance. It's so terrifying that it may even stop the wind from blowing. She speaks loudly and mouths even louder abuses. Like mother, like son. Shankar, too, can't express himself without mouthing foul language. In Mita's childhood, she hadn't heard even the slightest swearing, so the constant cursing here pains her deeply every minute. The woman, the mother-in-law, does not act as a motherly person either. She behaves like some cheap heroine before her son, making Mita wriggle silently. But she's helpless as when fat Shankar sweats it out in all his stoutness at his jewellery shop in BB Ganguly Street, there's nobody but Mita and her mother-in-law alone by themselves at this Bagbazar house at each other's mercy. But it wasn't always like this. Mita heard that years ago, a family used to live on the ground floor of this house, paying a meagre rent of sixty rupees. However, they are no longer there, as the mother-and-son duo caused such chaos that they eventually drove the family away. As a result, the once rented and now abandoned room of this house has been left in oblivion with piles of souvenirs heaped in like broken furniture, useless utensils and gadgets, torn ropes, and leaked pipes, one shattered bicycle supposedly from Shankar's childhood days, all decked and decorated inside. Mita has often felt a certain amount of uneasiness when sometimes her mother-in-law obstinately stares at her. She shudders. She chokes. She wonders why her parents chose such a house to marry her off. But then maybe there was nothing to choose from either. Since her father retired as a Senior Accountant from Authentic Pharmaceutical, he often remained disturbed by the thought of finding a way to marry off the twenty-six-plus, still unmarried, Mita. After all, her father was already burdened with her ever-suffering mother's health issues and her unemployed brother's lack of income, all while trying to manage with the meagre provisions from his retirement benefits. So, like the quintessential Bengali father of a young woman, he did what was common—he quickly arranged her marriage through a 'Want a Groom' advertisement in the newspaper. There,

"32/5'-4" and no dowry" declaration attracted him the most towards Shankar. Mita, too, naturally gave in. After all, in her twenty-seven years of youth, romance was still elusive despite having all the desperation and urge. Somewhere, in some way, it had always stayed vague, tangled deep inside in the web of restraints.

After Another Couple of Years

"Ohh... these days and nights of wailing are so bloody annoying! ...Get the windows closed." Shankar roared in anger, lying in bed. Mita rises, puts the jug down from its usual position at the window rack and closes it. She did it silently as she knew Shankar's target was not the baby of the neighbourhood but Mita herself. Nowadays, he couldn't even stand her existence around him, and Mita accepted that. She knows protest will yield nothing. Their neighbour Dipen had a son out of a yearlong wedlock. He wasn't a particularly beautiful child, with a complexion as murky and cloudy as his father's. Yet, Mita's mother-in-law and husband have continued to blame her for standing 'fruitless' to this day. After returning from the child's rice ceremony, gifting a minuscule gold piece shaped like a ring to the baby, the mother-son duo continued passing comments to the housemaid, Haru's Ma, targeting Mita under the cover,

"Whatever ugly the look may be, but their descendants are the ones who will keep their family undying, unlike us."

There were no shorter efforts, though, and experimenting in the last couple of years, including making rounds to the doors of a number of gynaecologists. Then there were unknown and unnamed offerings and vowing to many unknown and unnamed Gods and Goddesses, charms amulets tied and untied in Mita's waist, neck, and arms. But that bore nothing. Meanwhile, since last year and a half, Mita has been feeling her mother's ailment of indigestion and heartburn inside her. Recently, the burn spread further throughout the whole body. As a result, the pain-bearing body these days appears like the trunk of a lightning-stricken thin betel nut tree. Hairs thinned, dark circles deepened around the eyes; now, for days, Shankar and she even stopped touching each other. Mita feels rather relieved getting rid of brushing another equally lifeless body. Meanwhile, their growing distance has seemingly gladdened her mother-in-law. Perhaps their childless status also thrills her. Mita doesn't understand what pleases her anymore. But what she understands, funnily enough, is that she herself has grown a huge tolerance to everything. Even pinches of salt on her injury don't burn her any longer. Mita remembers, as a child, watching steam engine drivers working tirelessly by the fire, shovelling coal. When she asked her Railway employee uncle in amazement about the pain they must endure, he explained their remarkable tolerance to heat and burns.

"Uncle, how could they work by fire for so long? Don't they feel pain out of heat?"

"Perhaps they felt it in the past in their younger day. But now extreme endurance taught them to ignore the pain."

She remembers how she listened to her uncle's smiling response to her astonishment. Though not anymore.

Now, she kept watching the ceiling fan swirling tirelessly at a determined pace of its own. It cares a fig whether one tries increasing or decreasing the speed by the regulator. Mita looked towards her husband,

"Should I serve you food?"

"Nope. I already had something outside."

Shankar kept his eyes closed while responding.

Mita can understand. The unpleasant *aroma* of what he had consumed had already filled the air inside the room. This happens often nowadays. Mita didn't want to extend the discussion. She switched off the light and closed the bedroom door in preparation for sleep another night out. Nowadays, Shankar is returning late at home. Initially, she asked for a couple of times, but Shankar gave a common answer, "There's some work pressure." Mita never felt interested in asking for the details thereof.

Shankar fell asleep. His mouth remained open, and the foul scent from the open mouth fans out all the more inside the room. Mita turned away towards the wall and tried watching the point light of the plugged-in mosquito repellent. This has now become a routine job of watching this light until the eyes give in to the darkness at a distance from the dancing light. Once the darkness ushers, the light fades out from before the eyes.

Today also, the darkness was about to win the race with light when a shrill moan broke the spell.

"Mamata.. Urgh.. ahh. Mamata, please, take a while more, you bit. You have got a wonderful .." with Shankar's every moaning, hair on her hand arose, the pores burned in a fiery rage. Mita controlled her immediate urge to leap out of bed. Instead, her sharp nails bit her pillow sharper. Shankar kept murmuring some unknown Mamata's name in his dream a few more times in the night.

***

"Na.. No..! Are you mad? How can you plan to heap all the lunatics of the world in here, in this house? What if he makes a mess of the house?"

Mita's mother-in-law was yelling in the courtyard downstairs while her eyeballs were fixed at Mita standing upstairs on the veranda.

"Not at all, boudi, there's no worry about it. I took care of all his morning chores before coming out. He always alerts me when there is a nature call. So, just for the daytime, I am requesting that you let him be here. He will sit by himself as long as I stay outside. You needn't have to fear about it.

Bending over the veranda railing, Mita got a glimpse of a lad sitting at a side of the wet, damp washing platform by the tap side, where surrounding him, her mother-in-law and Haru's Maa were debating. But the lad didn't seem to care, though it was about him. Head dropped down; he was carefully scratching with his toes on the ground on the watery platform. Mita understood that this was Haru, by whom their housemaid was known to them. Haru is a mentally challenged young man. He couldn't even stand without someone's help.

In the middle of this hot debate, suddenly Shankar appeared from the latrine. Dropping the iron pail with a thud on the ground, he inquired, "What's happening here at this early hour of the morning?"

His mother submitted, "See, Haru's Maa is pleading with me to allow her to keep this chap here every day during her morning hours duty shift."

Shankar, "For how long?"

Getting a chance to speak, Haru's Maa begged, "Only for a few days till I can arrange something. Haru disturbs nobody. Actually, my husband has got a morning shift duty, and thus, we are facing a challenge of where to keep him all by himself..."

Shankar paused for a while and then ordered, "Let him be here, but see to it that he doesn't create a mess." Uttering those words like a Hero of the scene, he got busy in his work – filling the pail, emptying it in the toilet, washing, bathing. His mother felt that it would now be meaningless to extend the debate anymore left for the kitchen. Permitted to keep Haru here, Haru's Maa grabbed the lad by his shoulder to make him stand and then took him away slowly, content at heart. Meanwhile, Shankar was busy cleaning his mouth, gurgling and spitting, oblivious to the scene around him in the courtyard. Mita felt bad; she didn't want to throw even a second look at her husband. He appears like a worm-like dirty creature to her. She entered the kitchen where her mother-in-law had already kept water to boil to make tea. Finding Mita there, Mita's mother-in-law vented out her anger,

"Have you seen how that shrewd Haru's Maa took the chance on my son's kindness and threw Haru's responsibility upon us? Just wait and watch now how I take revenge. Let him make one single mess, and I'll kick him out of the house."

Mita felt a very bad taste in her mouth. Maybe out of indigestion. But she chose not to say a word.

"Had Shanku not said anything in between, I would have kicked the rascal out long before. The cunning, outcast maid... she has clearly taken advantage of my son's soft corners... Pass on the cups, please."

Mita passed on the cups still without making a comment, and her mother-in-law went on,

"Shanku is soft-minded since his birth," her mother-in-law continues with a sense of pride, "Once in his childhood, he gave away a new crisp dhoti of his father to a beggar. Lastly, I saved it after finding it. He is still so childish. Till you came, I still used to feed him by my hand."

The lady felt so content telling this while she prepared tea for everyone. But then, after finishing, when she looked up and laughed, her pan-stained teeth looked horrible. Mita stayed quiet.

"Go. Give the cup of tea to your husband."

Mita wanted to refuse her but controlled herself. She took the cup and walked through the long veranda with the reddish-brown-coloured liquid. She thought for a moment about whether a pinch of poison could change the colour of the liquid.

Shankar was busy applying powder on his bare chest when she entered their bedroom. He was in his towels. Then he sprinkled body spray under the armpits, behind ear lobes.

Mita silently kept the teacup by the side of the dressing table and was about to leave the room when Shankar called,

"Get me my red kurta."

Mechanically, Mita followed his orders. She drew the red kurta out of the wardrobe and kept it on the bed.

"Listen, I agreed, considering her helplessness. The poor soul she is, I was forced to take pity upon her." Shankar slipped out of the towel into his lungi, balancing the cloth by biting one corner of the lungi. Meanwhile, his voice sounded weird. Mita looked like a lifeless machine. Shankar took the cup and sipped. Mita took a glimpse and kept imagining how the face would have disfigured under the influence of poison. Films often show a poisoned person always getting hold of their own neck first, then the eyeballs pierce out, and slowly, the whole body kneels down on the ground. Will Shankar act alike?

Meanwhile, Shankar took a couple of long sips of the warm liquid and then, humming some songs, opened up the newspaper and commented, "What the fu**… Only news of murders and rapes are published all over the newspaper; there's nothing else in here… Nah, Na, Nope... Um hmm," Mita understood the act of kindness displayed by him earlier had made Shankar feel so great about himself that it was going to take time to subside. Mita quietly left the room, allowing him the space.

Shankar finally left for his shop after half past ten. After lunch, when her mother-in-law goes for a nap in her room, the whole house is drowned in a strange silence. Downstairs, though, one can hear the sound of cleaning utensils. It's Haru's Maa. Meanwhile, the last night's feeling of burns increased inside Mita's body. She was surprised as she thought her tolerance had let her defeat all her burns. But yesterday's incident was more intense, more insulting, intolerable, and against dignity. Mita tried to console herself, lying face down for some time. Feeling unrest, she got down and took out the suitcase that she had brought during her marriage from above the wardrobe. But where will she go? Last year, after his first stroke, Baba never returned. Ulcer made Ma incorrigibly bedridden. Her brother is fighting a lone battle, renting out a portion of their house and tutoring students days and nights together. Mita put back her suitcase. It feels like a handful of sand is choking in her throat. She drank some water. The unrest is getting at her head. She got out of her room. She descended downstairs. There, by the entrance door, the pale and lanky lad was sitting silent. Going by the stature, one can easily understand that he is of a good height. Head full of well-oiled frizzy hairs, unkempt beard, and moustache. The face has a naïve, childlike expression. If not talking, none can make out that the lad is a handicap. Haru was scratching the ground with his toes and murmuring gibberish. At first, he didn't notice her. And then her existence surprised him. He keeps looking at her, wide-eyed. Mita shuddered deep inside before those eyes, and neither could move from her position for some moment. Then, after a great deal of effort, Mita was finally able to break the spell and ran away.

That Day

Since yesterday there's been a problem with the water supply in the locality. The leftover water from bathing stored in the bathroom has been finished by Shankar and his mother. After Shankar left for the shop, even Mita's mother-in-law went out to Shovabazar to meet an old friend at lunch who recently came from Delhi. So she will not return before evening. Mita spent long hours lying in bed. She was feeling the summer heat. The thought of taking a shower reminded her that there was not a drop of water there in the bathroom. But there's some water stored in the open tank downstairs by the washing platform where Haru's mother cleans utensils. Haru's Maa will surely finish the water by the evening. Mita didn't want to waste her chance before Haru's Maa emptied the tank. She rushed down. There is dark, cold liquid flowing over the thickened layer of moss covering the tank. Mita immersed her fingers. Within seconds, it filled her heart. She knows that this is what is left for the whole house to use for today and maybe tomorrow. Mita knelt down by the side of the tank. She took out a mug full of water and poured it over her head. The whole body got numb by the coldness. While one more mug of water was running through her body, soothing every burning pore, suddenly an "Ohh" sound came out of her throat unknowingly. Haru is sitting at the stairs of the entrance. Bare-chested. Wearing pajamas rolled up to the knees. Looking directly at her, frowning. Mita had forgotten about his existence completely. She quickly covered her breasts with the towel. Then again, she pours water over her head. She only wishes to finish all the water in the reservoir. Not a single drop she wants to keep for anyone. So, she keeps throwing mugs of water over her head, all over her body. Haru kept staring. Suddenly, he becomes restless. Haru then started acting like an impatient feline about to jump on the prey. Mita suddenly did the unthinkable and threw the towel cover from over her breasts. She then keeps splashing water upon her body, directly facing Haru. The water keeps running all over her. The wet saree tightens around her figure. She closed her eyes. But Haru's stares could still be felt upon her. She kept splashing water, mug after mug.

After using the last drop, Mita stayed put standing, drenched, shivering, with closed eyes. Slowly, she got back her poise and opened her eyes. She was feeling tired; her chest kept pumping heavily. The whole body started feeling sticky. But so are Haru's lips, and saliva can be seen accumulated in the corner of his lips. Mita suddenly started feeling repugnance. Then, when she looked at Haru again, her heart sprang in disbelief as she saw Shankar standing there in the same position. His eyes are burning in rage. But those are futile, helpless anger of a poor soul.

A Body Full of Ash

Here I am, lying inside the electric furnace. Just moments ago, I was placed in it. When the crematorium attendant, the *dom,* trolleyed me inside the open mouth of this burning hot furnace, I got terribly frightened. I even felt like jumping up and running. But there's no scope. My whole body was wrapped in a bandage. The morgue did that. They operated my whole body, took out the innards and stitched the corpse back. Even my forehead is sewn.

The *dom* attending my body intended to steal my eyeballs. But someone stopped him. I don't know them, though. Neither could I remember their faces. Maybe my friends or someone else. I am unsure. While lying in the morgue, I witnessed how the crematorium attendant Dom took away the eyeballs from the corpse of a teenage girl with a strange skill, pressing the socket of the eyes with his thumb to lift the balls out. But when he came to me to repeat his skills, someone resisted. What will he do with so many eyeballs? Sale those? Sale eyes or vision? Can they sell someone's vision? He appeared intoxicated as he smelled of alcohol. When a rat was niggling out meat from my right thigh, he shooed it off lazily and then came closer to attempt to press and push out my eyeballs. His attempt was unsuccessful, though. Thankfully, for someone's intervention! I don't remember, though, who intervened. But I can remember last evening. I was walking by the rail lines, and then there was a spot of light that could be seen in the middle of the darkness. It grew larger; it came nearer.. then a sharp whistle.. the metallic sound of the wheels, over the flesh of my body. I was run over. It didn't bleed. The bodies run over by trains don't bleed. That's a strange thing. For the rest of the night, I lay there alone on the rail line. My body's upper half lay in between the lines and the lower part outside. On my back. Dew drops washed my body all night. I kept reading about the constellation in the night sky and admiring the fluffy and chiffon-thin clouds floating in the dark blue space. It felt good as if I had been lying like this for a long time. In childhood, I often used to lie there in the open field, observing the darkness up above, dotted with the stars. There was a breeze flowing, lights glowing from the stars. I used to feel melancholic. I used to feel desperate to travel to the stars. Across the planets. Across every heavenly body, space objects. After drenching deeply in dews that night, my body was carried away in a sack the next morning to the morgue.

Meanwhile, inside the furnace, my bandage already burnt down to ashes. I am sure that by now, the crematorium air is filled with smells of burnt human flesh. The fire is all by me, though I can feel no heat. I have been lying on my back since yesterday. Suddenly, I felt like turning sides. But as soon as I turned, I was astonished because, at the adjacent furnace, I found another person burning alongside me. Though I didn't notice the person earlier, going by the scene, I understand this must be a man. He is burning comfortably, lying as if he's enjoying every moment of it. Suddenly, the man felt known to me. Really! I felt sceptical at first; perhaps everyone looked the same after turning into a corpse, or possibly all the burning bodies appeared identical to each other. The man's rib cage looks to resonate in a rhythm with leaping flames. While he is looking up at the ceiling, his silence is clearly laced with joy. Then he yawned lazily and turned toward me.

"Baba... you!"

The words came out of my mouth in extreme surprise.

"Why did you come here?"

He remained silent and kept gaping. I know him. This is what he did as long as we stayed together. Dumb stares, wordless, expressionless, which I knew lifelong. Initially, it used to irritate me a lot. But later, I started feeling a particular pain for him.

"Baba, are you in pain?"

Baba tried to smile lightly in reply, but his lack of training never caused him to dish out a good smile. Therefore, he could only manage to open his mouth slightly. As a result, three glistening white teeth showed up. Ohh!.. I thought, but these three teeth were not there for long. He always wanted to get false teeth fitted in the empty space but could never express his wish. Then, when he did that? Also, his clean, shaved look! When did he make that? He's looking dapper, though, in his apparently salon-groomed avatar.

"You got your false teeth finally?"

He nodded. Then, raised hands to show a wired white squarish object. A hearing aid! I keep getting surprised! When did he manage to get all these? Because, till last evening, I saw nothing. When I left the house, he was eating wet puffed rice from a bowl. Wet, because it's tough for him to chew those dry in a toothless mouth. Meanwhile, I noticed there's another thing Baba is clinching with his left hand. Ohh! Is it a spectacle? Yes, a golden spec. But I have only seen a pair of shabby black dirty glasses on his nose for all my life. He managed that, too! And now he came all the way to display before me everything! I got angry. I started thinking, what should I show him back in response that I have managed by now? What can be that? Suddenly, I discovered a red plastic ball and a cricket bat lying down in the ashes where minutes before there were my legs. And Ohh!... there's even a toy train. I found a heap of storybooks, too, lying on my chest, costly chocolates, drawing books, colours, everything, all that I dreamt of all through my life! How did these come here? The things that I have longed for, as long as I lived? All the things that we always wanted to buy but could never gift each other in life! Has Baba been silently taking a look at all these objects over me till now?

Baba was a light-man at a local cinema hall. I went there twice to watch movies. One was Netaji Subhas Chandra Bose. The other one is the African Safari. Once accompanied by Maa and once with Sadhana Aunty. I remember there was pitch black darkness in the theatre hall when we entered there, but still, we didn't bump or fall since my light-man Baba skilfully showed us the way to our seats with his guiding lights. I felt proud that my Baba knew darkness; he could see darkness when people couldn't. Later, I realised that Baba could only see a limited amount of darkness, the darkness that was stored inside a theatre hall. In other cases, he remained as helpless as me, and there he bumped, he fell. Even I could manage to touch Krishna in all my blindness, kiss her, untie her in the darkness of the planetarium. I realised when you get training, light or darkness means nothing to you.

The business of the local cinema soon started falling with the entry of cable lines into the market of mufassil and peri-urban areas like ours. The owner started screening adult movies in search of profit and to attract viewers. Posters of popular Hindi movies are displayed outside, and Southern adult movies playing inside the hall. Young people started crowding. Some of my friends, too, had joined the crowd. Baba still used to work pointing light to seats to viewers, his head hung down in embarrassment.

He was breaking inside into dust, something that I could understand clearly. It was a losing battle. Ultimately, the hall closed down. Baba stopped going to work and stayed back home. Day by day, Maa became sicker and angrier. Perhaps because Baba maintained a peculiar relationship with Sadhana Aunty, a distant cousin of my mother. In my childhood days, Aunty used to come to us regularly. I got lozenge, biscuits and chanachur as gifts every time she paid a visit. She talked more with Baba than Maa. Initially, Maa ignored that, though she started disliking it later. The result of her growing dislike fell upon me badly. I started getting a lot of scolding and beating from Maa whenever Sadhana Aunty was around. Therefore, I too started getting angry with Sadhana auntie's presence in our house because I understood I would get thrashings from Maa afterwards for unknown reasons.

Sadhana Aunty had a strange profession. She used to clean telephone sets at different offices all around Kolkata. There were fixed clients of hers where she used to pay weekly visits. Two hundred or three hundred, that's the rate per client. And a fifteen hundred monthly income in all. Aunty was an early riser; she used to wake up at four in the morning and catch a train at 5.30. Then, after going back home, she could finally go to sleep by midnight. I once asked, "Aunty, why you chose to remain unmarried?"

The wrinkled face, wrecked jaws, and ramshackle tooth line, Sadhana Aunty smiled back to reply,

"What would have happened to those two then?"

Aunty had a younger brother working at a noodles-making factory. He had asthma, so he died early, leaving his wife and son. They remained Aunty's burden all through. But she took pride in them. Her face used to glow talking about them. I could see the light clearly.

I understood my Baba and Sadhana aunty had a platonic relationship, only at heart; there's nothing physical in it. Flat chested, her clavicles protrude more prominently than her breast; her snuffling voice, her rickety hands with a couple of thin bangles and hanging safety pins, all are still clearly visible in my mind. Then there was a black ragged sidebag where she used to carry a bottle of spirit, cotton balls, napkins, and a shiner – all the objects needed for her work. I had this knack of smelling the spirit bottle from her bag. Baba used to scold me for that, but Aunty supported me, "Ahh... let him be."

Maa had epilepsy. While she had seizures, Baba used to treat her by inserting a spoon in her mouth, rubbing iron keys under her feet, and making her smell shoes. One day, Maa suddenly died. She drowned in the pond while going for a bath alone. She had a seizure in the middle of the water. Baba always prohibited her from going to the pond for a bath, though, and Maa had always listened to him till that day when she disobeyed his order. I don't know why! Her body kept floating till Baba arrived. After her death, Sadhana Aunty came to our house just once. It was during our period of mourning for the death. I was dressed in all whites then as per the rites. She went away, never to return again. After that, I found Aunty buying fish at the station adjacent to the market one evening; Baba was accompanying her. They were buying rohu fish. It was Baba's favourite. I fled the scene before I could even determine who was buying for whom. Aunty used to live in our next locality, and Baba used to go there to meet her. I knew that, and I always supported that. I like the idea of two loners seeking respite in each other's presence. I could imagine that their meetings were both intense and dispassionate at the same time. But Krishna and I were the opposite. I used to find freedom while being physically close to her. She had the scent of the wild woods, and that always numbed my senses at the end. She is like a primitive forest where, for times together, I keep searching for the source of her wilderness. She used to laugh at my lunacy,

"This is a known field to you; what more can you explore?"

"I'm still not sure about that."

"You are out of your mind."

Really… I don't know what I still keep searching for in her; her breasts, her shoulder, her navel, and every pore on her body is already explored, but even then, I don't know what I kept probing. And Krishna, too, was equally passionate about me. She once told me, taking me in her arms,

"You, your body is like Buddha to me; illumination oozes from everywhere, every line of your body."

Listening, I felt like a real God. I couldn't imagine that, except for her, any woman has ever explained her man as a Buddha in her life. I felt myself as generous as the sky before her. Krishna was in love with me, my art. Unfortunately, even after not having good drawing books and colours and brushes in my possession, my passion remains in paintings.

Krishna was in politics, though. That is, in active politics of guns and bombs. With the same fingers that she brushed on my body, she pulled triggers in protests, too. It was an astonishing act of opposite poles. I even asked her, "How could you pull this off?"

She always laughed silently. I kept insisting,

"Do you think that you can change society in your own way?"

She insisted, "There's no harm in putting in effort."

"Harm isn't there in your efforts, but to you."

"You're a coward. You think like one." Her voice was stern, and eyeballs fixed upon me.

I accepted. "Not only me, we all are so. Living in fear. Fleeing from life. I paint. You shoot. My father visits Sadhana aunty. Every act is out of fear. To flee from someone somewhere."

"These aren't the correct examples of fleeing."

"Of course they are."

"Alright. Everyone has the right to think as they wish to."

"Will you stay with me, Krishna?"

"Am I not already?"

"That's true, but I want you more than that, for every single moment, with me. Marry me."

".. No."

"Why not?"

"Because I am scared of that."

"Scared! Why?"

"I really don't know... Neither do I understand the reason... but.."

"So, when you keep guns in your bag, that doesn't scare you? When the police run behind to catch you, that doesn't scare you?"

"Those are my compulsions because I don't have choices; I don't know anything else."

I knew her vulnerability. She has similar problems to me. She has lost her father. Her brother has physical disabilities. Her mother suffers from ulcers. She runs her family on her party's monthly pension of fifteen hundred.

"You live a social reformer's life only for the sake of earning a living. You should be ashamed of the fact that you take money to sell ideology."

"No, I'm not ashamed. I'm not ashamed to live my life."

We still met even after quarrels. We went on trips to Gadiara and Digha. Once to Rimbik. I still remember how Krishna embraced the bark of a moss-ridden tree and closed her eyes in pleasure. I could clearly understand her intent of cuddling a man's broad, hairy chest. Her closed eyes were throbbing in excitement and deep pleasure. Later, I tried a lot to sketch her pleasure but failed to express that correctly. I remember the name of the lad... Saikat. He was a comrade in her party. Saikat was handsome and eloquent. I met him through Krishna. He left medical study and abandoned his rich family, happiness, and prosperity to join militant politics and live a life of uncertainty like Krishna. It's very tough to assess after all, who will select what kind of living? I was lost in my thoughts. But the moment I got back to my senses, I found my burning father lying in a lazy posture, reading a newspaper. Golden glasses were on his eyes, and an expensive cigar was burning on his lips. There is a cup of piping hot tea by his side. He is looking so happy and content. His lower torso was already burnt in ashes, though. So did mine. My ribcage has caught fire. I thought, *let it be*. And then I called him "Baba."

Baba looked up at me. I threw a direct question, "You loved Sadhana Aunty, don't you?"

Didn't he hear me? Why does he keep staring silently? I repeated, this time louder. And even louder – a couple more times. But he stayed silent. Why did he stay silent all his life? I kept thinking… Why is he scared to answer a simple question? Umm, why does he always live in fear? Why does he act like a runaway man? Can't he confess that he is in love? Love or not, at least he could say it for the sake of saying it. Does it require that much valour? Does he think that I don't know anything? One evening, when Maa wasn't around, I saw Sadhana Aunty break down before him, saying, 'I have ruined my whole life, Suku-da.' That was the only time I found Aunty in tears. That was the only time I saw my Baba touching her rickety hands. That was the only time I observed the tender person that my father actually is, concealed behind the unkempt, untidy, apparently callous avatar of him that he shows before the world."

I finished my thought in one single breath. But I couldn't say it louder. I didn't want to breach the privacy of a very simple man, his vices, his vulnerable points. Instead, I asked, "You still haven't told me why you came here? How?" Baba tried talking. His lips moved slightly apart. Though he didn't utter anything, I could feel that he was actually asking me back the same question.

"I used to think before that one often gets used to the unfulfillment of desires in life. But no, I am wrong. You could never get used to that. Can you listen to me? It's just not possible. For the whole life..."

Before I could finish, Baba turned away. I got angry,

"You can't turn away this way from everything every time; you have to listen to me. You are answerable to me for my situation."

Meanwhile, the fire caught up with my head. One of my eyes burst out loud. It annoyed me. I shouted out, "I couldn't get admission to art college, all because I had to make sacrifices for you. I had to give almost all of the income that I earned from private tuition. Have you ever queried about my desires? Do you even know that yesterday I turned thirty-two? Did it at all concern you that yesterday, I was busy drawing a picture all day long? It was of Sadhana Aunty. I am not sure why I portrayed her, but I miss her. Can you do anything about that? Do you know why she disappeared after getting diagnosed with cancer in her stomach? She was not at all an escapist, so why did she escape? Her sister-in-law took up the work of a cooking maid as his son is studying in the eighth standard now, and she needs money to continue his education. I remember Aunty once confessed, "Babu is a talented kid, and he wants to be an Engin... Ha Ha... Do you get it? He means to become an Engineer." I still remember how proudly Aunty was laughing. Baba, do you really don't know where she has disappeared? Why did she flee? Why her escape didn't affect you? Are you scared to express? Are you suppressing anything? Baba, do you know I miss her? I never admitted it before you because I felt it was fruitless to admit such things before you. You can do nothing. I only learnt from you to get defeated. You only taught me the lesson of a loser. I have only seen you reading books on theology and the afterlife, and this always made me hate you. You have lived the life of a worm all along. Sometimes, I thought of borrowing a gun from Krishna and gifting it to incite you to take some desperate steps in life. Baba, can you run from life? No. At least I understood that much before you. But you didn't, till the end. Throughout your life, you ran aimlessly, like a cat trapped behind a closed door. I learned this analogy from my friend Anshu.

Anshu was desperately attempting to get a government job. He studied day and night together and sat for competitive exams multiple times. I followed him for some days. He succeeded in his target. I failed. He is employed at the Writers' Building now. The day before yesterday, he took me with him. We had egg rolls together. Then, lighting a cigarette shyly, he added, "Next month, I am getting married. You have to be with me at least two days before." He continued thereafter for hours. But Baba, believe me, even though I thought so, I didn't envy him the least. Actually, there is no heartburn inside me. I felt like a damp wall. It scared me afterwards. Had I lost my normal feelings? Did I even forget to be jealous of someone? By the way, you have been turning away from me for a long time. Are you sleeping? Can you even hear me? But I know you're only acting like you did throughout your life. Acting of hearing nothing. Acting of being unmoved before everything. Can you turn to face me once? Please? Can you tell me something, Baba?"

My neck caught fire. When Baba turned towards me, I found his lips on fire. The moment he opened his mouth, I found fire hissing inside his mouth. He might have uttered something, but it was inaudible.

"Can you speak louder? A bit..."

Baba tried to speak, but there was fire gulping his face. Both of his eyes burst in extreme heat.

"What happened? Speak up. Why can't you speak?" I insisted, raising my voice. There's fire coming out of the blank sockets in his skull and the open neck. He pressed the leaping flame inside with his hands. Then he raised a piece of paper. It's a paper torn out of some exercise book. There, someone has scribbled in untidy handwriting,

"I really don't want to die before them; it would have been shameful. Please, believe me, Suku-da."

Really! Sadhana, Aunty, did you even choose the path of an escape? Even you feared life? Baba, why are you showing me this after so many days? Baba, you loved me too, right? I knew it always. I remember when Maa used to throw away my drawing books and colours, you used to pick those up and return them to me, hiding from Maa. Baba, you even loved Maa, right? But why do you always fear expressing your feelings?

Baba, do you know Krishna was pregnant? We met after that. I knew it was Saikat's child. But an unmarried pregnant woman may tarnish the image of their party; that's why they drove her out of the party. Krishna never told anyone about Saikat and her relationship. She even didn't admit that to me. Neither did I ask. Driven out of the party, she came to meet me. Her eyes were looking beautiful that day. Soon, she got a job in a toy factory, where she used to make toys for lions and tigers. I remember standing there long after Krishna left the place. It was a windy day. I could smell milk in the wind that day.

How long have we been here inside the furnace? Is it more than an hour? Baba, why are we not completely turning into ash? There, your limbs and torso have burnt down to ashes. So is mine. But the head... Ohh... When will this all end? Baba, why are only the two of us burning here? Why there's no one else? By the way, why are you not telling me how you ended up here? Don't you want to say that? Are you feeling shy? Baba, do you know when the train was close by, and there was no chance at all to flee, there was a sudden urge inside me to get back to life? Really. Bloody hell! Did you feel the same? At least admit this! I believe so. Do you know, even seconds before, I never thought of backing off. What about you?"

Meanwhile, I found the fire caught hold of my father's head. The leaping flames are hissing, and a peculiar sound is coming out. The same is happening with me. It's like a monotonous ringing sound of beetles. The brain caught fire. The skull cracked with a thud. And with that sound, I leapt and sat back on my bed. I am profusely sweating all over. There, in our tin-shaded small room, the ramshackle bed lays before my eyes. The night is almost over, and it's about to dawn. In no time, a thin light ray, along with the misty cold of early morning, entered the room through the small window between the small gaps in the curtains. I looked beside them. My father was sleeping like an innocent infant. As I turned up from the bed, perhaps I heard my father's sleepy voice,

"There's ash sticking at your back. Rub it off."

On Sundays

Uff... I was terrified at the beginning, but then I won't blame myself either! I'm boarding a plane for the first time in my life, so I think my fear is pretty normal. Isn't it? When it suddenly whooshed up the sky above, I was terrified to my bones and grabbed him as tightly as I could. I was sitting by the window to witness the world outside. He kept his hand upon me and finally found some respite on his touch. Oh, are you wondering about whom I'm talking?

He is my hubby, dear. He is a frequent flyer, though, unlike me, flying twice or thrice a month to Delhi, Mumbai, and other places. His office sends him. He had even visited America a couple of times. I have decided that I will join him the next time he plans to visit there again. I will force him to take me. I'm dying to visit the country. My husband works in an MNC. He is '29/ 5'9", fair, handsome, Brahmin.' He is so fair that I have never seen another man with a complexion like his. He has got a headful of shiny black hair. When he shaves, his cheeks shine with a light greenish gleam. He looks so dapper, then. He always smells so good; his fragrance spreads on me, too, when I touch him. I don't know how he could always smell so lovely because even though I myself use so many perfumes, I never smell like him. We're now travelling together to Mumbai. From there onwards, we will be touring Goa during our honeymoon. Hi-Hi! We're just married. Post *Asta Mangala,* completing the eighth auspicious day of tying the knot yesterday, we are going on a honeymoon today. We had to hurry because he wouldn't get many more days off after this. This is the first time I'm going so far from home, so I'm shivering out of a mixture of thrill and fright. I am trying hard to control my emotions and remember calling Maa back home after reaching Mumbai. My poor mother is all so concerned about me. By the way, the plane's interior has kept me mesmerised all along. The air hostess is equally enchanting. She just got us some coffee. Is she showing some extra care to my husband? No, I don't want to believe that! I again move my eyes outside the windows. Ish! Everything outside is already looking microscopic. We have reached a great height by now. Roads-cities-hills-rivers-sea-people everything is far, far away... I'm 'under twenty-three. Beautiful, convent educated...' and this thought delights me inside. I quickly closed my eyes, blushing.

***

My husband has got a large jewellery shop on BB Ganguly Street, and a very popular one. He advertises a lot about his shop. The shop's glass walls bask under white and yellow lights all through the day. My husband is '43/5'1", which is certainly unmatched by me; neither does he match my height. But I ignore that. And then his complexion... yes, I ignore that too. Fat that he is, he looks like a... but I always stop before comparing... Dhurr, one shouldn't be that choosy in life after all! The whole day sitting in the hot and humid shop, he sweats but still hasn't installed an air-conditioner there; yes, he's that miser. I have always seen him sweating profusely at the back of his neck, under his arms, and inside his hair. He has beautiful curly hair, by the way, like Lord Kartik, with albeit greyer sideburns. He wears a long, heavy gold chain, one which hangs from the neck to the navel. Four thick gold rings are there on his left hand, and two more on the right. All are fitted with costly gems. I, too, wear a lot of jewels. Above everything, what I boast of is that my husband has got his own house. How many men can own that nowadays? Yes, the house is huge but old. The sleepy building is always filled with a lazy dampness all over. The staircase remains wrapped in a thin shit of darkness. In the square courtyard at the centre of the house, there's nothing to notice other than a big heap of uncleaned utensils lying in the want of a good wash, in silence like a boring summer afternoon always. Only when the housemaid arrives do they make noise to let others know that people live inside this house. Actually, the house has many joint owners who stay away, so most of the rooms remain locked. The people of this house are pretty conservative, and they don't want their ladies to go out by themselves. Here I'm about thirty. I'm 'WB, Goldsmith, fair and beautiful.' Even though they had declared 'No dowry required', my father was still compelled to pay them handsomely. My husband, being busy counting notes and measuring gold all day long, has turned into a peculiar character, humourless, unromantic. In the night, he's like… No, I don't want to discuss that. Before courtship, we had 'letter communication along with photographs.' In one of those letters, I included a photograph of myself wearing a green saree. This was the same photograph I had previously shared with several other potential grooms. Fortunately, my husband liked it. Thereafter, it was quickly followed by rounds of discussions between the families, thus resulting in marriage. My in-laws don't know that I was once divorced. We have never disclosed it, and I'm sure they won't be knowing that ever. Because I've been married off from my maternal uncle's house at Uttarpara. At my birthplace, Diyara, none of my neighbours knows that I've remarried. So, there's no risk of news leaking. My in-laws believe that I'm their first-hand property. But I still fear hiding facts. I have a six-year-old daughter whom I miss a lot! I close my eyes in all my nervousness.

My current husband has an annual income of six lakh. His previous wife 'died by accident.' But I care more about the fact that, at this young age, my husband owns two buildings in the city. One of the houses is given out for rent, though for a long time. He's a computer engineer, 30/5'6". His wife died only a couple of years after their marriage. I don't know the reason behind it. I don't even care to know. Rather, I feel quite comfortable not showing any interest. My in-laws advertised for 'Divorcee required, but not a widow.' Their ad bore the words 'homely, slim, min. graduate, loving and beautiful, contact by phone between 7 am-9 am.' Finding the ad, I immediately made my father call them. Their family liked me every inch, by my height, figure, skin colour, hair, nails, teeth, gum, everything. This time, I haven't hidden the fact that I'm a divorcee. Why should I? After all, they have asked for one. And then I was not at fault because my first marriage was a love marriage. I married a boy from my locality. My friends warned me about the boy, that he is a bad company and that I'm only ruining my future by marrying him. They wished me to leave him, but I would rather go with him instead, leaving my well-wisher friends behind. However, after a year and a half, the boy left me and our infant daughter instead. As a result, I now had to stay with my parents, the way an ideal homely girl stays with her baby after a failed marriage. The homecoming was indeed not sweet, but it was important for my daughter's future, her schooling, and her upbringing. I never blame my parents, as I only blame my fate. Love is not only blind but dumb, too. After my return, every day, I witnessed my father's wrecked stationary shop, which only managed to earn us half a meal a day; I witnessed my brother in the second year of college struggling to meet the two ends to cover his educational costs. The earning from the shop and interest from investments in the India Post were only miserly drops to meet our sea of demands.

I've not hidden a single thing from my current husband. They, too, have declared 'No Dowry', and they literally went by their words. Just the shankha-pola and a saree. They took a gold ring, though, after much persuasion by my father. My husband has bought a new car only a few days before our marriage. A silver-coloured hatchback. The car has got an admiring look, I must admit. I've asked him not to tear the plastic cover of the seats. After all, the moment you open the cover, it becomes old. The city of Kolkata has a lot of dust flying around. The day after our bou-bhat, we went out for a joyride in the new car. It was a scene to watch when the car was zipping past the red road by the Victoria Memorial. I was mum in wonder. My husband was driving. There was a saxophone playing in the car's stereo system by then. He introduced me to saxophone music. The tune created magic amidst the fast-blowing wind. I shuddered inside in romance-laden excitement. But beholding all my excitement, I understood that, in another couple of days, my husband had almost no attachment towards me. I tried not to bother myself about it; who knows, he might have some secret lover in his life. Who knows, he might have to marry me out of some compulsion. Or else he might have some other pathological problems! Does his previous wife die because of any of these reasons? – Let bygone be bygone, I thought. The fact and the matter remain that we're not in a conjugal relationship in our married life. Neither did I show any interest in that. After all, I, too, lost my appetite many moons ago. I care a fig about anyone else's interest upon me. My in-laws advertised for a 'divorcee, liability-less person', and here I am. I closed my eyes and murmured that my daughter was not my liability and that I was living free from her.

I never ever thought of leaving my banal life in West Bengal and travelling to the USA. I still don't know the name of the place where I'll be living abroad. But that doesn't bother me either. My in-laws declared, 'caste is not important, and a divorcee with a child doesn't matter.' They only emphasised on a bride 'interested to stay abroad, smart and under thirty-five' and we had a quick "registered marriage" as per my in-laws' wish. Thus, we boarded the flight to America. My husband is older than my expectations. He's fifty-six. But he's a pure American. I heard that his grandmother was a Bengali. I communicate with him in broken English, but I firmly believe that I will teach him Bengali soon. He's an established businessman, previously married. His last marriage lasted only a year. He already has a son, a twenty-eight-year-old young man, who doesn't stay with him and I haven't seen him till now. I am pretty sure this haggard is not looking for a life partner but rather is in search of a housemaid whom he could depend upon abroad. But I'm unmoved because this marriage has allowed me to admit my daughter to a good school. There, my child uses beautiful books and learns computers from such an early age; it makes me very happy. It pleases me when she tells me stories about her new computer lessons. Every day, she rides a shining big school bus to her school and has cakes, cookies and chocolates in her lunch; hi-hi, these elate me. I sometimes feel funny when my young daughter has got her own room at this age. Although she couldn't yet accept this new man in my life as her new father, I believe she will adjust to everything one day.

But I'm a little sceptical, deep inside, because I still don't know the man. I have heard stories about people here frequently changing their life partners. This man, though old, is quite active in bed, and I have to compromise a lot with him. I don't know after days whether he will be bored of me. I am afraid that my daughter and I might be forced to leave our home in an unfamiliar country. So, I compromise. But I long for my own country, too, in my thoughts.

Nah, this time, I'm really fortunate. I've got a husband who's pretty direct in his behaviour, a straightforward man. He remains immersed in books, his students and such all day long. He's a government school teacher, earning thirty thousand a month. No, it means a sum, I think! He decided to stay a bachelor all his life till his friends forced him to marry at the ripe age of forty-two. He is strictly ideological and religious-minded. I, too, am from a pious Brahmin Hindu family, vegetarian, broad-minded, under thirty-four, Bachelors of Art. But truly speaking, I couldn't complete my graduation because there were papers where I failed. But I'm not worried as nobody insisted on seeing my mark sheets. We're disciples of a renowned guru, same as my in-laws; I'm reasonably pretty in appearance. He being a '5'7", government service holder, and a divorcee with a child' at first made me happy, but then … providing a Box No. in place of a contact number disheartened me. I have lost a lot of money in paying stamp duties and sending a number of coloured passport-sized photographs while applying for marriage proposals, which were never returned to me. So, past experience taught me that ads carrying 'tel no." are better off. At least you get to know the reply on your face without much dilly-dallying. Even if postal addresses are provided, sometimes I send applications to test luck. I give tuition to schoolchildren of lower classes, three in all. But the earning of five hundred-and-fifty makes me struggle a lot every month in paying my daughter's school fees, books, uniforms, transportation, stationery, daily expenses, etc. I don't know what more I can do yet to make ends meet. It pains me now to ask for money from my father.

This is my routine on Sundays. Remaining absorbed in the middle of hundreds of ads of "Brides wanted." My investigative eyeballs remain fixed there in combing, screening, selecting, and ticking off. My worrying mother keeps asking in between, "Got anything meaty?" and I keep responding as lightly as I can, suppressing my own depression, "Nah, nothing that meaty today. Let's wait for the next week's edition."

As the day progresses, I start feeling weary of searching out at least a single potential ad from amidst the Sunday matrimonial page. My eyes started paining; the dot pen lay tired from me on the mattress, and it even failed to scratch a mark anymore. But, as the ads demanded,

I remain a homely or a working, under twenty-three or under thirty-five; I remain fair or dusk complexioned, beautiful or fairly pretty; I remain one with roots in West Bengal or East Bengal; I remain a Brahmin or Muslim or Sunni or Vaishya or Shudra, I remain a rationalist or a spiritualist, I remain a convent educated or a minimum HS passed, I remain a first hand or a widow or a divorcee, I remain available for those demanding 'contact by phone between 8 to 10' or to those asking 'contact with a photograph by post.' I suit myself everywhere; I become everyone, and I remain in every possible way it is being demanded. But I am not devoid of responsibilities; I am not without liabilities. I have a six-year-old daughter whom everyone has advised to send off to a boarding school. They say it's not uncommon at all, but I can't agree to do that. I'm determined not to do that. Because more than she, I'm a bigger liability to my daughter. My daughter never lets me out of sight, even for a second. She studies in a government school and every day returns in sweats and tears; she misses me, loves me, becomes anxious the moment I'm not around, and becomes nervous if I'm late to be by her. I don't know why she's like this, but I know I'm scared to bone when she's not around.

As the evening rolls in, my daughter wakes up and announces, "Ma, I'm going out to play with friends." I fold back the newspaper, keep aside hundreds of brides wanted ads inside it, and get up to face my daily fight in life. This fight will take place again next Sunday.

Two Men Is a Company

I

The plump man moved his bulky body to bend and spit gutka-laden gob in the waste paper basket at the side of his desk and announced, "Listen, since you've come with a reference from Bimal babu, there is no need to interview you." Go and understand the work that you need to do properly."

"O...Oh...Okay, Sir..." Atanu stammered; he found himself at a loss for words. His heart started thumping.

"You go downstairs at your designated seat. I'm sending somebody who will explain to you what you must do."

Atanu stood up and said, "Thank you, Sir..." He tried to look normal, though deep inside, there was an intense joy dotted with little nervousness and doses of an unknown sensation. He climbed down the stairs from the fourth floor to the ground floor office. But one will always think twice before calling this old, dilapidated building an office, where numerous dingy rooms jostle together amidst the karaoke of distractions. Firstly, clotheslines from wet towels to petticoats are lined up in the way from the fourth floor to the ground. Then there are unattended children wailing for food distracting your eyes, sour smells of vegetable peels and tobacco packets, torn plastic sheets piling up as wastes from the family kitchen distracting your nose, and sounds of moaning machines from workshops distracting your ears.

The abnormally steep staircase covered in permanent darkness leads Atanu to his new office, muscling out a philosophical indifference from his soul, let this be a proper office or not, the truth is that, from tomorrow onwards, he will be regularly coming here to work, proudly telling family and friends, "I'm on my way to office," or "I'm already late to office." Stepping out from the stairs to the central courtyard of the building, the surroundings again attacked his olfactory sense with a pungent odour; there's a toilet there, or instead, one may simply call it a urinating hole.

Atanu peeped there; it was a doorless nuke covered in sheer darkness. A small dry tank filled with rubbish of the world stands at its entrance while two high pedestals demarcate that the spot is a loo. The pedestals, though, clearly look unused for many years because the place around them and the entrance are being used more frequently by busy people who want a nature call. A killing smell made the surroundings heavy, but there, two seemingly unperturbed labourers still could be seen having their lunch together from the same plate of dal rice.

Atanu started feeling nature's call, but the surroundings were so discouraging that he hesitated. Suddenly, someone called him from behind – "Come with me."

The man who made the sound appeared from the darkness behind. Atanu saw this man working at a computer minutes ago, up in the office owner's room. Surprisingly, then, he didn't even care to throw a glimpse at Atanu.

Atanu took a good look at him. The man appears to be in his forties, but his hair and unshaved beard, which are mostly grey, bring him an untimely oldness in his appearance. The eyes are as dull as a dead fish. He's wearing a yellow terrycloth shirt with brown trousers, which, with months of unironing, took the shape of a pyjama instead. There are cades on his feet. This made his getup look so saucy. But Atanu thought, this man was just the appropriate colleague for this office.

Atanu asked with an open smile, "You're the one working at the computer upstairs, right?"

"Hmm."

"Accounts?"

"Yes."

"What package they use here?"

"Tally."

What the heck? This man replies to everything in monosyllables.

"Okay, come with me."

"Sure, let's go." Atanu followed the man to the office room. The downstairs office is the showroom whereas the fourth floor one is the back office.

There's spotless white linen spread over the mattress inside, with a couple of pillows to welcome customers and clients. At the corner of the room stands a mighty iron chest marked with a pious swastika mark in orange vermilion. Above the chest lives a clay model of Lakshmi-Ganesha in duality.

"Take out the deposit slip book of Axis Bank from there please." Atanu took that out as told and remarked, "Don't be so formal with me."

"It's alright."

"Does this lane only have thread business houses like this one?"

"Hmm."

O God! What a man he is! Atanu silently handed over the slip book.

"Do you know how to fill cheques?"

"Sure." Atanu followed the man's shortcut answering style.

"Then fill these up," the man handed him a bunch of cheques. Atanu felt amazed, the first amount being of three lakhs and seventeen thousand. He shuddered. It's so amazing that a piece of paper, merely five inches by three inches in size holds such a huge weight! None of the amounts was less than two lakhs, and there are eight cheques in total. That sums up to around twenty lakhs.

The shudder returned to his fingers.

"Are you finished?"

"Hmm," Atanu is determined to answer back in that man's style only until he behaves properly.

"Bimal babu referred your name?"

"You know him?"

"He often visits here," the man paused and then added, "Did you join here as an accountant?" he clearly sounded very hesitant and disturbed.

Atanu thought, at last, this man was falling into place. It gave him a sense of pride because he assumed, since he, too, had started responding in his monosyllabic way, the man finally decided to change his way and started talking in complete sentences. He forgave the man and gave back a big grin, "Yes. But there's just a lone computer for the two of us."

The man smirks strangely, "Do you think the owner will keep both of us together? If you stay, surely, I will be sided."

Atanu tried to say something back but couldn't. The pale stares on the man's dead face resisted him. He felt uncomfortable before the stares.

Atanu changed the topic of discussion, "Dada, I still don't know your name?"

"I'm Samir Bhattacharya."

"Okay, and I'm Atanu Sanyal."

"Wow, we both are brahmins," the man showed his teeth while throwing a burst of disgusting laughter and asked again, "Where do you stay?"

"Hindmotor. You?"

"I stay in Andul."

"O God. That's quite far."

"Yes, true... Sit here; I'll be back in a few minutes."

After Samir is gone, Atanu silently puts the unused slips back in their place. But as he looked out of the window, he saw another tall, equally dilapidated building. In a hole in its wall, swarms of cockroaches were crawling over a heap of wastes comprising vegetable peels, oven ashes and human excrement. His head started spinning at the scene.

How can he work sitting in this hell for days together? Atanu almost cried when he heard Samir again, "Come, let's go. Come... Quickly... What happened?"

"Ahh..."

"Are you thinking about something?"

"Why the place is so dirty? How do you people stay here?"

"Why? Have you already started hating this place? Yes, initially you will feel that, but later you'll get used to it. Everyone does."

What the heck! How can that be true? Atanu doesn't believe him. He asks, "Where do you want me to go?"

"Boss wants you to go to banks. He asked me to show you those."

"Bank? Why should I be shown those? Does the Boss want his accountant to even run to banks?"

Samir laughed cruelly in reply, "You came to Burrabazar to work. So, get this in mind that you'll have to do everything whatever is asked for. You've to keep accounts, collect money by visiting potential business parties at their places, go to banks, and if situation asks for, even ..." Samir didn't elaborate and pushed him on his back, "Come, let's not waste time in talking."

After walking together for five minutes along MG Road, Samir suddenly asks Atanu, "Are you in relation to Bimal babu?"

Nah-Na. I tutor his son."

"Oh," he paused.

Atanu thought of those days when he felt lost wanting a job. One of his student's father, Bimal Sen, happens to be a renowned Advocate. He knows a lot of people. It took Atanu sometimes to win over his own shyness to one day ask Bimal Babu as submissively as he could, "Uncle, can I say something?"

"Hmm, tell me. Is my child bunking classes again?"

"Na-Na, that's not the case, I mean..."

"What is it then?"

"Can you arrange some work for me?"

"You mean a job?"

"Yes, truly speaking..." Atanu threw up everything before Bimal babu, whatever he had rehearsed for the last five days about his family condition, his elder sister from a failed marriage, his ulcer-ridden mother, his poor father serving as a neighbourhood priest and his half a dozen tuitions, none of which can bear their comma stricken family expenses. Within a few minutes time, he drew a neat picture of their struggling life.

"Do you know computer?"

"Yes, I know accounts-related works."

"Okay. Good. Prepare and share your biodata."

One and a half months went by in silence after that. And then again, Atanu asked, "Uncle, you have not found anything for me, have you?"

"O, do you know computer?"

Atanu sounded disappointed, answering the same question, "Yes, that I know."

"You got any biodata?"

"Yes."

"Okay, come tomorrow around seven in the morning."

Atanu reached half an hour before.

Bimal Babu handed him a piece of paper bearing someone's address and asked him to pay a visit to the place at around eleven in the morning. He said he had already informed a man there about Atanu. The man is his client. A thread trader. He may not pay handsomely, but Atanu will get a job for sure.

Atanu felt elated; Bimal Babu's voice was really assuring. Sometimes, words sound like the prettiest thing in the world.

While returning home, he stopped his cycle to check the address once. It read,

Banwarilal Kejia. 184/A Jamunalal Bajaj Street. Suta Patty.
Burrabuzar.

***

Reaching Chittaranjan Avenue, Samir said happily, "We've been permitted to travel by bus today."

"Okay, but to where?"

"To the State Bank at Ganesh Chandra Avenue."

"Well... But what do you mean by *permitted to travel today*? What do you do on other days, then?" Atanu felt inquisitive.

"On other days, I walk. Bother not, later you too have to graze around Kolkata on your feet. But why worry today? It's your first day at work, after all." Atanu's heart jumped upon hearing these words. I hope he doesn't mean that!

Samir continues, "On my way home often, I can't really feel my legs. Then, thankfully, my daughter used to take care of those at home. A waist pain has also started with it. You ..."

Samir has to stop because a bus has arrived. The conversation couldn't extend inside the crowded bus. The two men could merely look at each other between scores of passengers.

II

The house where Atanu lives still looks the same in its damp ceilings, flaking walls, and cracked-up floors, as it stood together for years. But the residents inside have changed in their moods. His parents and elder sister are all convinced by now that Atanu has turned into the wonder lamp of Aladdin. The more it is rubbed, the more there is the supply of stationery, fuel, milk, fish in meals twice weekly, timely payment of electricity bills, and other luxuries. Atanu's father, being the priest in the local temple, always brought fruit offerings from temple to home, but now those started filling Atanu's lunch box. Since none in his family ever went to fixed duties at offices, adjusting the biological clock in this life has become a challenge for all family members, and they're struggling happily. Rice-dal-curry before going out from home, roti-vegetable-sweets for the tiffin, and oodles of affection every day are loaded with Atanu's journey to the office. It embarrasses Atanu sometimes he wants to shout at them to stop because his office is not that elite; it's a building worse than their house, standing in between a heap of waste and his life there is not of some collared professionals, rather more of a labourer. But then, deep inside him, his turmoil and protest get consoled with a rationale that a workplace is a workplace where you go to earn. Whatever or wherever it may be, the workplace is feeding Atanu's family.

The Burrabazar is a strange place. One never gets to know the place correctly, the crowd here, and the ecosystem here that runs from eleven in the morning to seven in the evening, non-stop. Atanu thinks, all day long, how the people here laugh, cry, shout, push, hug, come and go, tread past intrusion of cockroaches, packs of rats, heaps of wastes, unperturbed. And then there is a man called Samir, whom, for many days, Atanu couldn't understand. One day, while returning from their office, Samir suddenly remarked, "As a Bengali man, I don't want you to work in this environment. This one is a completely unfit place for you."

"What do you mean by unfit place?" Atanu frowned.

Samir answers in a sad voice, "The people here mistreat Bengalis. They treat you like dogs, and employees don't last long here." Samir added, "But you won't get to understand that in your initial days. It will take some time to realise."

Atanu silently tries to think about Samir's intentions. Meanwhile Samir continues,

"You may think I don't want you to be here. I'm sure you may think that too. But that's untrue as I like you. You're young and energetic and can create many opportunities in life. I've ruined my life here, so I don't want you to do the same. You have got time. Try to explore opportunities elsewhere..."

"Try... elsewhere..." Atanu laughed, hearing Samir. "Trying for the job" is a strange phrase in the world, and he doesn't want to go deeper into discussing it. Atanu instead changed the topic, "For how long are you working here?" Samir silently thought for some time, put some tobacco in between his lips and then answered, "It's about nine years or so. Actually, I already had my back to the walls when I joined; I was helpless fighting with poverty."

"Didn't you try elsewhere?"

"I have tried but failed miserably. After that, I hardly have the scope to apply somewhere else after working so hard here all day long. That's the reason I keep on poking you to explore for other jobs. By the way, do you have a girl in your life?"

The sudden question stumped Atanu. He paused and then replied, "Yes." But he doesn't know why he lied.

"Oh! Then it's a bigger problem. What's your age?"

"Twenty-eight."

"Her age?"

"She's still studying. MA in History. Final year." Atanu keeps lying, unfazed.

"O God, she'll start pressing for marriage soon," Samir added, "Is she the only daughter in her house?"

"No, she has got a brother."

"That means the same as me. You won't get property share from your in-laws. So, take this from me: before losing anything more in life, go and join some other jobs."

Atanu marked that this man keeps pursuing him to leave the job! Why is he doing so? Out of fear of competition? Did Atanu disturb the man's safe life by coming here?

Atanu holds his silence. He started analysing his lies; why did he confess to a love affair when, in reality, there was none? In his college days, there was a girl whose beautiful eyes are still there in his memories. But that you can't call love. But it's also true that the old memory still moves his heart. Is the girl still there somewhere?

"At your age, I was such a womaniser, bloody hell! I don't know why girls used to find so much charm in me then. Locals knew me as a famous flirt because of my appearance and act. One day, while romancing one of my partners, I got caught red-handed by another and off! What a mess was created that day... Huh! Huh! Huh! He clapped and laughed at his own joke.

Atanu stared at him with an open mouth. How a passive-looking man suddenly changes in his own melodrama. With an attire composed of grey hairs, wrinkles wriggling all over his forehead, an unshaved beard in untidiness, a couple of teeth missing in the mouth, and holes at the corner of his eyes, and despite that, how a man is claiming himself as a big hit with the girls! Is every lie of the world this hollow, this helpless, this handicapped!

"Come, we've got to go there," Samir showed Atanu the entrance of a house. There is a cemented central courtyard inside, centring around godowns and shops crowding together. By one of the corners of the courtyard runs an iron stair case, which the two started climbing on when Samir advised, "If you decide to stay, then know all the places well. I won't be with you every time."

Walking through a long corridor on the second floor of the building, both of them entered a room decorated similarly in white mattresses and white pillows like their office. A few people were sitting there discussing serious things in a complex Hindi dialect that Atanu failed to understand. None cared about them, and neither did Samir pay any hid to them. The two crossed the room and entered a second room, smaller in size. Atanu saw an overweight young man, perhaps of Atanu's age, sitting on a mattress and talking over the telephone. He has adorned himself with orange vermillion on the forehead and thick gold rings on all the available fingers in his hands. Samir and Atanu took off their slippers and sat on the corner of the mattress, waiting for this man to end his telephone call and attend to them.

After five minutes or so, the fat young man finally finished his conversation over the phone and looked back to Samir, grinning in his gutka-stained teeth.

"Look, the orderlies of Banwari have arrived at my doorsteps," there's clear insolence in his voice.

Samir laughed indifferently, "As you may think."

The young man took out a packet of tobacco, took his time to tear and gulp every little grain and then looked at Atanu, "Ah-ha! A new recruit?"

Samir replied, "Hmm."

"For how many days now... Huh, Huh, Huh?"

His cheeky laughter irked Atanu to the bones all the more when Samir joined the man in the laugh, too. Samir looked at Atanu and said, "See what I said; everyone knows that. Our boss's behaviour never lets anyone stay on the job for long..."

Meanwhile, the man took out a chequebook from his chest, wrote a figure in it, tore it off from the book and extended it, "Banwari was losing sleep over a paltry sum of sixty thousand! I pity him! Or was he thinking I would steal his money? Huh!"

Samir again sheepishly smiled at his words, took the cheque filled in an envelope, and put it inside his handbag.

"Sir, we're taking a leave."

"Sure."

Atanu followed Samir to exit the room.

On the road, Samir starts lamenting, "What a heck of a life I've got, but this was not like that always as once I was such a desperate dude. None could gather the courage to slam me then, not even Banwari. He respects me because once, I sternly protested in a raised voice against his mistreatment. Do you know, in my younger days, once in my own locality, there..."

In the crowded street, the ever-scared worm called Samir Bhattacharya's lampoons got lost, and Atanu started thinking about the long-lost girl whom he had almost forgotten a couple of days ago. Is it possible to suddenly meet her now in the middle of this crowd? Can she recognise Atanu, then? What will she ask him? What will he reply?

Atanu, immersed in his thoughts, was about to lose his way too in the crowded street when Samir pulled his hands, "Oye, are you lost? Never forget your way back."

III

He wakes up early in the dawning hours. He feels confused as to why such thoughts from the past are eating his mind now! There's no denying that what he told Samir was an utter lie, so why are his dreams now laden with the same lie? Atanu can't even remember the girl's name... or is it, Hema? In the college, perhaps, he heard people calling her by that name. She doesn't look like Hema Malini though, nor do Atanu like Hema Malini so much that he will try searching the actress's face in his secret lover. The thoughts are turning into sheer jokes.

He could see himself in the jam-packed streets of Burrabazar, carrying large collections of money in his handbag, walking nervously while thinking about the girl, then expecting her to appear from amidst the crowd. He keeps imagining that she walks up to him and holds his hand and then both zips past, sailing through the swarming streets. Atanu didn't even feel surprised, as if he had expected this to happen. Atanu couldn't laugh at himself as he was prepared for this to occur.

Suddenly, Atanu uttered a swearing and pulled him back from his dream-laced thoughts. He opened the windows to the February dawn, hazed and wet in a wintery sheen. Then he closes it back. He rubs his eyes and wail inside, "What's happening with me?"

In the office, Samir repeated his everyday question, "So what've you decided?"

Atanu twisted his lips and replied, "Dhurr, I'm not finding any satisfaction here."

Samir taunts back, "Oh, that's early! You've just not seen enough here!"

"Neither do I want to. No man can work here."

Samir's dull eyes started glittering upon hearing Atanu's frustration. But then this question-answer game has also become an untiring routine job between the two men when they stay in each other's company.

"I guess yesterday you got some bashings from the boss. Right?"

"Hmm."

"What was your fault?"

"Oh, it was a negligible mistake. I made an error in giving the correct command while reconciling the Bank Statements. It is just a minor outcome of the dearth of practice. But he was like..."

Samir was startled, "You sat at the computer?"

"Yes. Why?"

"When?"

"When you were not around. Perhaps you went out to City Bank."

"Na, Na. You're not supposed to handle the computers when I'm not around. Your errors can delete all data and create a cadaverous situation."

Atanu knows Samir's concern is not about the data loss but about job loss. He panicked because Atanu might get more value from the boss. Till now, Samir has always turned Atanu away from using the computer.

"Never touch the computer in my absence."

"I never touched by myself. Banwari insisted."

"Then deny it on his face. If he scolds you for that, then I'll handle it afterwards."

Atanu acted about his false irritation, "So be it."

But Samir persisted, "But what did he tell you?"

"He mistreated me, insulted me."

Hearing this, suddenly Samir's voice sounded very satisfied, "Take this as just a start. If you stay, you've to silently take a lot more of these bashings. If only I would have a financial condition as sound as you, I wouldn't have given a second thought before resigning."

Samir always treats Atanu as a fortunate and rich compatriot to him. Atanu doesn't know why strugglers always think others are far better than them. But Atanu never protests on his face. Rather, he relishes Samir's misconception about him.

"By the way, what's happening between you and your girlfriend?"

"Nothing much."

"Didn't she ask about your workplace?"

"Of course. And I told her."

"What was her reaction?"

"She asked me to resign."

"Hmm, it's quite natural for her to react like that. I, too, would have done so only if I had not married earlier and had a child right after."

"How old is your daughter?"

"She will be five this year. I have a younger brother, too. He is a special child. Didn't I tell you about that? I'm under unimaginable pressure in life."

"Try your luck somewhere else. May that pay."

"Dhurr, when can I make time for that in between balancing my work and family life? When I reach home at the end of the day, I can barely muster enough strength to simply roll into bed. How can I try?"

In between their conversation, the phone rang. Samir picked up and replied, "Hello, yes, boss. Nah, it hasn't reached yet... Okay... I'll tell them so." He keeps back the receiver.

"What hasn't reached yet? What are you talking about on the telephone?"

"It's puri... Oh, perhaps you don't know about that. Here our boss distributes puri and vegetables to beggars every Saturday. This circus is organised here once weekly... Huh!"

"Circus! Why?" Atanu expressed wonder, to which Samir chuckles, "Wait and watch."

Meanwhile, two Bihari lads entered with baskets of puri and a tub full of vegetables covered in towels.

"Why so late?"

"We haven't got enough men today at our shop."

"This excuse won't land you anywhere in the future. Our boss will otherwise take stern steps if the next day you are late beyond eleven in the morning."

The two lads silently nodded and went away.

"What is this all about? The odour of the food is churning my stomach."

"Just make a wild guess. Or open the lid of the pot and see for yourself."

Atanu checked to find the puri and curry and wondered, "Such an elaborate arrangement! Wow! But for whom?"

"Wait and watch."

As the clock struck twelve, a crowd of beggars started lining up in the courtyard. Mostly women, they start jostling in the lane in front too. They come in groups before their ground floor shop; Samir is distributing Puri vegetables to them packed in sal leaves. Taking four pieces of puri with a spoonful of curry in each pack, he hands that over, with a shouted instruction, "Whoever received food immediately leave and let others come in the front."

Someone in the crowd is heard begging, "Boss, please give me another spoonful of vegetables." The crowd resonates, "I got less, too, give me more." "Here, don't be miser to me, please, boss."

"Should I pour the whole tub before you now? Will that satisfy you?"

"Boss, we have been waiting in the queue for a long time now."

"Then get lost. Nobody called you."

"Boss. Can you give me two more puris?"

"Why should I?"

"Boss, see, he has taken twice."

"Oye, whoever is cheating me is actually making the life tougher for the others because they will lose their food in that case."

"Nah, I didn't take the extra plate for me. It's for my neighbour."

"Neither I took any. I just arrived now, Boss."

"Boss here, two of us are together; give us two plates."

"Well... Where's the other one? Oh, you mean this milk-feeding infant. Can infants eat puri-vegetables? Are you trying to make a fool of me." Samir still allowed two more puris to the mother of the infant.

Atanu was witnessing all in a baffling state of mind when Samir suddenly asked, "Come and help me out." Then a voice from the crowd flew towards him, "Here, our new Boss, we're three of us here. Hand us our share."

Samir rebukes, "Don't try to impress. Atanu, don't give more than four pieces to anyone even if they insist," and then quickly gets busy with his distribution work.

Atanu keeps watching Samir in amazement; a distressed man in poverty that he is appearing like a patron, like a king before this crowd of hungry beggars. Suddenly, someone has whacked a magic wand over the scene. Atanu admired the transformed avatar of Samir.

Samir declares after some time, "Leave. We're out of stock."

The leftover crowd demands, "Then pay us some money instead."

Samir replies, "Come after some time."

"Well, don't make us wait long."

"Don't try to lecture me; I'll do what I can; get lost." He turns to Atanu and instructs, "Go and see inside; behind the chest, there's a bag full of coins. Pull that out."

Atanu dragged out the heavy bag while Samir shooed a couple of stubborn vagabonds, still loitering, threatening not to consider them for giving money.

Atanu opened the bag and found heaps of metal coins, some even obsolete. He wondered whether the obsolete coins should be considered for alms, too, but Samir insisted on keeping them all under consideration as people in want don't discriminate against free gifts.

Samir sounds like a leader and a preacher. Is this the real man hiding inside the man Atanu generally witnesses the rest of the week?

After finishing arranging the coins in separate piles based on their value, Samir asks, "What can you make out?" Atanu shrugs in ignorance.

Samir explains, "Our boss likes to herald his kindness through charity works like this. You could say this is kind of an effort of atonement for oppressing poor souls like us."

"Does everyone do the same here?"

"Some distribute alms, some food. Our boss does both."

"Wherefrom so many beggars have arrived?"

"From Kolkata and beyond. Brother, the whole nation is begging after all. Huh-Huh-Huh!"

Atanu observed in awe how the beggars started coming in a well-organised queue and took their share of money from the piled coins. None tries stealing extras. Samir gave him a snubbing, "Don't waste time on watching. Instead, attend your own work."

In less than half an hour, the beggars vanish after taking their shares and keeping half a dozen obsolete coins. Atanu showed that to Samir, but Samir ignored it and got busy with work. Atanu was too immersed in checking the sales register.

Suddenly, a kid's voice was heard, "Uncle taking two coins." Atanu finds a bare body 6-7-year-old boy in a loosely fitting half-pant standing there with an old woman. The dirty-clothed woman shouted at the boy, watching him taking the two obsolete 10-paise coins. She uttered a peculiar term for the coins, "Kochi paisa." It sounded funny to Atanu's ears. He couldn't hold his laugh, but Samir remained serious.

IV

Everybody is dragging through a short-lived but large life filled with truth and lies from every day.

– Atanu's pen stopped here. Then he wrote next – *honestly speaking, people live happily under the shadow of their own lies, helpless and weak.* Atanu closes his diary. Atanu is writing his diary again after a great many days. He had almost forgotten his green diary, selling himself in the crowd of strange people all day long. Tonight, he suddenly remembered, dragged it out and started writing in the diary after many days. Atanu sleeps alone in a separate room. While his elder sister sleeps with their parents in another room. There is a door separating their rooms, but the cracks in the door panels let each other know if the other in the neighbouring room is still awake. Noticing the light from his room, Atanu's mother advised him not to be late to sleep. But Atanu couldn't sleep; tiredness couldn't let him sleep. The moment he closes his eyes, problems from the world around crowds before his eyes. The crowding chokes him. Every day, he decides to leave his job, and every day, he changes his decision. It reminds him that three living beings are waiting for his income to quench their thirst. Atanu wants to gather experience and shift to a better office. But where is such a job? Where are the people who offer him such a job? Where is the girl whom she dreams of every night? Does she even remember him? Bizarre thoughts usurp his mind and scare him. Atanu quickly switches off the light and closes his eyes.

"Do you know I'm losing my job?" Samir declares.

"What?" a startled Atanu looked at him.

"Yesterday, I heard Banwari talking to somebody against me. He will not keep me here."

"Dhurr... that's not possible."

"But why not? When he pays me twenty-seven hundred, he got you in just eighteen hundred. Why should he bear me anymore? But I feel so scared and lost now! There are so many at my home to feed!"

"It's impossible; Banwari can't drive out an employee of so many years."

"He can. He is very unkind."

"But none can match your contributions."

"There's nothing that stops in the want of anyone. Oh, I'm feeling so abandoned!"

Atanu stared at the man, the one who was distributing food among the beggars like a king the other day. Today, he's again wriggling back like a worm. Atanu felt a lump in his throat. He tried to attend to his work instead.

Samir again asked, "You haven't got any job anywhere else, right?"

Atanu nodded in denial.

"Have you searched?"

"Yes. But failed." Atanu lied. Both become silent. Then the phone rang, and Samir took the receiver.

"Yes, boss, okay boss, sending him."

Samir looked at Atanu and asked him to go to Banwari on the fourth floor. Atanu suddenly observed a glimpse of excitement on his face. Why so? Is Atanu mistaken?

He murmured, "But why will he call me?" to which Samir shrugged, "I presume you must have made some mistakes at work."

The owner doesn't interact with Atanu much; he generally sends his instruction through Samir. Then today, what happened?"

Atanu climbed up to the owner's fourth-floor chamber nervously, "May I come in, Sir? What happened, Sir?"

"Hmm. Come in. What happened, Atanu? I heard you're not working properly."

"Me? Why?" Atanu fumbled in disbelief.

"Listen, brother, you have been employed here for Bimal Babu's reference, but if you can't perform, then that will be a big problem."

"But Sir, I couldn't..."

"Yes, I heard that you're neglecting duty hours."

Atanu was stunned at this allegation. Who can blame him like this?

The stout man Banwari suddenly broke into laughter, "Brother, don't let all these nonsenses disturb you; rather, work hard. I have already started liking you, and in the future, I've decided to make you work all by yourself. Samir is already a heck of a haggard. Understand all he knows as quickly as you can. Okay? Now, you may leave."

"Okay, Sir."

Atanu was leaving when he heard the owner's voice again, "Listen, don't talk about our discussion with anyone."

"Okay, Sir."

While climbing down the stairs, Atanu was in shock at how Samir could falsely put blame on him and provoke the owner against him. How a close colleague like him can put a dagger from behind? The more he thinks, the more he turns into rage.

There in the room downstairs, Samir was possibly in more anguish than Atanu. Atanu looked directly into his eyes. There is an intense excitement mixed with guilt in Samir's eyes. Before Atanu's furious eyes, Samir quickly recoiled and relented. Atanu didn't utter a word till Samir gathered the courage to ask, "What happened? Anything serious?"

"Nah, nothing serious."

"What's that supposed to mean?"

"He just inquired about my work. Nothing more."

"Really? No. That can't be. Please tell me what happened?"

"I told you already, nothing serious."

Samir fell short of words; he only kept frowning in disbelief. After a pause, he made a final try, "Please, please, I'm really excited to know what actually happened up there between you two?"

"Seriously, nothing mentionworthy happened upstairs. Were you expecting something exciting to happen, you mean?"

Atanu's question silenced Samir. None talked a word anymore after that.

Around seven thirty in the evening, both were walking on the MG Road on their way home up to Howrah station. Usually, they walk the stretch together. Since the afternoon event, Samir has not been talking and behaving like a holed-up animal. On the contrary, Atanu wasn't angry with him, but he felt a certain amount of discomfort working together. After a long pause, he was the first to ask Samir, "What's keeping you so silent? After all, today is the final day; you're getting an opportunity to talk with me." Samir was staring at him.

Atanu smiles, "I'm leaving the job."

There was an apparent disbelief in Samir's voice now, "W-hat! I mean, why?"

Atanu noticed that and tried to remain as unmoved as he could. He replied, "I actually didn't tell you, but then Banwari insulted me very badly. He said that I didn't know about

Accountancy and that I neglected my duties every day. It's proving to be fruitless keeping me in his company."

Samir's eyes glittered back in excitement, "Really? So, starting tomorrow, you won't be coming?"

"Even after all these? Do you think I'm that much shameless! There are hundreds of jobs available in the market. What happened, and why have you stopped walking? Come, let's move ahead."

"Huh-Huh-Huh!" Samir looks like an excited kid in the middle of a pool of gladness, "Didn't I tell you before, this man is cruel? He destroys people's lives. I know I've ruined myself, but..." Samir keeps repeating the dialogues that he has uttered scores of times already. Atanu kept watching the helpless liar immersed in his madness. He found a strange comfort in watching.

They both reached Howrah Bridge, walking and talking. There, the crowd is pacing to catch trains from the railway station. A cool breeze is flowing from the Ganga. After a long pause, Samir's head remains hung. Atanu was about to say something when the rough, pale-skinned hands of a hackneyed man held Atanu's hands in all the wetness of sweat and tear, "let bygones be bygones; the truth remains I really like you, brother."

The Winged

"Last January, it felt colder, ain't it?" Anushka sounds curious.

Krishnendu was busy rubbing his palms to raise body heat. Not only did he fail to light the cigarette with his trembling fingers, but it even flipped from his lips soon, as he felt too weak between his fluttering jaws in the cold. But finally, he overcame the struggle, held it tight between his lips, lit it, exhaled some fumes, and doubted her, "What are you saying! I'm finding the cold more bitter than the previous year. I'm missing my hand-gloves."

"Dhusss, you forget that the last time there was knee-deep snow everywhere around the hotel due to the whole night of snowing. But, this time, where can you see that much snow around?

"Listen, madam, snowfall always mitigates the cold. This year, the bone-chilling wind is actually proving a killer from even under these bales of woollens and leather jackets, caps and mufflers. Look how I'm shivering."

"You're getting older; hi-hi-hi," Anushka laughed, freezing vapours came out of her mouth when she talked. It was dawning a new day on the heights of the mountains in Sandakphu, and they were witnessing the sunrise together with a few more crazy spectators in the open, staring to the east. In the beginning, chunks of clouds started rising from the depths of the valley, accumulating there all night, racing to reach the mountain peaks. Next, it's the turn of the first rays of the sun. The clouds soon started shining, and the sky soon witnessed a beautiful rainbow at dawn. The sun then wands a magic stick to play a maddening spell of illuminating spectacle. Fascinated, Anushka forgot to use her camera and stood numb while Krishnendu whispered in her ears, "After witnessing such a scene on earth, I can even die." There's the mighty Kanchenjunga on the horizon. Other ranges like Kumbhakarna, Three Sisters, and even a pint-sized Everest were visible, framing the stage as the sun cast spell after spell, presenting the most mesmerising show for the earthly spectators.

"How fortunate we are! I feel like the king of heaven."

They stood there until the whole world started basking in the broad daylight of the sun again, putting down the screen on the charming game of its rising for the day. Krishnendu asks, "Let's go back."

"Anushka, you still haven't replied to my question; which one do you like the most?" Krishnendu is now sitting on the beach, witnessing the sunset of the day.

"Of which you're talking about, Krishnendu?"

"I mean, the Sea or the Mountains? Which one is your favourite?"

"What's your favourite?"

"Umm...Hmm, I asked you first."

"I know, but I couldn't describe."

"Why?"

"The Sea remains inside my heart."

"Oh, and the mountains are mounted over your chest."

"Stop it, you savage!" Anushka mocked, anger in her voice, but her eyesight kept sailing over thousands of waves in the sea. She calmly adds, "I hope you're right to some extent; the mountain, indeed, is my heart. Now tell me about your choices?"

"For me, Sea is the mind, and Mountain is the soul." They smiled lightly at each other when the ripples in the wet beach caressed their feet.

"Krishnendu, I suppose you like incomplete things. Is it true?"

"Which incompleteness are you talking about?"

"Emptiness, Hollow, Zero, how should I explain you?"

"Oh, then incompleteness supplements completeness."

"Wow, that's a phrase with a very deep meaning. Where have you learned that?"

"From the Upanishad."

"You're studying Upanishad?"

"Na-Nah."

"Do you remember earlier when we went to the desert and faced that sandstorm?"

"Uff, of course, how could I forget that! A calm and quiet sand field turned into turmoil in minutes. It was an unbelievable experience." Anushka looked at Krishnendu. The lights of the setting sun illuminated Krishnendu's facial profile and his whole body, lounging in the glory of the golden shine. Not only he, but the whole earth is bathing in an aureate glimmer. Krishnendu remarked, "Nature plays different music based on different landscapes, and you witness it in. For example, by a mountain spring, one can't miss hearing the sound of santoor, while in the middle of the forest, there's the staid sound of metal."

"Well, what can you hear now?"

"Sarengi. Of Sultan Khan. Close your eyes; you will hear that too."

Both closed their eyes and listened to how the sound of his sarangi flowed through the scratched landscape of yellow sands and rustling winds. Anushka reminded, "Today will be a full moon night."

"We will get to see a full moon night for the first time in the desert. Can I bear the extreme beauty of it?" The sun was setting in between their conversations, and the darkness was oozing in, drip by drip. Waiting for the inevitability, Anushka holds Krishnendu's hands tightly.

Then Alas! A power cut took place on the office floor. And with that, the amazing nature scene in the computer screen saver disappeared. With that disappeared the dreaminess of the two IT employees of a renowned MNC whose favourite game at the recess period was a game of imagination, of visiting various places sitting in their office chambers.

"Wah, it's all ruined now." Krishnendu rued. Anushka remains silent, still sailing in her leftover imagination.

"You haven't got a power backup with your system?"

Anushka didn't want to respond to Krishnendu's query and break her overwhelms. Meanwhile, the beeps of the power backup system inside the office floor keep blaring from all corners.

These two people play this game every day during their recess period. Krishnendu taught this to Anushka. He assured them she would soon fall in love with this game, though Anushka didn't quite fancy this childish game at all. But in between the routine of long stretches of work and going back dead tired dozing, all along in the office vehicle, entering home and unknowingly having dinners at late hours and dropping into bed like a dead body from Monday to Friday, this game has kind of breathed life in Anushka. It's not that Krishnendu hasn't proposed any other solutions other than this foolish game. He offered day-outs to places like Bakkhali or Gadiara for the two, but Anushka never liked the idea. Instead, she chose a weekend of pure sleeping and recharged her body and mind for the next week's life battle. During the weekends, she sleeps, watches TV, flips through magazines, thinks unnecessary thoughts and sleeps back. Anushka is a convent-educated girl from the peri-urban Srirampur. She did her BSc. Honours commuting daily by local trains to the Presidency College. Her father died after her college Part II exams due to a heart attack, leading to a halving of the government pension and a permanent frown towards her from the beautiful newlywed sister-in-law. It was really tough to search for a job, failing interview after interview till, on a friend's suggestion, she sat for the screen test for a fresher's job in this current company and succeeded. Her smartness and fluency in speaking earned her the job. But then, in the initial months, when travelling back home on the last train of the day started scaring her, this boy Krishnendu offered a solution.

Krishnendu, the tall, dark, handsome man with a pure Oxford accent, introduced himself to Anushka on the second day of her joining. From day one, the man's steep nose, back-brushed hairs, elongated fingers, enticing eyesight, and such deep details made Anushka's head spin. But the funny bone that he has unknowingly freed the introverted girl in her, and she transformed into a carefree, open-minded Anushka before him. Krishnendu's roll of laughter started to drench Anushka's soul more often. His description of the numerous solo trips to faraway lands fascinated Anushka. She wondered once,

"Aren't you scared to go on solo trips to unknown places?"

"No, rather I feel scared to return to this city of crowds and traffic, long hours of office work after my trips to the unknown places."

"Why do you plan a return then?" It was a foolish question to ask, though, to Krishnendu, who has the burden of a retired father, an ulcer-stricken sick mother and unmarried sisters upon his shoulder.

But to her foolish question at first, Krishnendu, smiling a strange smile, had replied, "Let the time come; I will not return for sure." And then, in a roll of laughter, he sang Rabindranath,

"I know, I know, my Friend –

Your arms are there always for me."

It was an indescribable sensation that she felt that day. She asked herself later, whose arms Krishnendu had talked about. Is it about her? Anushka withdrew. But Krishnendu remained the same easy person. He offered her a solution, "Anushka, don't take the risk of journeying late at night to return to Srirampur daily. Rather arrange your stay here in some ladies' hostels or rented accommodation. Their company offered Anushka a good monthly package, and she managed to find herself a single-room flat at Ultadanga with Krishnendu's help. She never cared to thank him because, by then, they were more than friends to care for any formalities. Krishnendu was always there by her during office hours, but Anushka still longed for someone's support in her loneliness in her new rented accommodation. So, her mother started visiting her at times. Anushka wanted to call her permanently at her home, but her elder brother never let her do that. Now, sometimes she feels really scared. Krishnendu understands that. He says, "Go and stay with your mother for some days." Anushka refuses that. Krishnendu gives a Plan B.

"Stay by yourself then, away from the office job. You need some break."

That's true because she is overperforming nowadays, and that has earned the company accolades, too. But she disagreed again.

"Staying by myself throughout the day in that lonely rented house is also an impossible task."

"Then I will join you."

"Really! Will you come and join?"

"I don't mind."

The fright of loneliness made her forget societal norms and restrictions.

"Why do you remain bogged down in office life?"

"I don't have other options."

"Or you don't want to explore other options? Do you know, exploring options opens up the road to new desires?"

Krishnendu's game had opened the horizon of new desires inside Anushka. She keeps thinking about the open sky, green forests, and high mountains. Her dreams and desires jammed up with reality and her objective. Anushka thought she would tell Krishnendu that she had decided not to play the game of imagination anymore. However, with the rising work pressure, she only had some respite when playing this game with Krishnendu.

"Madam, will you come here by me, please, for once?" Krishnendu kept calling, but Anushka was too busy at work. She has been recently promoted to the post of Team Leader. She was too busy with the data. But then Krishnendu's voice entered her ears after much effort. "Umm, are you calling?"

"Hmm, for ages."

"Can that wait?"

"Maybe, but if you come, it will help both of us."

Anushka couldn't avoid Krishnendu's call. Neither can she move her eyeballs from the picture that Krishnendu showed from his computer. There is a white bird with a long, narrow beak diving into the blue water to swim. The wings are still spread.

"I called you to show this."

"Good."

"Can you name this bird?"

"No"

"Arctic terns. Migratory birds. They can fly all over the world, from North to South, with the support of these two wings. Can't you find grains of snow-sand-smut of the planet, global forest-sea-hills and the world's geography on those two wings? I pray I could be like this bird."

Anushka laughed, "You should have been a poet. I have heard that poets always live in their imaginary world."

"No, dear, you don't have to be a poet. We all have wings, but we forget to unfold and fly. I can teach you that."

"Don't start this again," Anushka quickly moves away from this man with a laugh. She knows he's crazy, but those are not lunacy; Anushka loves his nuances. But she couldn't waste time liking or loving someone else's shades and nuances now. She has got work in hand.

Krishnendu came to pursue Anushka again during the lunch hours, but Anushka strictly declared beforehand, "There will be no game today."

Krishnendu nodded, "Okay," and then added, "Just for a special reason, can we play it for ten minutes."

"And what's the special reason?"

"The reason is today is a Friday, and we will be playing only for the last day of this week. Moreover, I won't be around in Kolkata for the next two weeks to disturb you."

"Why won't you be around?"

"Because I'm spreading my wings."

"To where?"

"Not that far away, though, to Lava. Actually, when I went there a few years ago, the weather was not good. So I decided to visit again."

"Solo?"

"Would you like to join?"

"Do you care about my wishes?"

"O, I have got strong wings. If you can hold them strongly, you can have a tour of the world with me."

"Then leave me to myself; I'm better off at my home."

"So, you don't want to play the game?"

"Okay, let's play, but strictly for ten minutes."

Before starting, Krishnendu asks, "Do you really like the routine life that spanned between your office and home?"

"See, Krishnendu, I had to struggle a lot to reach where I am. Once there was no ground under my feet, and at that time. I got to know all my so-called well-wishers. I understood that nobody helps you in distress. So, I don't want to lose my job now and willingly fall in agony."

Krishnendu heard her minutely and then nodded, "I can't totally agree with you. Because when you say that you get to know others in your days of distress, you are wrong. Because in your days of distress, you actually get to know yourself rather than others. Do you think you did that? Do you think you now know yourself?"

"No, I'm not sure about recognising myself. But please leave the serious topic."

"So be it. Topic changed. Have you seen the pictures from my previous Lava trip?"

"Umm...Hmm, I don't remember."

"Wait," saying this, Krishnendu shares an album folder from his desktop with Anushka. They then opened it together at Anushka's computer to watch the pictures, each of which bears hazy backgrounds, misty forest scenes, wet roads lost amidst thick clouds, a monastery and a little museum covered in fog and rain. Krishnendu continues commenting in a whispering tone – "This is the jungle of Lolegaon. It was raining there then, and you could hear each water droplet falling in the middle of complete silence. There was a mysterious fog dancing all around you. That was the first time I admired the beauty of haziness. I have witnessed clear blue sky, lush green forests, and glimmering white peaks on the horizon many times in life but never witnessed wisps of thick fog hiding everything around me. I won't be able to explain to you the thrill and romance of the situation. I was having a sense of standing in the sky between clouds.

Anushka again moves to a trance under the magical spell of Krishnendu's commentating and the visuals running before her eyes.

"How was your ten-minute trip to Lolegaon, madam? Fooding is free on the trip, by the way." Krishnendu laughed, broke her spell and offered her a share of his lunch. "Come back... madam."

"So you have decided to go; it's final?"

"Yes, so I decided."

"Do you know you are a bad person. You are eating my brains; you're ruining my life."

Krishnendu laughed again, "No, I still can't do that. You still couldn't spread your wings. But try to be by yourself for some days in my absence. Save these photographs in your folder and keep watching those during your free time."

"Are you mad! I won't look at those! I won't do anything you suggest." Anushka nods her head strongly.

"I thought that you would follow every bit of advice I give to you..."

"Get lost, will you..!"

***

The week passed, followed by countless days, but Anushka could do nothing except silently long for Krishnendu. He called once after reaching there, but that was his only call. Undoubtedly, that speaks about his irresponsibility because Anushka, on the other hand, remembers him every moment, between her work, during recess, and amidst her loneliness at home; she is seriously feeling the big difference between his presence and absence. He told her to unfold her wings, but did he mean that Anushka doubted that; do humans really have some invisible wings hidden inside their limbs? Then again, how could that be unfolded... Anushka feels like going mad in crazy thoughts. But neither could she forget his insensible ravings nor focus on her sensible office work. She misses the non-sense work that she used to do in company of Krishnendu. She decides to confront Krishnendu the next time they meet and make him understand clearly his sheer callousness in not calling her and making her wait.

Anushka's birthday is on the twenty-eighth of February. But does he even remember that? It's only a couple of days to go. Lost in thoughts, in between her office works, Anushka accidentally opened a folder full of photographs that Krishnendu clicked and shared. Photograph after photograph, she scrolled, and they started commenting about their backstories to her ears in a whispering magical voice like Krishnendu's...

See the lushness of green in me? Would you like to hide in the middle of that, see the blue of the space above? Won't you sail there, here, watch the flow of water, or care to dive deep down? Nah! Lunacy will surely catch up if she continues playing this game by her any longer. She needs crazy Krishnendu by her. She can't bear his absence... Uff!

After silently bearing another couple of unbearable days in the biting loneliness of a distressed maiden, Anushka finally finds Krishnendu at the office on the twenty-seventh. Anushka quickly acted to be busy at work, not seeing him. Krishnendu comes to her and announces, "Here I've arrived."

Raising her acting skill considerably, she lackadaisically replied, "Well, I can see that. So, should I be happy?"

"Yes, because I'm a day early."

"Early from what?"

"What's this? Don't you remember that I've got an invitation to attend your birthday tomorrow, dear?"

"Oh! So, you remember that?"

"How can I forget?"

"Okay, but I still didn't invite you."

"That doesn't matter because had you invited me formally, then I would have thought twice."

Anushka couldn't hold her false seriousness anymore and giggled, "Promise that you will really come."

"Undoubtedly."

"Well, I will see."

"I have clicked a lot of pictures this time. I will show you those tomorrow."

Waking up the next morning, she could feel happiness dripping like dew drops on green leaves, like palm juice on earthen pots, thus filling the depth of her mind. It was her birthday, and Krishnendu promised to come. He actually never stepped in here after helping her to rent it. Initially, she invited him a few times to come to her new address, but he always turned her down, saying, "Wait for the right time. I'll surely come."

Is today the 'right time?' but then what if he doesn't turn up? What if he breaks his promise? Still, Anushka didn't want to lose her hope. She switched on her mobile and found three missed call alerts from her elder brother. Possibly, it was to wish her for the special day. Should she call back? But then she thought that calling someone to take a birthday wish looked like a foolish idea. In her childhood, her mother used to prepare puddings; today, the thought suddenly flashed in her mind. Here in her rented house, Anushka has employed a cook, and she plans to instruct her to prepare Krishnendu's favourite dishes. But then she doesn't know what Krishnendu loves to eat. The boy perhaps doesn't have anything favourite other than touring places. So fried rice and chilli chicken would be a nice idea to treat him, she thought. Thereafter, the day went by, arranging the room, supervising cooking, doing other daily chores, and eyeing the clock every now and then, in between. But there is no denying that nervousness remains laden in every work, and with that, a sense of worry, doubt, and restlessness keeps driving her throughout the day. Slowly, the evening ushers in the wait and after that, finally, when the clock hand touches nine, Anushka gets angry with herself. What a waste of a day she did sitting at home by taking a leave from the office, amidst so many unfinished jobs that she neglected for this irresponsible boy. When it was as late as ten in the night, the doorbell rang. Anushka was shocked, "Who can that be at this late hour?" But her shock turned into an unexplainable ecstasy when she opened the door, where a very well-known face was standing in all smiles.

"At this hour?"

"Or else, when had you expected me? I remember that your birth time was quarter past eleven in the night, and in that way, I'm still quite early."

"Did you plan to stay that late?"

"If you allow."

The sensation that just took place on hearing this is not at all known to Anushka. Suppressing this alien feeling inside her, her eyes started following Krishnendu, roaming around the room. She tried to remain calm and normal and asked, "What would you like to have?"

"Tea."

In two minutes, Anushka brought tea for both from her flask.

Krishnendu looks at his watch and declares, "An hour more for you to be born."

Anushka says, "You've lost weight a lot; aren't you taking care of yourself?"

"Dhuss... leave that, rather answer to me; how was it without me in the last ten days?"

"Fabulous!"

"Really?"

"Of course. There was none to disturb me in between my works."

"And the photographs... Haven't you seen them?"

"Which photographs? I don't know what you're talking about." Anushka tried to play act, but it proved to be overacting because she was caught before his deep, probing eyes. He joked, "Ghost photographs!" and laughed loud.

The conversation went on until the deep of the night making Anushka wonder whether Krishnendu at all had plans to leave for his home. What if it's too late to leave for Krishnendu? The alien feeling again ushered in and gave her a peculiar sense of joy.

"Ehh, it's past eleven. Quickly take out the cake."

"Where will I get a cake?"

"Oh-ho! I forgot to take that out; here it is." Krishnendu took out a cake box and a candle from his office bag and added, "I was skeptical about the number of candles to buy... I mean, I couldn't quite remember whether you are turning forty-two or forty-five this birthday, so I brought just one."

Anushka concealed her smiles while taking the cake and the candle and replied, "I will be sixty-nine."

Both laughed, and Krishnendu prodded her, "Be quick, it's time to cut the cake. Bring a plate and a knife."

Anushka rushed back with a plate and knife, her heart bursting with happiness. They blew the candle together. Anushka invited him to cut the cake with her and said,

"Today, we were both born together." An intense feeling of elation starts flooding Anushka when she holds Krishnendu in her arms.

They cut the cake together, sang the birthday song together, and partied together with an imaginary crowd of well-wishers around. Then Krishnendu took out a gift meant for the birthday girl. She unwrapped the gift with delightful gazing eyes and found a CD with a piece of paper inside with the writings, "In the wait of the day when you unfold wings."

"What's this? A blank CD?"

"Let's find out, bring your computer."

"Shouldn't we have dinner before that? It's very late already."

"Let that be. Play this first."

Anushka took Krishnendu to her bedroom the first time an unknown man stepped in there. Again, it raised the hairs on the back of her shoulder. She conceals her excitement. Anushka switched on her laptop lying in a corner, and they inserted the CD into the computer to play when Krishnendu asked Anushka to sit on the chair while he offered to stand behind her. The CD starts playing hills in lushes of greenery, clouds sailing in the blue deepness of the sky, the dancing Teesta river, deep forest, setting sun, maids from unknown mountain tribes, Kanchenjunga, one after another.

He whispers, here I give you the best moments from my life. Anushka's heart throbbed like a baby bird in Krishnendu's company, but she tried to hide her feelings. He whispers, "All the scenes are from Kalimpong, Delo Park, and Suicide Point." Anushka chips in, "Why does such a beautiful place have such a strange name?" "Because a couple from the local tribes committed suicide here to ensure their bondage in the afterlife." "Issh..." Anushka shudders.

"Can you imagine in their last moments of fall how they were holding each other's hand in a journey to the unknown?"

"Is it possible to think of love in such a moment?"

"Maybe, I don't know. I only know that when we do that, we won't fall, we will fly, we will sail through the ether of romance."

"I feel scared, Krishnendu; what if I lose my way to everything that I have earned?"

"What have you earned to lose? If you've really earned something, you won't lose that life long. Isn't it true that…"

"S-i-l-e-n-t!" Her fingers covered his lips, and then his arms embraced her from behind. It was like a trance. She's completely under a spell of charm. Rest, as they say, has been history.

After missing the date of her periodic cycle this month, Anushka started feeling discomfort all through her body. There's an unfamiliar feeling in the lower abdomen. As a result, she couldn't focus on her normal work, but though her life started changing, Krishnendu remained unchanged, normal, and indifferent. Anushka started avoiding him and started to remain buried in work even during recess. She tries hard to do soul-searching as she starts feeling she's becoming an alien to herself. Soon, the head of her department called her to alert her of her inattentiveness, mistakes at work, and negligent behaviour. The company warns her that underperformance may lead her to lose her job. Anushka shuddered in fear. She only murmured, "Sorry, Sir," and fled from the man. Coming back to her seat, she vowed to get out of every thought which was not related to her job, her profession. In between her and the career, there is no life, no friends, no relations, nothing.

"Anushka, what has happened to you?"

"Nothing."

"Then what makes you keep a distance from me?"

"Work pressure, of course."

"Is that the only reason?"

"Yes. And moreover, if I lose my job and I'm unable to handle the pressure, then there's nobody to take care of me." Anushka stressed something: Krishnendu understood jolly well, and he took a leave from her. Anushka felt bad, too, but she was helpless as this crazy boy was becoming her only priority, and that was harmful to her career. So, this is the only way for Anushka to forget everything and look ahead in life.

Meanwhile, the discomfort in the lower abdomen has only increased day by day. It could be felt even in the middle of business at the office. She tries to think that it's only because of extreme work burdens, unstable food habits, irregular sleep and mental pressure. Soon her rationales couldn't stand because even when she rested or slept, the feeling kept driving her crazy. She couldn't sleep well or rest freely. One day, she stood before the mirrors in the house, stripping completely to have a look at the strange, swollen underbelly. She couldn't believe her eyes at first. She tried hard to remember what happened that night when Krishnendu stayed with her, but all her efforts were in vain as she could remember nothing. She does not understand what happened to her usually strong memory. She can't even take the help of Krishnendu. She buys the preg-test kit to check, but no positive result has been obtained either. It confuses her even more as the swelling keeps growing. She fears getting caught before her acquaintances will only get her wrong before them. She stopped wearing fitting clothes and started choosing more loose clothes. She keeps thinking all the people around are only looking at her abdomen, and she keeps pulling the end of the clothes to cover the engorged belly time and again so frequently that it turns into a bad habit. The thought of getting caught in someone's hand was driving Anushka mad. Here, the swelling never takes the name of stopping and keeps growing and growing at an unbelievably faster pace. In no days' time, the abdomen becomes so full that one can't hide it under even the most oversized clothes. Anushka thought that, in this condition, she couldn't go back to her mother either, so it would only be wise to take leave and sit at home for a few days. She cursed Krishnendu for everything. She books a doctor's appointment at a faraway nursing home.

Nowadays, Anushka has been standing before the mirror several times. The strange feeling inside the abdomen has gotten stronger. She prays that she must have a peaceful abortion of her pregnancy. She has decided to leave the job in this office permanently and move somewhere else. It won't be wise to stand before the man once again. Anushka couldn't eat a nimble the whole day. She's feeling like throwing up every grain of food she has inside her. There, through her abdomen, something is trying to push out. She goes to be crazy with herself. She is in a rage, and she can't remember any of the incidents that happened on her birthday night.

The pain made her go nuts that night. It only increases, and it becomes a challenge to maintain a sense of tolerating the excruciating pain. She soon raised her legs, pressing her knees on her chest. The clock chimed midnight when Anushka was yelling in unimaginable agony, moaning, biting her lips in a kind of pain totally unknown to her. Soon, she started frothing in her mouth when the quintessential woman inside her let her know that the water had broken. The bed turned into a mess. But like every distress has an end, Anushka too could feel in the darkness of the bedroom that from the dark world of her womb, a dark something is coming out through a tunnel to the world. Something got released finally, and Anushka couldn't even open her eyes for some time together. And then she tried to raise her body, pressing on her elbows, and what she found? What a strange scene unfolds before her! What a bizarre piece of life has just been born out of her! An organism which looked like, not a human, not like a primate, but a bird... What was the name of the bird she saw a few days back, the bird with huge wings diving in the blues of the water? The bird which flies across the world on its strong wings? She couldn't remember the bird's name. The strange part is that its eyes are totally like those of humans. The way of looking is so known to Anushka. She keeps shuddering with an unexplainable emotion. The little birdie repeatedly tried to unfold its wings. It keeps trying and failing but never fails to try. Anushka carefully cut the naval thread to free her offspring. She whispers in its ears, "I know you; I've known you for years." The rest of the night, she told so many stories to her child till she went to sleep.

In the morning, someone arrives at the door, and the busy ringing of the doorbell wakes Anushka up. She was still tired but dragged herself up to the door. She was feeling completely empty, totally hollow in mind. Before opening the entrance door, Anushka once again looked at the newborn she gave birth to a few hours ago. It is growing restless and unable to balance itself on both its wings. It touched her by its beak. Anushka touched its back lightly and said, "Wait for a few more moments before I let you fly to the horizon." She opened the door to find a restive Krishnendu standing there.

"Come inside."

"I don't want to disturb you, but I just came here to say..."

Anushka was too tired and cut him short, "Please come inside."

"How are you?" Krishnendu sounds confused and affectionate.

Anushka pointed a finger on her lips and then gestured him to follow her to the bedroom, "I had to show you something. There, see, by the window pane... it's our child... born last night."

Both fell silent after that amidst the darkness of the bedroom. Nobody knew what the parents of the newborn witnessed, but they decided to open the window and free their offspring to the open sky.

A Few Many in an Island

At least tonight we have to sleep together in the same bed. There are no other options. *We* comprise of me, my wife Siuli, my childhood friend Jayanta and his wife Kajari. The room that has been allotted to us has a solitary bed, though bigger than what all four of us required together to lie down, probably meant for half a dozen users. But still, it causes a certain level of discomfort between two couples. After all, there is a pair of men who have known each other from childhood and a pair of women who have been sheer strangers to each other until now. The room is full of dust, filled on the floor and covered on the furniture. There's a tin-built bedside table with a glass to drink water. There's a finger-sized, half-burnt candle nearby to light up the evening darkness. The attached bathroom is something that could make anyone feel disgusted. I was the first one to enter and felt the same because there were cobwebs everywhere, brushing against my face, and numerous families of spiders and cockroaches seemed ready to attack. The most terrible part was the dirty commode, still bearing the signs of the previous user. Since the user never cared to use the flush, I couldn't gather the courage to do so either. We immediately called the office and requested that the toilet be cleaned as soon as possible. Unfortunately, the office did not heed our request. Instead, we were fortunate enough to quickly receive four sets of clean pillow covers, a white bed sheet, and a mosquito net. We made our beds ourselves and sat on them, completely stumped by the situation. None of us could manage to utter a word for a long time due to exhaustion, anguish, and annoyance.

The room was stuffy, and there was a power cut. The war-torn ceiling fan hung like an old, haggard figure. Siuli was the most annoyed among us; the summer heat, the tiredness from our journey, and this unimaginable welcome at the hotel had caused her face to redden abnormally with frustration.

Jayanta was the first to break the silence, coughing slightly, "Let bygones be bygones. This can happen to anyone, so there's no point in dwelling on it. It's only our fate to blame here for all this." Upon hearing these words, Siuli finally lifted her face, as she had been blaming herself and feeling responsible for our troubles.

Actually, it happened because Independence Day, which was a Friday, brought two extra holidays with it. Siuli and I were looking for a three-day getaway. Meanwhile, I happened to meet Jayanta on the street and discussed my intention to find a peaceful place for a holiday. He then suggested visiting this lonely hamlet, a place that hardly anyone visits throughout the year.

"Where?"

"Sagardweep."

"You mean Gangasagar?"

"Yes. I was told that the beach is excellent and completely devoid of crowds."

"That's a great idea then."

"Can we join?"

"Of course. No problem."

"But what about lodging?"

"Why don't you find one for all of us? I'll try, too."

"So be it."

I didn't have to give much effort after that because the moment I told Siuli about the place over the phone, she assured me that she had got sources to arrange lodging there. Her aunt is a member of the Janaseva Sangh, and the Sangh has a grand facility established there in Gangasagar. So, When one carries a letter of recommendation from a member, accommodation will be guaranteed to him or her, free of cost.

Great news indeed, I thought. Siuli arranged a letter from her aunt, endorsing our names and clearly mentioning, "Provide two good rooms for them." Her aunt even called the local authority of the Sangh to double assure the arrangement. Then, today, in the early morning, we took the pain to first catch a bus from Esplanade to Harwood Point at Namkhana. Then, from there, a huge vessel took us sailing across the waves of the widespread Ganga to the Sagardwip. After the vessel journey, only after hitching a trekker ride for another thirty kilometres, we finally managed to reach the ashram lodge at around three in the afternoon. But reaching the place, to our utmost astonishment, we witnessed there a huge mob of hundreds of people already queuing up before us, demanding rooms for lodging. What's all this fuss about, we thought, because, except for the annual Gangasagar fair, one would hardly find even two dozen people together here around. But we soon learnt about the reason for crowding. It may not be the time of the Gangasagar holy bath, but it is Rakhi Purnima and many from outside Bengal, mostly Rajasthan, take this auspicious opportunity to bathe here at the holy Gangasagar. The Maharaj from the Ashram told us in a cold voice without moving an inch of his oversized body, "More than one room cannot be allotted."

"What! But we're four from two different families!"

After a quick look at all of us, the unmoved Maharaj consolingly said, "Bear the hardship for a day. I'm giving you a big room. Here, we have to serve a whole crowd. Can't you see?"

Now, who can carry on arguing anymore or expect to win anything more after this? After taking possession of the room, Jayanta lamented, "We hardly have any option now. But let's explore our luck in the evening."

On the way to our room, we found that the ashram courtyard covers a huge area. Jayanta and I were walking ahead of our wives, who were busy in deep conversation. I was surprised to find my usually 'choosy' wife mixing so easily with Jayanta's wife, Kajari, whom she met for the first time in her life. I soon got a taste of their strong bondage when I taunted Siuli in between their talks, "Your aunt hardly has any hold here as a member." To my disbelief, Kajari protested and shot back instead, "Don't blame my friend Siuli. Nor is her aunt at fault. Nobody has control over time and destiny." I could only manage a sheepish smile and fled the situation.

After a cursory visit to the cleaner at the toilet, we had some cautious and short bathing sessions, lunch from an outside shack and went back to the room. It is fairly hot inside, and the ceiling fan can hardly provide us with any comfort because the whole of Sagardwip is powered by electricity only between evening six and ten at night through power generators. This news was unknown to us all. We are staying in a corner room on the ground floor where just opposite our window is the cowshed of the Sangh, sending us the deadly odour of cow dung and horrific moos of the huge Australian cows round the clock with the minimal breeze flowing. A visibly upset Siuli offered a walk to the sea beach while Kajari advised to take some rest before moving out. I silently admired the growing closeness between the two women. A pun from Jayanta reached my ears in between, "Considering the situation, we may have to spend the night by the sea."

Siuli then requested Kajari to sing, but Kajari exclaimed, "Who can sing on such a hot, sultry summer afternoon?"
Now I joined them, "Why? Didn't Rabindranath write anything suitable for such moments?"

Witty Kajari answered, "Of course, he wrote, but it's barred to be sung sitting in front of cowsheds and the air around strongly smelling of cow dungs." We all laughed. In between talks, my eyes got stuck on Kajari's hands, and they looked rickety. The skin on her hands is also white-pigmented. Her whole body is so, except her face. She had been found with the disease a couple of years ago, and her father was left with no options but to spend a lot of money in treating the skin disease. However, his efforts failed. Now, she always hides her body and hands under full-sleeve dresses, even in summer. But since now she has slipped into a half-sleeved nighty, I could see her bare hands, spotted all over. I shuddered inside because the scene was quite odd. Then, I found that Jayanta was observing what I was looking at and how I was quietly reacting. I felt bad and quickly tried to change my mood and asked, "So, when are you all planning to move out? The summer is sulking here inside!"

Kajari requested to be left alone to get some more rest due to her persistent backache. Jayanta readily arranged for her to rest in one corner of the common bed allotted to us in the room. She crawled to the corner on all fours. I shamelessly lay down in another corner in shorts, baring my two unshaven legs, which I would have otherwise hesitated to expose before any other woman. But then Kajari is not a typical woman before whom a man would feel unsure or hesitant. Perhaps her appearance lacked the right kind of appeal to captivate men, or at least in my case, I could only muster a feeling of pity, mixed with moments of discomfort and shivers. However, I fail to understand my wife Siuli's feelings. She is a regular salon-goer, with manicured and pedicured beauty; how could she mingle with a person like Kajari with such ease?

I have never been fortunate in my encounters with female companions, despite being a daily passenger on public transport all my life. I never had a beautiful female co-passenger. I'm not unattractive, nor short, and I don't have crooked teeth or hair growing out of my nostrils; I even have a stable government job. Yet, I remain devoid of romance in my life. I married Siuli through an arranged marriage because her uncle and my father were colleagues at the office. But Jayanta, Kajari, and I used to be neighbors.

Soon, the day ended to usher in the evening, and we had to wake up from the bed. Kajari informed, "Have you guys noticed that there is a beautiful water body there behind this building with cemented banks to lounge around? Let's go there."

Jayanta and I quickly consented and came out of the road to give the ladies a chance to change and get ready. I hurried Jayanta, "Let's go to the water body."

Indeed, there's really a beautiful water body with cemented embankments and seats.

"Let's sit there."

We sat, and I immediately took the opportunity to throw my question to Jayanta, the question which was bugging me now for a long time,

"Listen, Jayanta, aren't you seeing that Kajari's health has drastically fallen?"

I tried to put it as casually as possible, but Jayanta responded in his trademark calmness, "It's not clear yet as doctors couldn't find anything major till now. They only asked the two of us to stay happy and not get tense because all of her essential readings were normal. But yes, in spite of that, she's losing a lot of weight. After our marriage, when she used to have frequent stomach upsets, I always monitored her food habits and ensured that she always had home-cooked food with less spices and oil. But still, I don't know why this is..."

"All of you had such blatant food at home?"

"Yes, otherwise she gets hurt if she's served food separately..."

"That's okay, such food is healthy anyway, but one thing I would like to ask you but you shouldn't get angry."

"It's okay, go on."

"Actually, I wanted to say, is there any psychological problem, like depression?"

"See, because of her pigmented skin and her weight reduction, people already ask her a lot of questions or show unnecessary sympathy or curiosity in our life, and that creates a lot of tension. I tried counselling her whenever I got the time, and I had faith in her; I always believed that she was the same person that she used to be many years ago. Even before my mother..." Jayanta had hiccups after continuously narrating his past emotions, but his eyes were dry.

I tapped his arms, "Leave that; everything can take backseats if you two are happy."

Jayanta sounded doubtful, "I am not sure about that too. But you two seem to have a very strong bond."

I tried to laugh but only managed to throw a sound like spitting and said, "Sure, but leave that."

"You've been married for four years now."

"Yes, something like that." I tried to avoid everything when it came to me.

"Now, don't waste time. Have a baby."

"Everything will happen on time."

"No, but later, it may complicate the process of having a baby."

"Let's see," I tried to shrug off, while in the water, a dark silhouette of me kept dancing.

"Let's move from here," I was more interested in fleeing the scene.

***

We hired a cycle rickshaw and combed the whole area in search of better lodging. But unfortunately, everywhere every facility is booked till tomorrow. We felt utterly confused, as we had a plan to spend three days here, but in such a room, neither of us was ready to stay for such a long period. We will surely check out of this room tomorrow, I thought because I'm the one who is most irked with everything here now. By the way, Jayanta doesn't know how much I was inclined to have a baby after our marriage, but as luck had it, after days of trying, no results were obtained. Even the gynaecologists in the city couldn't be of any help to me. It was learnt that the problem lies with me because although Siuli has the capacity to be a mother, I, Saibal Chatterjee, have got impotent sperms in me. Since knowing this, Siuli strangely started avoiding me, although we had no problem sleeping together. I may be impotent by sperm, but I'm no lesser than a man physically. But Siuli thinks sleeping together and bearing no child out of it is sheer farcical.

"Why farcical? Can't I have a demand of my own? Am I not a human?" But Siuli never responded to my questions but offered her body before me like alms offered to beggars. I felt myself belittled as much as a street dog. Since then, we haven't been able to sleep together. These days, when I hear of someone childless, like me, it gives me a certain level of uncanny pleasure. Then, under the influence of my dark pleasure, I keep hurling uneasy questions to such people as, "Why don't you have a child? Do you have any problem with having children? Don't you know that you'll face problems later if you don't take up the matter now? The game proved so comforting to me that I never stopped it, but it proved very irritating to others. I got a few rebuffs for this, but that never deterred me from my way. For example, I had already asked Jayanta the same question at least half a dozen times. Jayanta, poised as he is, answered with a heavy heart, "Now, it's not possible at all. She has lost a lot of weight. Let her get well."

I enjoyed his way of replying and his present condition.

While returning to the ashram from our failed hotel hunting, we wished to visit the empty sea beach again at night, but our rickshaw puller stopped us from doing so. We had our dinner from the same shack and went to the ashram for our night's sleep. There are hundreds of people taking shelter in the courtyard of the ashram. Tomorrow is a full moon, and hence, there is no dearth of light in the sky today. Siuli offered to stay in the courtyard for some more moments under the open sky. She took us to the pond behind.

Kajari begged her husband to accompany her to the temple steps.

So it was decided that while Jayanta and his wife Kajari would go to the temple, they would let us go to the pond bank. There in the pond, the full moon has thrown its shadow and the moonlight is brushing the back of the fish shoal underwater.

I whispered, “So calm, so peaceful.”

Siuli only said, “Hmm.”

“But our time of coming proved to be a bad time.”

“Why? It's a full moon night!”

“I mean, I'm talking about the room; it's very uncomfortable to stay with another couple.”

“But one should adjust because everything can't be controlled.”

“That's not what I meant. I mean to say, the idea of four of us sleeping in a bed on a hot summer night is very claustrophobic in itself. Ain't it? Whereas, see, there is a cool breeze blowing outside.”

“Then we can spend the night outside.”

You can't answer that, and hence, I chose to remain silent. Then I changed the topic, “Kajari has had a huge weight loss. I feel sorry looking at her. You two, however, gelled well.”

“Yes, we gelled well. But you shouldn't be talking about her weight loss.”

“Nah, but I took pity on Jayanta's fate.”

“You don't have to because he's a composed man, someone very rare in today's world.”

Perhaps Siuli said the right thing. When Jayanta offered to marry Kajari, she was already suffering from her skin problem. Jayanta is a librarian at a government school in Hooghly, but he is not very good-looking. He has uneven teeth, a hump in the back, thinning hairs and all such ugly features. Kajari was a potential singer shining in Rabindrasangeet, and Jayanta was a fan of her singing. When Kajari was diagnosed with the disease, she abruptly stopped going out for singing programs. We have prodded Jayanta a lot to propose to Kajari, but Jayanta always used to say that Kajari wouldn't accept his proposal. But finally, when he proposed, Kajari did not have many options open, as the skin disease had spread on her whole body by then. She accepted Jayanta as her husband, though we all knew that if not the disease had stumped her, Jayanta wouldn't have got the chance to even propose to her. I always think about how Jayanta reacts now while sleeping by a pigmented black and white Kajari and whether Jayanta repents for his decision. I know neither I can ask him nor can he reply to me because that would be incorrect.

"They are very good together, ain't it?" Siuli asked me, lost in thoughts.

"Maybe."

"Why, maybe, don't you see that?" Siuli got angry after hearing the nonchalance in my voice.

"Do you judge everything by its appearance?"

"Yes, if you can judge it in the true sense, unlike trying unnecessarily criticise everything."

"What is this? Why are you making a fuss out of this?"

"Why shouldn't I?"

"No, you shouldn't. Looking from the outside, don't people think of us as a strongly bonded couple, too? But is this the case?"

"Well, who's to be blamed for that?" saying this, Siuli at once left me in my company and went away.

At night, all four of us were forced to sleep together. It was a stuffy night, but to my surprise, I found Kajari sleeping peacefully and snoring. Jayanta and I kept talking and whispering to each other, but after some time, we were out of topics and were compelled to go silent. Beside me, my wife has been silent since our evening interaction. I can feel that she is lying still but not sleeping. The unbearable night passed at an agonisingly slow pace, and finally, I couldn't take it lying down and left the bed and came out of the room. There was a light breeze outside and the song of the sea. The surroundings look strange in the veil of darkness and moonlight. I was lost when suddenly I felt the presence of Jayanta beside me.

"It's too hot inside, and I couldn't sleep at all."

"Hmm."

"Kajari is very interested to witness a sunrise by the sea. I've decided to show her the sunrise here, and then let's go catch the bus to Kolkata. What do you say?"

"Sure," I answered shortly and added, "The journey this time proved restless."

"Yours may be restless, but not mine; I got rest tonight after a long time," Jayanta winked. The end of the night moon brushed a layer of moonlight on his unpleasant-looking happy face on this opportunity.

I understood but still asked in nonchalance I asked back, "What do you mean? When could you rest in between the running?"

"Since we all slept together today, I earned a holiday from her."

"O God, you do it every day?"

"Don't ask. Kajari has a very odd habit of doing it regularly. If I stop her, she feels sad, tensed, agitated."

"Why?"

"I don't know. I had to perform even amidst tiredness and in the middle of my sleep. If by chance I show signs of lethargy, she immediately turns gloomy, stops talking and keeps repeating that I no longer love her, I'm intentionally avoiding her... What a peculiar condition I am in!"

I heard and laughed. I don't know how my teeth shone in the moonlight before him. I could hear myself telling him, "Good, good, and why would you rest at this young age? Keep going." Then I promptly changed the topic of discussion, "But do you know why Kajari left singing? She has such a beautiful voice after all; she was building a good career in singing, too..."

"I can't tell her anymore; I did enough. Since marriage, she has not practiced singing even for a day. Whenever I insist, she avoids me. Nowadays, I've started thinking perhaps she left singing because of me." We both fell silent.

"Jayanta, it's dawning, but look at the condition of the sky; I don't think we can witness a sunrise today." Jayanta shrugs; his face looks as suffocating as the morning sky. I insisted, "Go and call Kajari. She wished to see the sunrise. Let's go then."

"Umm... Yes... okay." Jayanta turned when I called again and held his hand,

"Sorry if I had turned you off."

"Don't be. I don't mind." Then he added, "I'm losing my fight, Saibal.." he pressed on my fingers, "Hardly had I thought that my life would become so hard," and then he quickly entered the room, leaving me behind. I turned towards the exit gate. They catch up with me. Let me go out first. Already, the morning is proving to be very disgusting. There's no light, no air.

***

The sea is a long twenty minutes' walk over the beach. It's a green field full of grass, beyond which is a sand-filled bank of the sea. The place is unlike other beaches in the world. I've never seen such a scene anywhere else. And everywhere, it's devoid of any humanity, lit up by the dim light of the day, cloudy and breezy, ripples of waves touching the beach. Coming to such an open world from the claustrophobic corner of the lodge, all of us fell at a loss for words. Kajari announced, "I'm too tired to walk anymore. I need some rest." Jayanta showed a dune on the beach, "Let's go and sit there." There are greenery of cactus trees and unknown shrubs. There's a backwater lake close to the sand dune.

Today, from the beginning, we are loving our silence more than words. All but Jayanta sat over the sand. We are looking at the sea in our silence. Our minds mingled with the sound of the waves.

Our bodies dissolved in the sea breeze. Dark clouds are hanging over the sea.

"Seems like it will rain; see the clouds," I told him.

"Maybe," Jayanta sounds unmindful.

Meanwhile, Siuli suddenly asked Kajari, "Will you keep my word? Just for today?"

"Tell me."

"Sing a song for this morning. Will you?"

Kajari remains silent.

"Not for us, but for you. Or else, for the sea in front, or for the clouds above..."

"What will I get in return?"

"Nothing, possibly, but what if in the coming days, you rue that you could have sung but you missed the chance."

I watched both the ladies talking to each other and realising something about each other. Jayanta looked at them just for once and turned away.

Kajari said in a low voice, "I easily get tired these days; I lost practice."

"Stop at the moment you get tired."

"Okay..."

Kajari's "Okay…" didn't turn Jayanta towards her; rather, he just sat on the sand where he was standing, looking the other way.

"What would you like me to sing?"

"Whichever is surfacing in your mind."

So, Kajari straightens her back and closes her eyes. Suddenly, a drop of rain from nowhere fell on the ground. All of a sudden, we heard Kajari after many many years,

"Why do I go crazy, moment to moment, why does my heart want who it wants?"

My heart sprung and I found Siuli closing her eyes.

"Why paint the dawn sky with such colors"

Raindrops increased in intensity, but I could see Jayanta sitting straight and stoic, much like a dead coconut tree. After a long long time, Kajari is singing, enjoying, immersing in it, "If you did not imbue my soul with poetry, then why does the sky gaze so intently into my eyes..."

The sky suddenly bursts open with the crack of the lightning, followed by a torrential rain. But amidst sharp, intense raindrops, we forgot to stop Kajari; Kajari didn't remember to stop. Neither could we move from our seats as if we got glued to our positions. Kajari continues singing, repeating the lines. Amidst the sound of lightning and gusting wind from the sea, I hardly could hear her anymore. Amidst the heavy pouring of rain, I could hardly keep my drenched eyelids open anymore. And then an unexplained feeling of crying ushered. In between the rain, the warm tears got my senses drenched, my soul sopping. Nobody could see me crying in the rain, though, but I knew for sure that all four of us were actually crying. Crying and talking to our tears.

Self-poisoning

I

Perhaps it's raining somewhere close by. The wet vapour coming out of the coldness of the ground announces that each minute. Braja suddenly broke his silence and instructed the rickshaw puller to stop. The man thought Braja stopped him because he might have to attend nature's call. He advised, "Finish it quickly."

Braja felt amused as the poor rickshaw puller completely got him wrong. Braja didn't try to correct him, rather he pulled out his wallet and announced, "Here, take your money. I reached my destination."

The puzzled man expressed disbelief, "But didn't you asked for the Housing?"

"Yes, but now I have changed my mind."

Listening to his whimsical passenger, he murmured in his irk, "Blame my luck that I always have to deal with such drunken passengers!"

Blimey! At least in the last couple of weeks, Braja didn't have a pinch of alcohol and still this man is calling him a drunkard. Braja is pleasantly surprised.

The Delhi Road is otherwise empty at ten in the night except the flashes of light from the speeding cars. The roadside has rolled down into a canal where the whites of the water lilies are shining under the dim light of the night sky. There are sparks of lightning in the far-off horizon. Braja first stood calmly for some moments and then opening his slippers from his feet, sat down over it. His bare feet felt cold, but he still sat idly without any reason. Slowly, the lightning spreads till above the head and the sky reddens silently without anyone noticing, while Braja sat unmoved even after it started raining. Braja got drenched as drops of water drained through his body, making their way to the canal on the roadside, the leaves of the banyan tree which can be viewed standing at a distance over the walls of the graveyard started shining being washed by the rain. His vision got hazed in the middle of the rain. Then suddenly a car's headlight flashed, almost blinding his sight. He tried to eye the car which pulled the brake just a few yards ahead. Someone, in a raincoat and holding an umbrella alighted and came towards him. Braja found himself in a trance and out of his sense when he could only vaguely figure out his surroundings, but couldn't see anything clearly.

"Mister, what are you doing here?"

Braja looked at the man asking but couldn't reply.

"What are you up to?"

"Well, what do you want to know?"

"That's what I want to know, what's going on here?"

"Nothing"

"What Nothing?"

"Well I'm merely sitting here, doing nothing."

"That I can see, but why so?"

"Just like that..."

"You are not supposed to act smart. Stand up."

Braja followed the instruction.

"Where's your home?"

"Dankuni Housing"

"What do you do?"

Braja didn't answer.

"What happened? What do you do?"

Braja wished to tell many things but could only manage to whisper, "I don't know."

"What?"

"Nothing."

A second person shouted out of the car, "Don't mess with us, otherwise you will land in jail."

"Board our car." Braja didn't want to listen but the shout was stronger, "Be quick, immediately board the car."

***

Only after a long time passed, that Braja Chakraborty slowly found himself out of his trance. He tried to raise his head, but it felt really heavy. Someone has put a bed sheet over his body. It must be Arati. Braja's eyes felt really heavy.

"Why? Can you say why? Why you all are doing this to me?"

Braja turned his head to watch his wife silently. Arati is crying. She came beside his bed. Without a word, Braja just put his hand over his wife's hand. The rain has stopped by then outside.

II

Mr. Banerjee from Alpha Ceramic Company called this morning to remind him about the car he had kept with him all this time and seemingly forgotten to return. Banerjee, though, put it mildly by asking about his son first, "I heard about his son. It's a sad story, and I'm really sorry. How is he doing?"

"He's alright."

"Where have you admitted him?"

"In a private hospital, there."

"Oh, okay. Do let us know if you have any problems."

"Thanks, bye." Braja didn't want to extend the discussion. He had totally forgotten that their company car had been lying with him for the last three days. Being an Excise Inspector, Braja has unknowingly made it a habit to get hold of different company cars and use them for free for his personal use like going for shopping to travelling to Kalna to check the health of his younger uncle, who has recently fallen ill, to go for free tour to Digha for a couple of days. Braja, now let the car go.

Arati asked, "Why did you let the car go? How will you travel then?"

"Why? Like others. By train, and then by bus."

"Why are you doing this?"

"Arati, I'm doing nothing. To tell you the truth, I have done nothing so far."

"Please control yourself. If you yourself couldn't stay calm in this crisis, then how would you take care of me?"

"No, I'm alright."

***

While waiting for the train amidst the crowd at the Dankuni Railway Station, Braja looked around. The station has changed in the past few years. As the arrival of the train was announced, he prepared to board it along with the crowd.

"Braja-da, Hey Braja-da"

Braja turned back to find his neighbour Samir standing behind him. Samir, a childhood friend, is a couple of years younger than him. He has got a fairly successful stationery shop in the locality.

"What happened? Are you going to travel by train?"

"Yeah."

"How's Sajal doing?"

"He made it."

"When will he be released?"

"Not sure."

Their train entered the platform. Braja was thinking of boarding on another compartment to avoid Samir. But Samir held his hand and said, "Come. Let's complete our discussions inside the train."

After that, it was some moments of violent pushing and shoving inside the crowded train till Samir expertly made way for Braja to stand. Braja thanked Samir because he couldn't have managed in the middle of the office-going mob alone. In the stuffy, sultry interior, Samir tactfully made the nervous Braja at least stand in an advantageous location. Braja remembered that Arati repeatedly warned him, but he didn't give her an ear at that time for some unknown, unexplainable reasons.

"Why all of a sudden you chose to travel by train?"

"Just like that."

"I couldn't make time to visit your son; after all, he is such a good boy." Samir paused.

Braja turned away his face. Sajal, indeed, was good. Perhaps he was in standard seven then when Braja was promoted to the post of Excise Inspector. From that day, everyone in the house turned happier, but since that day, also things started to change rapidly. The overall mindset of the family changed along with the furniture, appliances and prosperity. Braja still remembers the first day he took the bribe; he was hell scared that day all through. While returning home, he continuously feared being followed by some invisible stranger. In a couple of days, he got caught in the hand of Arati, but Arati only casually said, "How can you become so irresponsible to put bunches of notes under the bed?"

Braja shuddered in fear, but Arati never asked any more questions.

Since then, Braja kept taking bribes. As the douceur increased, the invisible man following Braja vanished one day. The bank accounts multiplied as a new apartment came up in Salt Lake under the name Arati. The house has been left empty since, but Braja is planning to shift there after retirement. Amidst happiness and joy, Braja and his wife never could see when Sajal's upbringing changed course. They, however, got their first shock on the Maha Saptami night of the Durga puja. In the middle of the night, when the Officer-in-Charge of the Dankuni Police Station called to inform that Sajal had landed in police lock-up, being prosecuted for drinking and driving a motorcycle, Braja felt a slap on his face. "Aren't you taking care of your son well? Otherwise, how is a minor getting drunk at this age?"

Braja found no other way than to digest the insult with his head hung down. After bailing out his son Sajal and his two friends, an angry Braja came back home and thought of teaching his son a lesson. Instead, he learned the hardest lesson of his life when he understood that his minor son had actually become too grown up to be controlled. He couldn't beat him, although he tried his best to keep him under strict control. But that was temporary. Soon, both went back on their own ways.

"Braja-da, please don't get too much bogged down with anxiety."

"Umm...Hmm, I'm alright."

"As a younger brother to you, I suggest that Sajal's friend circle is not good; try to take care of that." Samir fell silent, but his sign was clear.

Friends! Yes. He has seen Sajal's bunch of friends for the first time at Sajal's birthday party at a Park Street restaurant. That day, Braja had spent money lavishly. There were office colleagues, friends and highly placed officials on his guest list at the gala, and it was all good until around nine in the night when a group of Sajal's friends landed there packed in three cars. Within moments, the scene changed in the presence of the odd pack of young men and women. What the heck... Braja thought! He could never imagine people dressed like that, talking like that, behaving like that and felt too intimidated by their loud wishings of "Hi Uncle, Hello Uncle!" But Braja was still managing a smile until that girl walked up to him and introduced herself, "Hi! I'm Cynki." Then, Braja felt as if someone was swishing a whip on him. Dressed in knee-bearing ragged jeans and an oversized sleeveless netted shirt, the girl's mere presence gave him an overwhelming knee-jerk of his life. His son's girlfriend's pushed-up black brassier and deep navel peeping from under her shirt, the sultriness oozing from her pierced eyebrow and blue contact lenses and rudraksha beaded bracelet gave him such a taboo-filled uncanny twist up to his manhood that he will remember till his death.

Braja and Arati were shocked and shouted in shrilled voices when they discovered that the girl Cynki was holding a soiled snake in a plastic packet.

"O God! What's that?"

"Don't worry, Aunty, it's my lovely snaky. You know Suzu, Bijay gifted this lovely surprise to me this evening!"

Arati, helplessly in fear, could only manage to whisper to Braja's ears, "Take me home, can you?"

Braja, too, was in discomfort, but he had no option but to wait and watch the friend circle around Sajal, the Ricky Martin and Brittney Spears et al. gripping him tight like that twisted snake in the plastic packet.

That night, Arati cried, "Who are these people? How can they be your friends, Suzu?"

"Yes, they are my good friends. What's wrong?"

"You are asking me a question! Are they even humans? I don't want you to meet them ever."

"Don't be ridiculous. Leave me to myself."

Braja had to meddle. Otherwise, the quarrel would have been long-drawn. He consoled Arati, "Don't worry, things will surely change in the coming time."

"*Change*! How?"

No, there is no immediate answer to this.

***

"Braja-da, let's move closer to the door."

Braja returned from his thoughts back with Samir's intervention. There is a heart-stopping crowd pressure inside the train when it's about to reach the platform. Braja tried dragging his feet to match the crowd flow, but he fell short of breathing.

"Braja-da, are you okay?"

"Of course."

"This is how the public journeys every day, runs mindlessly everywhere. We only struggle. None of us know, though, about our destiny."

Braja remained silent to Samir's words. They exited from the gate together when Braja stopped by a soft drink counter. Braja ordered a couple of soft drinks for the two of them.

"I won't have cold drinks, Braja-da; I've been suffering from tonsils for the last few days."

So Braja took one and then gulped the whole bottle in one breath and burped. The poise came back at last.

"You must be catching a taxi. Let me take a leave then. "

"Where will you go?"

"Canning Street. I have to purchase some stock for the shop. Okay, bye."

Samir vanished in the crowd. Braja at first decided to board a bus, but then the train journey disturbed his self-confidence so much that he understood that it was not easy to catch up with the old Braja so easily. Braja therefore called a taxi.

III

It was still another twenty minutes left for the visiting hours to start, and Braja sat on the lounge waiting for his turn. The lounge area and the surroundings of this hospital have a soft, dreamy ambience imported from some outer world, much contrary to the real world outside. Braja keeps thinking, will his son talk to him today? In the last few days, the father-son duo had practically no words between them. But then, literally speaking, they stopped conversing many, many years ago. Sajal was admitted to a night college in Commerce. Initially, he would return around half past nine or ten. But gradually, it becomes half past eleven in the night. Then he started calling home to inform, "I won't return tonight."

"Why?"

"We had a party tonight at a friend's place. I will return tomorrow after college."

He was slipping out of control, beyond the reach of everyone who had raised him. Instead, his friends became his life. Braja witnessed Sajal's friends once more in the Nandan courtyard. It so happened that one day, Braja went to the Nandan area to meet a potential client at four in the evening. He was slightly early and, therefore, was lounging around under a tree drawing on a cigarette when he heard a known voice, "Hi! Uncle."

Braja recognised the girl with her pierced eyebrows, now dressed in a body-hugging black t-shirt and knee-length jeans pants and accompanied by a boy with a ponytail and a guitar.

"You are here?"

"Yes, to meet someone. What about you all?"

"Fine."

"What are you doing here?"

"Just enjoying life."

Braja tried to sound modern and advised, looking at her, "But don't waste valuable time."

To this, his eyes met the gleams of another pair of eyes covered in green contact lenses, "We never waste time, uncle; rather, time wastes us."

Braja Chakraborty, the indomitable officer before whom executives and top officials of the professional worlds wagtails to get importance, felt like a balloon out of the air, slapped on the face and then kicked on the butt. Looking at the way they went away, Braja couldn't help but utter in disgust, "bit..h," but quickly restrained himself; the young girl was his son's friend, after all.

An old man sitting close by perhaps heard his tantrums and chuckled, "Do you know her?"

"Hmm"

"And the boy by her side?"

"No."

Braja was not interested in talking but couldn't lose his attention either. The stranger went on,

"What! You don't know this gigolo? "

"What's that?" Braja frowned at this unknown piece of word.

"The girl is a rich brat, a spoiled product from an affluent family. And this boy from Hind Motor is already married. But he stays with the girl at her place as her kept. Bloody swine! What a shameful piece of shit he is."

***

The visiting hours had started, and Braja was climbing stairs with a heart full of expectations that his son would talk to him today. Tensed, Braja could feel his palms wet, so he clinched his bag tightly so that it didn't slip off his sweating palms. Will Sajal talk to him?

Braja peeped from behind the green curtains and watched Sajal sitting on the bedpan held by two nurses. He waited till a nurse called him inside.

Sajal was lying on his back again by then. He never looked at Braja. Braja sat silently for some time and then hesitantly asked, "How are you feeling today?" Braja touched his son's hands. They are cold. Sajal didn't turn.

Braja tried to request with a "Please..." but that never came out of his mouth.

A couple of weeks ago, Sajal returned home after half past eleven at night. That day, Braja couldn't hold himself back and confronted his drunken son, who was seemingly going to ashtray. He shouted, "You swine, don't you know the rules of this house? How dare you come back to your parents getting drunk at the midnight hours? Immediately get out of my house."

Intoxicated, Sajal couldn't even stand properly but roared back to his father, "What's wrong with it? Don't you do the same?"

"Shut up, rascal, you're playing on whims over my hard-earned money. How dare you! Get out." While shouting, he even shoved back his wife, Arati, who tried to defend their son.

"Don't show eyes to me, I give a damn to your house."

"Arati, this boy is a disgrace to our family. It's such a shame that we have raised him with our hard-earned money, wasting blood and sweat. Immediately drive him out of the house."

"Listen, don't lecture on hard-earned money and sacrifices as your money is only earned in dishonest ways, by cheating others. You have done nothing to stop me from going ashtray. You all have betrayed me and ruined my life." Sajal pointed fingers to his parents' faces and shouted in rage. Then he left. To this, Braja kept shouting madly until the sound of his son's motorcycle melted in the dead of the night.

Then, at one at midnight, a phone call came from PG hospital, saying that Sajal met with an accident on the Kona Expressway. Since then, only after another two days did Sajal come back to his senses and get a second life. He got stitches on his forehead and steel plates implanted on his fractured waist and knees. The doctor consoled Braja, patting his shoulder. "Don't worry; at least he will get back to his life. Thankfully, he will be on his feet in another six months. Till then, he will remain bedridden."

"Six months!"

"Yes, but consider it as a final warning. Maybe he will get the chance to change his way of living in this six-month period. Today's generation is completely reckless..."

IV

Braja returned home at seven in the evening, and Arati came running to him from the balcony.

"How is my child?"

"Doing good."

Arati paused and then asked in a low voice, "Did he talk?" Braja didn't answer.

"He didn't?"

"Uff, Arati, it hardly matters to me if your son talks to me or not. He has to only blame himself for whatever happened to him. There's no point accusing me."

Arati didn't argue. She went away towards the kitchen.

Braja was getting furious with his son. He doesn't understand why this boy is angry with his father when the fault is completely his own. When his father is still spending lakhs for his treatment, how could he hold his father responsible for his misfortune? Did Braja treat him in a government hospital and show any lack in the father's duty? No. Then why is the ungrateful boy showing unnecessary tempers?

Braja went to the bathroom. He stood inside the tastefully styled bathroom's milky white marble tiles, the glass enclosure of the shower and the big mirror behind the wash basin. He minutely watched himself in the mirror. His anger kept haunting every corner of his brain, and he grunted, "Let the whole world go to hell." He went on to have a long shower.

***

Arati was waiting with tea in the dining hall, but Braja came out of the toilet and opened a whiskey bottle instead, ignoring her. Arati didn't protest and kept watching him silently. Till his second peg, Braja didn't look back. On his third peg, he looked up to her. His wife was sitting there in a sleeveless yellow nighty. Her fair complexion is glistening on her shapely, rounded arms and shoulders. Arati still looks hot at this age despite having a college-going son. She still can move heads when Braja takes her to office parties. The alcohol started getting into his head meanwhile. He started feeling lighter.

Braja cleared his throat and said, "Today I met Samir in the train..."

Arati remained silent.

"I had a talk with him after a long time. He is a good boy but couldn't do anything meaningful in life."

"Stop drinking."

"Yeah, sure."

"Shall I serve dinner?"

"Nah, I already had it outside."

Arati left her seat; Braja lost his balance slightly, leaving his seat. But he is feeling lighter.

In the green light, their bedroom is looking soft and dreamy. Braja, after lying by his side for some time, closes in on Arati. Putting his face by Arati's face, he said in a consoling voice, "Don't worry; everything will fall into place soon." He then started touching Arati and unbuttoned her nightly playfully. To this, Arati rebuked angrily,

"What are you doing?"

"Why? What have I done?"

"You... You should feel ashamed of yourself!"

"Why?"

"Your son is at the hospital, and you…"

"Am I responsible for his hospitalisation? Why should I be blamed? Why?"

"You're really impossible…" a visibly annoyed Arati turned her face away from her husband.

"Oh… well... am I impossible! For all of your life, you mother and son duo lived life on my money, spent well, ate well and now blames me for everything," Braja keeps roaring in rage. He pushed Arati, "Listen to me, I have no more money to spare and keep your son in a good hospital. Tomorrow I will admit him to the Medical... Yes, I will do that. Then act as you like." Braja leapt out of bed. He is shivering in anger. He rushed to the toilet.

Sajal's room is on the other side of the toilet. The doors are closed. Braja slowly entered the dark room and searched for the switches. He forgot the position of the switches as he entered this room after a long time. First, he tried finding them on his left and then fished in the darkness towards his right to finally get the switches and light the room. First, it was the fan, and then it was the light. The bed is well-made and unused. There is a cupboard by the bedside. Braja went there and opened it after a minute's hesitation. There's a rack full of books, magazines, cassettes, and CDs. Unmindfully, Braja took out the CDs, most of which are of English songs, and few are Hindi. On a CD of Ricky Martin's music album, there's a writing: With best wishes to my son on his birthday – *Baba, two thousand and two.* Braja took out the CD and put it on the bed separately. Then there are CDs of Madonna, Michael Jackson, Daler Mehendi, Kanta Laaga, and Dhoom Macha De crowding the rack, but far off in a dark corner, there is a secret cassette with a hazy cover of Kishore Kumar's Rabindrasangeet collection. It has a faded writing *Baba on Suzu's Birthday, nineteen ninety-nine.*

While Braja took the return path to his own bedroom, he felt bitter inside his throat. Deep inside, somewhere, turmoil is felt. He quickly opened his bedroom door, but he was surprised to find a waiting Arati on the bed looking directly at him. She is sitting with her face on her knees.

Braja didn't speak. He lies down, facing away from Arati; the uneasiness is haunting his soul.

Suddenly, Arati could be heard speaking in a coy, lovey-dovey voice, "Aye, listen..."

"Hmm"

"Are you angry with me?"

"Nah"

"Of course you are angry," said Arati. Suddenly, Arati leapt upon a surprised Braja like a teenage girl burying her face on his chest, rubbing, cuddling, and kissing. Braja frowned with a confused look.

"You are my one angry darling," Arati sounded like a loving feline as she started caressing Braja.

Unprepared, Braja protested, "Stop it, Arati, I don't like it."

"But I like it, and I don't believe you that you don't like it..."

"Please."

"No."

"Stop."

"No."

There was no stopping of Arati, and after some time, there was no stopping of Braja. He was in search of something else, something more than her body, beyond her newfound vigour on top of her appeal and zeal. He kept searching till, at the climactic moment, he could hear Arati's helpless plea,

"Aye, listen, promise me that you won't be transferring my son from this hospital."

The Life We Live

I

Barry visited Shreya in her office after a long time. As per Shreya's calculation, he is paying a visit at least after a gap of three months.

"Hello, Shreya. How are you?" Barry pulled a chair from another side and sat beside her desk, uninvited, while Shreya acted busy on her computer and replied in between her work,

"I'm good. Where have you been for this long?"

"Umm... where... nowhere... I mean, I was here... I was at my home," Barry nervously keeps brushing his thin fingers within his rough, curly, greying hair and continues fumbling in search of words before Shreya and then finally managed to mutter, "I was kind of busy with work... but I will tell you later about that."

Shreya chuckles and whispers back, "So be it; tell me later."

"It's not a joke, it's a serious case, my life being in…"

"Oh, hey Barry, seeing you after a long time, I hope you're fine.." Amaresh threw his words casually while passing by.

"Yes, dear, I'm fine."

"Good. Good." Amaresh went on his way, biting on a piece of pizza.

"Is Shankar-da there in his chamber?"

"Yes, he's there. Go meet him."

Barry rose from the chair, pulled up his oversized trousers and hesitantly murmured, "Then let me go and meet him first. I hope you will be available later, too since I have got many things to tell you."

"Of course, I'll be available for you," Shreya grew worried inside because she started fearing Barry might jeopardise her work plans today, hanging around here for hours.

Barry walked to Shankar's chamber, Shankar Gupta being the boss of Shreya, the sexagenarian bachelor designing chief of the English daily, 'Wake Up'. The good man and a workaholic that he is, he remained unmarried for some reasons unknown to everyone in the office.

Shreya kept looking at Barry from the back and discovered that the slender man had grown thinner in his usual shabby and colourless T-shirt and baggy jeans. But before entering Shankar's chamber, Barry quickly returned to Shreya once again as if suddenly remembering something. He says, "Sorry, I forgot to ask, how your husband is doing?"

"He's fine," Shreya kept her answer short and immediately turned her back to him, but she got busy with her work. This little question always irks her to the bone.

"Very good, very good. I wish you a happy married life. Very good." Barry repeated the same words unmindfully, going on his way. Shreya then again looked at the pathway the seemingly unsmart and unmindful man went.

Shreya has known this man, Barry Das, for the last couple of years since joining this company as a trainee artist. She got introduced to this half-mad, untidy, middle-aged Anglo man in her initial days of apprenticeship and immediately got attracted to this tall, lanky, sun-burnt funny man with grey hairs. The first day she saw him, this narrow-shouldered, thin, wasted, bushy-haired man was talking with Ruku-da when he suddenly asked him about her, "Who's she?"

Senior artist Ruku-da replied with a smile, "Oh, she's Shreya, newly recruited to the company and like my daughter."

"So she has joined your department?"

"Yes"

"Very Good. Hello Shreya. I am Barry."

"Hello, Barry," replied Shreya and immediately Barry took out a couple of slightly withered saplings from his plastic bag and gifted those to her, "Here's some gifts for you. Do plant them today at your home. Take care of the soil at the roots while planting. Okay?"

The type of gift surprised Shreya, and Ruku-da laughed, seeing the surprise on her face, and whispered in her ears, "Take it and beware, this is only a start."

After Barry departed, Ruku-da explained that Barry always gifts saplings. Initially, he used to gift small fish in small plastic bags filled with water, but he has stopped now and is gifting plants instead. Ruku-da talked about this man in detail to Shreya, saying that Barry is a peculiar character who lives in the old Park Street area. Initially, he used to work at CESC. He then had a wife and a daughter. But all of a sudden, he started mingling with weed-addicted people. As days passed, his addiction, his friend circle, his lethargy and laziness quickly ruined his life. He started ignoring his wife, paid no heed to his job, cared less about home, and overlooked his child's health and food day after day. As a result, his Nepali wife left him with his daughter and started to live with his bachelor elder brother. The elder brother works in a bakery and used to live alone on rent at Ripon Street. Barry followed his wife to his brother's place, angrily barged into their house, but took a beating after being driven out by the locals. From there onwards, he left his job and started living the life of a vagabond. He used to come to this newspaper office for a long and, in his better days, drew quite a few freelance illustrations for the company. Shreya has seen his works, and she has found those to be bold, clear, and conceptual works. But his shortcoming is that he doesn't know how to use computers. He requested Shreya to teach him computers quite a few times, and Shreya tried to teach him too. But the man has lost the capacity to remember anything being high under the influence of weeds all the time. So, Shreya lost hope in him. Ruku-da, too, has asked her not to keep much expectation on the otherwise straight-thinking and simple-at-heart but crazy Barry, who couldn't even maintain his loving family due to his own vices and misfortune.

Shreya watched Barry coming out of Shankar-da's chamber with a sad face. Barry's facial expressions are always clear because he can't hide his emotion. He came and sat back by Shreya. Shreya at first ignored his presence and didn't take her eyes from the screen till Barry asked her,

"Are you very busy?"

"Hmm, but tell me."

"No, but for that, you have to spare a couple of minutes. Can you do that?"

Shreya turned to him with a question on her face.

"I'm in the middle of a big problem. Can you help me?"

"Me? Okay... What help?"

"Can you arrange a job for me here?"

"Me? Job... What are you saying, Barry? I mean, how can I…?"

"Do you know how serious kind of a monetary problem I'm in? Don't you want me to get a job?"

"Of course, but for that, you have to get Shankar-da to agree."

"I did. But he denied me, saying that I'm insincere, irresponsible, and forgetting things, so I'm not suited for his office. So it's now up to you to do something for me. Make a request to Shankar-da for me."

"How? Especially when he has already rejected your request once…"

"Because you're a sincere and good girl, he definitely cannot reject you."

"Okay… I will try."

"O dear, thanks... thanks."

Ruku-da was passing by, and he asked Barry, "How're you, Barry?" Barry was about to reply something, but Ruku-da quickly rebutted, "Stop disturbing the busy girl in the middle of her work."

Barry quickly rises from the seat with a dejected face and apologises, "Sorry that I disturbed you... Bye."

Shreya felt bad for him and looked up. Then Barry quickly came closer to her ears and whispered, "Only one more question... Do you know where I can get a good quality binocular?"

"What! No... I don't know anything about binoculars, Barry." Shreya felt astonished, but Barry indifferently said, "It doesn't matter; I will find it out myself."

After Barry left, Shreya's phone started ringing. She's surprised again, this time seeing the phone number, as the mobile screen is showing the landline number of her in-laws' place!

"Hello!"

"Hello, Shreya, listen, I'm going out on some work and I'll be late. The house keys will be at the neighbor's place. And ask Bubai to get his thing from the deep freezer..." The line got disconnected without Shreya even having a chance to respond. After the call from her mother-in-law, Shreya looked silently at the blank screen for a few minutes; an unexplainable rage was accumulating deep inside her throat, and she could feel that.

***

Shreya got hitched to this Bubai three years ago, but she feels that the marriage has withered for ages, and with that, Shreya, herself, has also aged for ages and will not die anytime soon to get rid of all the unrest in life. But as the thought numbed her emotions, another thought quickly marched in: why should Shreya die for no fault of hers? Why should she sacrifice her happy life for people like Bubai and his mother? But things were not alike, as before their marriage, Shreya was introduced to Bubai over social media. It was after seven months of courtship that twenty-five-year-old trainee artist Shreya decided to marry her online friend Bubai because she liked his Facebook profile, messages and half a dozen meetings they had between them. On receiving her marriage invitation, Shankar-da laughed, "What was your hurry? Have you checked everything about him before this marriage?" Shreya really had nothing to answer, so she only nodded with a smile. On the marriage night, Bubai served a message from her mother: "Listen, my mother instructed us to bear a child as soon as possible." His hand was already on her blouse.

Shreya protested the way Bubai served his mother's message and stopped him, "How could your mother issue a decree without discussing it with us? It's our decision as a couple, after all, isn't it?"

"Oh, why? Where's your problem to agree?"

"Don't you know about my problem? Don't you understand that I've got a career ahead which will get disturbed? No, I won't relent to your mother's wishes... No."

Her "No" had a solid metallic sound, which stopped Bubai from extending the debate that night. But he started pressing and forcing for it again and again, much to the annoyance of Shreya, "What's this, Bubai? Why are you pressing so hard? Why are you irritating me?"

"Even I'm feeling irritated finding your stubbornness on the matter. You know very well that my mother is a heart patient, and she wants to see her grandchild's face before something happens to her accidentally. And if accidents happen, then we will be repenting."

"Don't mind, Bubai, accidents can happen anytime; it may even occur tomorrow. In that case, you should have married a woman with a child to satisfy your mother's wish of having a grandchild at the earliest."

"Shreya, why are you crossing your limits? Do you think after bearing a child, you will lose your body shape, and that will affect promotions in your career, or else you already know that you don't have the capacity to conceive a baby, and you're intentionally hiding that from me?"

"It's meaningless debating with a mindless fellow like you. I know that it's my entire fault that I didn't recognise you as an unevolved primate before our marriage. Let you grow up into a human first, and then we shall discuss the matters like two mature human beings," an enraged Shreya told him, all the while thinking about severing all ties with the man soon. But amidst loads of disturbances, she has still spent three more years with Bubai in search of love and compassion. The days didn't go the same, as in between, after her job got permanent and after she got a promotion, she willfully went into Bubai's arms. But perhaps a night's passion or physical need is not enough to become parents of a child; otherwise, why couldn't Shreya become pregnant? Medicines, puja rituals, and astrology didn't help either. Neither Shreya's vital readings nor health reports find any fault in her. So finally, Shreya asked her husband, "Bubai, you go and have a check-up this time."

"Me? Why me?"

"Because you too may have a problem, you too may need treatments which can broaden our path to become parents."

"I'm fine; I don't need treatment. Don't show concern about me. Actually, I've a pretty bad luck that I got a partner like you."

"You should have a medical test. See, I've never denied any test myself. Instead of lame arguments, you need to test yourself medically. It's as simple as that."

"Oh... So you're trying to take revenge now by making me stand in your position!"

"Don't be foolish. Go and confirm yourself."

"I'm confirmed that I've got no problem in me."

"And since when did this confirmation come in you?"

"What do you mean? What are you trying to implicate? Don't think others like you."

"What do you mean by that, Bubai?"

Shreya has thought about a divorce many times, and she doesn't want to leave the office at the end of the day. She requested Shankar-da and others to transfer her to night shift, but none agreed to shift a newly married woman to night duties, "Do you want your husband to come and kill us?" They never agreed to her proposal, neither Shreya was sure about how her own family would react if she tells them about her plan to divorce. Her parents, relatives, and neighbours will discuss, "...But didn't she choose to marry on her own?" "Did girls of this age forget to cohabitate at the in-laws' place?" "Will girls nowadays ever compromise?" These queries are apart, and her mother-in-law has also got other strategies. She creates emotional scenes or acts scenically whenever a child is born somewhere in the neighborhood. Shreya bears everything silently. She understands that her husband and mother-in-law fear her working in the media, and that's why they don't try to mess with her in excess. A couple of times though Bubai tried to pursue her, "Why don't you leave your newspaper office job?"

"Why?"

"You could try somewhere even better where pay package is higher."

"Here I have got a very conducive environment to work; money doesn't count always for me."

II

"See what I've got," Barry opened his plastic bag to show a binocular made of cheap plastic.

He then puts a finger on his lips and whispers, "But don't tell this to anybody. I actually needed it badly."

"Alright," Shreya tried to cut him short; otherwise, he would have wasted her time a lot.

"Shreya, I want to gift you something. You are the best in this office, and so I keep gifting you, but I won't gift to anyone else; I felt bad."

Shreya knew which gift Barry was talking about. Of course, it would be saplings like always, but she's also inquisitive about Barry's bad feelings, "Thanks. But why so?"

"Last day, when I gifted plants to Ruku-da, he left them at the office. Do you know the plants died?"

"Issh! That's not good at all. Okay, henceforth, you gift me; I will take care of your saplings."

A visibly glad Barry said, "These are chrysanthemums; please plant them today in your home. I will gift you fertilisers for them afterwards. They will produce big beautiful flowers in the blooming season."

Shreya smiled. She plants all the saplings gifted to her at the balcony. The chrysanthemum of the last year bloomed beautifully. Although that doesn't guarantee these new saplings will bloom the same, Barry's cordial gifting always makes her happy.

"I will gift you another nice thing."

"Wow."

Barry handed her an envelope hiding from others' sight and said in a hushed-up voice, "Keep it in a secret place now; read it when there's nobody around. I'm taking a leave now."

Shreya laughed at this half-mad man's antics. Shankar-da came and asked, "Why did the crazy Barry come? What was he saying?"

"The usual things. He gifted some saplings, too."

Shankar-da laughed, "Saplings! Again!... He's crazy, half-mad. If he hadn't been insincere at work, I would have given him a job here."

Shreya keeps listening, but she doesn't answer. Shankar-da continues,

"But the man really likes you; he talks for hours with you. But beware, his wife fled from him."

They both laughed at the joke.

***

During lunch hour, Shreya took out Barry's secret envelope. It's an English letter written with good handwriting but in improbable language, as improbable and inapprehensible as the man himself. The paragraphs speak about a tragedy in a very unorganised, diffused way. The writeup funnily started like a notice with a, "It is hereby notified to..." However, the basic meaning that came out from the letter is that, Barry is invading the locality of his elder brother's, armed with his newly purchased binoculars, for the last few days, and what has come out of his little investigation is that his wife and child are both staying with his brother in the same room. Moreover, Barry's wife is now letting his brother treat her like his own wife, and Barry's child is calling him New Daddy. Shreya doesn't understand, though, how Barry could listen over his binoculars, what his wife and his child are calling the man. In the writeup, Barry vowed to come up with more proof and sue his elder brother. In the end, Barry has made a sketch of a two-storied building with a man and woman in it while a third man positioned on the road is looking at them with a binocular in hand.

"O God!"

"What happened Shreya-di?"

"Dhurr, nothing," she put back the piece of paper inside the envelope.

***

Barry appeared again at the office before Shreya in the evening, "Have you read it? Do you understand my situation? Did you understand the fact that I have proved in my letter that both my wife and daughter want to return to me but couldn't do so because of my brother?"

"Did anybody tell you that?" Shreya asked without turning to him.

"No, but I've realized that. So I've decided to publish my letter as a leaftlet and distribute that at the locality where my brother lives. Now if you can extend a little..."

Shreya turned and face him, "Look Barry, your realization is completely your misconception. Your wife and daughter left you because of your own faults. First you correct yourself, then they may return..."

"What's there to correct myself? Am I a bad person?"

"You're not bad, but you're not a normal man either. You don't have a job, you remain high on drugs, you don't have money to keep a family by your side."

"But if nobody offers me a job, where's my fault?"

"Yes, that's your fault too. You lack sincerity in work, nor are you regular. Correct these natures so that at least a job can be arranged for you here."

Listening to her words, Barry's eyes gleamed in excitement, "Can you ask Shankar-da and arrange a job for me here?"

"How does it matter? You will again drop out of a job and remain absent for months! Then, people will only blame me. I think it's pointless to refer your name here."

Barry turned sad. He broke down and then silently walked away.

Shreya felt terrible about him, but she couldn't find a way. She's too bogged down with her problems. But she admires that this man loves his wife very much, even after so many incidences.

***

"Why are you spreading dirt inside the house?" Bubai taunted when Shreya was gardening on the balcony, planting the newly gifted saplings in flower pots. She has acquired some garden soil from the ground downstairs and is now watering and preparing the soil for plantation. She was working, lost in her thoughts when Bubai's bitter voice broke.

"Umm, what did you say?"

"I'm saying why you got busy dirtying the house at this hour of the morning. Didn't you have better things to do?"

"Nah, I couldn't find a better job than this," she giggled and completely ignored him.

Bubai felt insulted but couldn't stop, "What makes you a gardener suddenly?"

Shreya ignored him and started talking with the saplings, "You will be alright by the evening, don't worry."

"Why are you ignoring me? Didn't you learn to respond to someone's questions?"

"Oh really! Do you want some answer from me? Okay, tell me."

"I'm asking whether you are collecting the saplings on your own or somebody is supplying you with these."

"Of course, someone is supplying."

"Who's that person?"

"You don't know the person."

"Still, the person might have a name."

Shreya was amused, "It's pointless to know the name of a person you don't know." Telling this, Shreya tried walking out on Bubai when Bubai held her hands in anger. Then, suddenly, in the middle of the scene, her mother-in-law emerged from the bathroom and got caught in the middle of the warring husband-wife. Having no other options, she quickly fled the scene, but Shreya knew she felt elated whenever she witnessed them fighting.

"Who's the sample? A man or a woman?"

"How does that matter to you? Leave me. Or do you want to enact a slum-like scene at this hour of the morning?"

"Oh, very well, I can understand that a man has entered your life. But why don't you ask your newly found hero to leave gifting mere saplings and instead plant a real child inside you if he's a real man."

Shreya glared at Bubai for moments and then rushed to the toilet to spit a lump of irritation, hatred and bitterness. Her head is spinning with a mix of fury, disgust and repulsion. She quickly turned on the shower to get wet till deep inside her soul.

III

"Didn't you have your tea, madam?"

"Nay, I won't."

"Should I bring you another cup?"

"No." Shreya couldn't continue talking with the office bearer, Bimal. She still has to complete four pages of the supplementary paper but couldn't write a sentence more. Her head seems to burst anytime soon in anguish. She's numb with fury. She's not feeling hungry or fearing being scolded by the seniors for incomplete work.

Shankar-da came, "Anything wrong? Why are you sitting silent? See, the sky is clouded, and it will probably rain anytime soon. Plan a candlelight dinner with your hubby tonight."
Shreya couldn't respond.

Barry came around four in the evening. His face is reddened, his lips swollen, his dress unwary, and his buttons torn. Ruku-da expressed surprise, "Hey Barry! What happened?"

"No, nothing serious," Barry answered, sitting on the chair beside Shreya.

But Ruku-da warned him, "Okay, but don't disturb Shreya today; she's very busy, and she's not well today."

Barry clearly felt confused; he couldn't understand what he would tell them next as he had got a lot of things to tell her.

But Shreya, without giving Barry a second chance, quickly asked him, "Listen, Barry, you always come to meet me here, but why is it so that you never invite me to your place? At least you could have invited me for a cup of tea, couldn't you?" Barry was totally stumped at this; clearly, he was not ready for such a thing from Shreya.

But Shreya keeps insisting, "What happened? Answer me."

Barry fumbles, "I mean…I mean, there's nobody else in my house, so..."

"Don't you yourself live there? Don't you know how to make tea?"

"Of course, but I mean..."

"I want to visit your home tonight. Will you allow me to?" Shreya's voice sounded clear.

Barry kept hesitating, "Oh... tonight itself, but…"

"Yes, tonight, after five in the evening. Yes or No? What do you want? Can I come and at least have a glass of water at your place?"

"O Dear! Please come; I never meant to hurt you; I mean, since I live alone so I thought you would feel comfort..."

"It doesn't matter. Write me your address here and get yourself ready at home to host me. I will be there in the evening after office. I love good tea. Get some salted biscuits to accompany the tea. Okay?"

Shreya was finding herself half-mad, almost as mad as Barry. She was not listening to herself all the while. Soon Barry went away with a parting "Please come" and a "Bye", and after some time, Shreya too left the office. While switching her computer off, she discovers that she has hurt her fingers unknowingly, perhaps with the nail cutter, and there's blood clotted on the side. But she's feeling no pain. There's no sensation of burning inside her.

***

From her office at the Esplanade crossing, it doesn't take long to reach Royd Street by the Taxi. Around half past five, Shreya left the Taxi in front of fourteen Royd Street. The atmosphere around felt like a sheer imagination, untrue and weightless, nothing quite touching the soul. She feels no external pain except an unexplainable burning sensation deep inside.

The place is crowded, mostly Muslim settlers dwelling in the lanes and bylanes amidst shops and souks. A naked infant was crawling through her way when she reached the end of the lane where the house of the designated address stands. She pushed a wooden door to enter inside and found a staircase covered in darkness. A boy came rushing down the flight, awkwardly eyeing Shreya while going away.

There Barry was standing where the stairs end at the first floor. He welcomes her dressed in clean clothes, "Please come, this is my room here." Shreya follows him to a room where the air is thick with a kerosene smell. Perhaps it was because of an attempt to quickly clean up the interior. A white bedsheet covers the wooden cot, which, on one side, piles up awkwardly, surely covering dirty pillows and unclean linens. There's a pump stove, bottle of fuel oil, tea leaves, sugar cubes, crockery, utensils, and water cask in the corner of the room. Shreya sat on the cot; Barry stood by hesitantly again lamenting, "I mean... since I stay alone here, I mean... since I left my family house, this being a rented property, it's very dirty... maybe you won't like it... maybe you're feeling bad about it..."

"Stop talking, sit beside me. No, I'm not feeling bad. Get me a glass of water."

"Oh sure," Barry nervously poured water from the cask and inadvertently wasted some on the floor. Shreya was eyeing around; she could see the only photograph on the wall, of Jesus Christ, calmly watching her from the wall. A mail train is running fast inside her head, inside her heart so fast that Shreya fears Barry might hear it. Uff!

"Shreya, I understand; you must be feeling stuffy here. Actually, I can't open the window; the shouts from the slum below will disturb you then..."

"It's okay. I'd rather you increase the speed of the table fan."

"So sorry, it's speed doesn't increase. Shall I make you tea?"

"Of course..." Shreya was feeling uneasiness because she continuously feared that Barry might hear the sound of the mail train speeding inside her. She recoiled within. It will be very embarrassing if he gets to listen to the sound of the turmoil inside her.

Barry is sitting on the floor, making tea on the pump stove. Shreya keeps looking at him, admiring the man in his head full of unkempt grey hairs, eyes full of childlike purity and unshaved chiselled chin with untold steadiness. Immersed in deep thoughts, she gripped the corner of the bedsheet firmly and hesitantly asked, "What happened to the corner of your lips? Why has it swelled?" Barry paused and then murmured, "I was beaten."

"Why? Who has beaten you?"

"My brother and a group of his men."

"But what have you done? Come here, tell me all."

"I had done nothing. I was only keeping a watch on them with my binoculars. Finding me, my brother attacked me with the men. But..."

"But, what?"

"My wife couldn't come out to save; she was watching from the windows upstairs and then moved away from there…"

"Issh Barry, there are clear cut marks beside your lips. Did you apply medicines?"

"No, I haven't. Shreya, since you like me, you can see my wounds; none saw it throughout the day."

"Barry, do you have any antiseptic to apply to your wounds? Give me that so that I can nurse your injuries."

"Nah, I don't have any."

Shreya pulled Barry by her side; she tried touching Barry's lips where there were cut marks. But she failed to touch him. Her hands didn't reach him there. She could neither see beyond a certain point, especially in the scenes around Barry getting hazed. Under the blanket of fog, Shreya's hands keep searching for a way to touch Barry. But her fingers couldn't find anything.

"But... But... I still believe my wife loves me. Yes, I know that... I believe that my wife was eager to come down to save me, but someone must have locked her inside. She moved away from the window because she couldn't bear the scene of me getting beaten up," Barry kept repeating while sitting by Shreya; he didn't care for Shreya's touch. And then suddenly, he leapt from beside her, his eyes being on the water boiling for tea,
"Oh! The water got boiled; I should stop that..."

The Fairy with Chopped Wings

I can call fairies. I got secret mantras to invite them. Every night, I call fairies at my place on my will. I have mantras written on coloured paper and carry them in my pocket, where there are myriads of mantras written for various types of fairies. The fairies come by night, stay with me and leave in the morning, taking back their mantras with them. But that hardly affects me as I have a never-ending stock of mantras in my anvil. I am not even sure of the size of my anvil. I just sit and invite fairies from the cosy corner of my room, and they drop in. They hover over the city sky, and hearing me, they drop in through doors or the windows. They have got wings of varied shapes and sizes. Large, small and medium. Some come to me flying from a long distance, and some just check in from some adjacent places. They can't ignore my call and come rushing in because they respect me and fear me since I can do anything with my mantras.

They entertain me in the best ways they can by singing, dancing, or playing the flute. But I know they fake everything and try to fool me into learning my magic mantra of controlling them. But so far, none have been successful in fooling me. I would lie to you if I say I have liked none. Among them, especially one fairy, Lili by name, has been my favourite. Perhaps Lili is not her real name, but I keep calling her by that name because I like it. Although I don't like the same fairy every night, I keep calling Lili. There is a peculiar odour in Lili's skin, a grassy aroma. The aroma that floats in the air of a foggy field. But Lili's saliva tastes the same as others. This thought often mystifies why all fairies taste the same in their mouths. Is it because they keep by the side of their Lords like us? Lili had her home at... I forgot the name of the place. But it's somewhere on the outskirts of the city. I used to lay back at my fourteen hundred square feet home and drink wine while she kept singing and dancing around in the dim green room light. I sometimes sprinkled mantras on her in excitement, and she shuddered in thrill, hugging me back tightly. I could smell her grassy aroma then, and that gave me an instant high.

Other fairies have gold wings, silver wings, and wings of red-blue-pink colours. Only Lili had green wings. I asked her the reason, and she answered with a laugh,

"I don't know, but I like forests."

When she flapped her wings, sometimes while sitting by me, I noticed that the feathers that fell off from her wings accidentally looked like leaves. However, fairies customarily don't leave anything while leaving their Lords, so I have got no feathers of her wings in my possession. I have liked green since my childhood. I don't remember much about my childhood, but in the snapshots of my memories, I can remember my village, the thatched roof of our hut, and the wide paddy fields behind it. It sounded a shrill melody when winds blew over the lush green of the paddy fields. It was then that I understood that air and scent can be green. And so can be parents-siblings-friends. In my school, when I drew scenery, my teacher laughed at me because I coloured trees, cows, the sky, and everything green. I felt awry because I had really seen everything around in green. Even my teacher's affection and love appeared green to me. He loved me because I was a good student. After school, I started studying in college in the city, living in a student mess. The student mess became the incubation centre of the new me, where slowly, the green in my eyes started fading off when I started travelling to forbidden places, watching newer colours. The lights around the village help one see their surroundings, while the city lights teach one to look at oneself only. The intensity of city lights covers everything. I started losing attachment to my village. However, I was always honest with my studies and my career. I always believed that one day I would reign over the city, and to reign over, I knew that I required a very strong foundation of knowledge and study. After passing college with flying colours, I never looked back to my home. After spending days in some odd jobs gathering requisite experience, I started advancing in my career with the power of brain and brawn. I kept rising higher until I reached the twelfth floor of the high-rise building in the southern part of this city in fourteen hundred square feet flat. From the balcony of this flat, I amusingly watch city life as if it were ants crawling on the ground.

My history couldn't pursue me long because it soon lost pace to me. It gave up, and I walked away, and I moved miles ahead. I can now find none behind my back. Fortunately!

I used to think that I had many things similar to Lili, but then love always drives one to look for similarities in the loved one. Does Lili do the same? I don't understand Lili's feelings. In our emotional moments, I often asked Lili about her past, and she told me a different story every time. I could understand that those were mere fabricated good-time stories of childhood. But although every time the places and characters of stories changed, one thing always remained constant: there was a huge forest beside the house. She always explains the extent of the forest by stretching both of her hands as much as she can. I could understand the real existence of the jungle in her otherwise made-up stories by her way of telling. But then, in made-up stories, she only drew pictures of her dream, and dreams can be true in life, isn't it?

I always fell for Lili's narration of geography rather than her history because then she looked more attractive. And in this way, one day, I fell for her, perhaps for her made-up story or her green-coloured wings or for her grassy aroma. I am not sure which of these drove me crazy for her. And then one day, without getting high, I asked her, in my complete sense,

"Would you stay with me?"

But Lili left me and flew away at once. After that, I looked for her at many meetings, parties, bashes, and carnivals. Throughout the night, I chanted my mantras persistently in rage but couldn't call her back. I was surprised at my failure and my mantras. Did I enjoy my *unsuccess*?" I don't remember.

Days passed. Other fairies brought news that Lili now stays with someone. She refused me, but she stayed with someone else by marrying. The news of her marriage couldn't exude any reaction out of me. I was spending my life without her when one day I found her in a shoe shop at Gariahat, selecting shoes for children. She was carrying a child in her lap and a man by her side, one tall and lanky, dark and rusty young man of around thirty-five. I could understand the man to be her husband. There were no green wings on her back, but the dark and oily-skinned back of an underrated woman was displayed there before my eyes. I was looking at her. She looked back but couldn't recognise me. I found her pretty. I found her child's meaningless laugh prettier! Radiant! A fairy with chopped wings... A wife with chopped wings... A mother with chopped wings..! Dhuss!

Other fairies told me that Lili's husband is a painter, but the family does not have much income. I wondered whether her husband knew about her fairy life! My fairy informers couldn't answer me either. I wondered why Lili left her multi-toned, fairy-tale life for a poor and monotonous life. I found the man quite unattractive. I thought he must be wearing underwear with holes, and Lili might have to wash his torn underwear. This made me more surprised about Lili's selection in life. I tried inviting Lili many times with my mantra just to know what made her choose a different path in life. Actually, during her fairy life, I once asked her, "So you must be having a wonderful life, isn't it? Because you don't have liability towards anyone." To which she laughed and, cuddling my hair, replied, "I don't know if I'm having a wonderful life now, but I believe one day I will live like I want, and I will happily return to my liabilities."

I couldn't understand her replies. I couldn't understand what she meant when she told me she wanted to live the way she wanted. In an effort to forget her, I used to invite fairy after fairy every night, but in vain. I found fake aromas in their bodies. I couldn't smell natural grass in anyone's naked body. I got angry. In a feat of rage, I drove them all.

Unknowingly, age caught up with me. My anvil of mantras increased, but my capacity to throw mantras at will was greatly reduced. I started getting nervous; I started getting afraid of making mistakes. I started becoming unbearable to myself. My increasing tummy, dark circles, weak vision, and slow movements were dragging me down. My fourteen hundred square feet kingdom was no longer filled tightly with the 'Great Me' that once used to be. I started making noise while walking just to let me know that I was the same me. A feeling like a loser—a fear of the unknown—was replacing my confidence, and life started losing colour before my eyes. I started losing sleep and started taking heavy sleeping pills.

Then, one day, suddenly, I had a dream that I was flying high through a green sky with my wings making great noise while flapping at high speed. And then I found another girl flying by me, but I could hardly see her face. My vision faded, and all my efforts to look closer and recognise her went in vain. Then I woke up nervously, and the thought of Lili came to my mind. I started missing Lili. Then I used all my secret mantras to invite her. I used up all my powers to call her. I knew deep inside that she wouldn't turn up, but still, I kept trying. My voice broke, and I fell ill. Then I, don't know why, started feeling very happy inside. The day I gave up and stopped my efforts, she turned up. Surprising me, she came dragging her body through the cornice of the terrace and leaping into the room through the window with a lot of effort. Saggy and malnutrient body. Amateurish Makeup and blooped face paints, gawky look in unmatched saree and blouse. The way she was panting, I thought she now needed all the oxygen of the world. I said, "Come sit." She sat and drank water from a bottle kept at a side. I could see her exposed midriff from under her saree; it appeared like the exposed tummy of a toad. I directly asked, "Why did you come?"

Lili smiled, exposing her paan-stained teeth, "Because you called."

"So you started taking calls again," I sounded bitter in my voice.

She sighed, "Huh, huh." And licked her lips to add, "I thought you forgot me."

I wished to reply that I was trying hard to forget her but didn't utter a word. I wished to ask if she still had the grassy aroma but instead said something else.

"You are looking like the shaved skin cheap fairies."

Lili smiled a leisured smile, "O really?... Aye, you have many contacts, so please admit me to a group where I can make good connections. Do you think I lost my skills?"

"How do I suppose to know that? What about your husband?"

"We don't live together anymore."

"Really?"

"Yes," she sounded tired.

"What about your child?"

"Does he have an option?"

"What's his age?"

"He studies in Class Three. He is an intelligent boy." I could see the expression of a winning mother's pride in the answer. She adds, "But he's very mischievous."

I faced Lili and asked on her face, "Last time I saw you at a shoe shop. Then you didn't have the wings. Then what's this? Did the wings grow anew?" I asked in a relaxed way, but the question hurt Lili. She covered her face and cried, stooping in front. I could see then that a couple of artificial wings had been pinned on her back. At once, I pressed and uprooted the wings. Some bad blood gushed out with those. I buried my face on her shoulder and finally could have a faint smell of the grassy odour from behind the back of her ears. And then I whispered to her, "Even I can't call fairies by my mantras. I have lost my magic. I know you came on your own."

A Delirium Born

My elder sister is deranged. Everyone knows that. So did I. But what I know more than that is that dementia hasn't routed her; like throughout the day, she remains the beautiful girl that she always has been. But with the evening coming up, she changes. She then becomes silent. She gets lost in her thoughts, watching the sky. Watching for hours together. Adrift. Unresponsive. And then, when the moon rises, she turns restless. None can make her go to sleep on a moonlit night. She keeps watching the moon, witnessing the white clouds bathing in the white beams. Then alone, she recites the eternal lines unmindfully to herself,

"There's the rain is coming. Let it rain. Pitter-patter raindrops, call the river tide, Lord Shiva came to marry three pretty brides. Lord Shiva came to marry.. came to marry.. to marry.. Hi-Hi-Hi."

Her shrill role of laughter startles me. She looks unknown. I shudder. Where's the rain? Who does she mean as Lord Shiva? I can understand nothing. So, each time, I feel shocked anew. I feel lonely. Sometimes, she remarks to me – "Sona, see, Lord Shiva has arrived. There he is."

My name is Sona. We have lost our father last year. He was an officer working at a very high post. He committed suicide by jumping before the moving train. When his dead body was brought to our house, my mother didn't cry. We did. Me and my elder sister. My father's face was tied with a piece of green cloth. I tried to open and see him for one last time. I was not allowed by people around. I don't know why, but I miss him and his face.

I don't know why Baba took his life. I don't know why Didi turned deranged. I am just a kid, after all, studying in Class Six. My Didi, when she was normal, sometimes went on trips with her uncle. Together, once we visited the zoo. She used to be very happy, especially when Ranjan uncle was around. Then, once, I saw Ranjan uncle making love to my mother. It felt bad. My mother scolded me, as she didn't want me to watch them. I was forbidden to discuss this with Baba and Didi. But still, I told everything to Didi as there was agony inside me after witnessing their scene. Since then, a lot of quarrels started in our house. Didi started to change. My mother works now. Ranjan uncle has arranged it; I know that. Together, they travel places. Ranjan uncle pays her money. I planned to tell her to stop taking money from him after I started working.

Ranjan uncle is a good painter. I, too, paint. However, I don't like Ranjan uncle. Not at all. I only love my Didi. I watch her while she stares at the sky, counting the stars. "One, two, three... Dhurr, it's so confusing; I'm losing it all," she cries, and then she turns to me to request, "Hey Sona, can you bring me the stars?"

I ask, "Which one?"

Didi points to one, "That one, there."

Then suddenly, I grew up and replied like a mature person, "Okay, not now. But tomorrow, for sure. Now you need to go to sleep."

She shouts at me, "Are you mad! They will be lost in the morning."

I remember my father's dead body was found in the morning by the rail lines. My mother never loved him. She used to call him a coward. I don't know the meaning of the word. My Baba called my mother a whore. I won't tell anybody the meaning of that word. My Didi keeps staring at the sky. She sees rain falling from the sky. She calls me, "Aye, Sonamoni." Her call makes me feel sleepy. I fall asleep and don't know how, but slowly, day by day, I grow up in my slumber.

I love my city drenched in moonlight. While returning home on a moonlit night through the serpentine ways amidst the tall buildings, suddenly, power cuts take place, and the world gets immersed in darkness. Only the silvery light of the moon painted the walls and the streets, and I started thinking of myself as the Alice of the Wonderland. I fell in love with my city. My city looks like an unknown maid to me; it is so loving. I romance each of the bricks and the pebbles and they pay me back with affection. They talked to me about history, about Mahmud, Shah Jahan, and Charnock. I tell them stories about my parents. They patiently listen to me. When they became upset, I could feel that. I didn't want to leave them upset; I wanted to be by them then. I feel the urge to melt into those walls. I know there's a different world inside them, and I always beg to explore that. Sometimes, I bury my face in the moss-ridden bricks; I embrace the oldness of the walls. But when I still remain busy feeling the history and the emotions of the heart of my city, suddenly, lights come back, and darkness fades. I feel forced to return home.

My mother left with Ranjan Banerjee. My Didi's hair is grey now. She's completely delirious in her loneliness. She often undresses herself. I have to dress her back. She imprisoned herself in her room, only at times moving to the window to watch the sky. She used to sing but no more. I used to paint, but no more. Sometimes, I had to leave her to go out to work by locking her inside her room. I have no job; I teach a few students. The rest of the time, I stay with my Didi; I stay with my city where the bricks and the pebbles, the streets and the walls, the moon and the sky are my world and with whom I talk. I always want to write about our conversations and our stories.

I thought of writing a story. I have to. There are thousand of words bubbling inside me, inside my heart, stomach, and intestine. I have to shape those in letters otherwise I won't have peace. But I am searching for a start. Then a scene appeared before me –

"Is Shyamal uncle home?" I asked a woman of around thirty-five or thirty-six.

"No, he's not," the lady looked visibly morose in her reply.

I suspiciously queried, "I mean when can I meet him…"

"Don't you know what happened with him?"

The question splashes like a whip on me. He was a good man; he wrote beautiful poetry; what could happen to him? My heart fluttered, "Not really... what happened?"

The lady turned darker in sadness, "He retired this month. So, there's no fixed timing for him going out or staying at home."

Shyamal uncle is a bachelor. He was a supervisor at an export company, while his brother is unemployed and dependent upon him, but married. This lady is the brother's wife. The moral of the story is: I understood that she is visibly puzzled about whether to treat his retirement as equal to his death.

Then another scene appeared,

My mother shouted loud, "You're a coward, good for nothing."

Baba hits back in a hissing voice, "Shut up, you whore! Go to hell."

I and my Didi tremble in fear, all the while in each other's arms.

One more scene,

"A bit more amount of money in this month would have helped," my mother remarked to Ranjan uncle while counting the currency notes he gave her.

He replies, "Manage with whatever is given. The market is very expensive, and I have to maintain the cost of not one but two families."

My mother still tried to argue, "A lot has to be spent on my daughter's treatment."

"That's something unnecessary, fruitless..." saying he started cuddling her like a pet cat he owns.

A fourth scene arose,

In a weird but sweet voice, Didi asked, "Can you bring me the star, please?"

Hearing her, I came out of a three hundred years old moss-ridden wall, finding her wholly undressed; I first dressed her up in a saree, then lovingly asked her, "Which one, Didi?"

"That one there, where it's raining, Hi-Hi, Lord Shiva's marriage, Lord Shiva's… Hi-Hi!"

Dialogues, loads and loads of dialogues like these, characters like those are driving me around like a crazy bull. I am madly in search of a story, I am spitting froth like a tired stallion, and I'm feeling numb at my feet. My age and life expectancy are shaking like the flame of a candle about to extinguish. Does the city have any other story to tell? Does it?

I could find none. The city before my eyes has no stories either. None of the citizens has done so in this dead city. There are only some characters disarrayed. There are only some dialogues disoriented. The sky, the moon and the moss-ridden bricks are all accidentally placed around. There's a bottle of poison kept before me. I couldn't bear my lifelong pain anymore. So, I decided to end it all. There's a notepad and a pen by the bottle I kept. Though Baba hasn't left a suicide note, I have decided to leave one.

What may I write? Sylvia Plath –

'Dying is art

I do it exceptionally well.'

At least I want to make my death famous, which is a great incident that ends with a poem. I don't know what will happen to Didi after me. Nobody knows. I can bear no more. I hate all betrayers of the world. Everyone has betrayed me so far. I wrote my poem in one breath. Then I took the poison bottle in hand. Suddenly, I remembered Didi. I kept the bottle back on the table and went to her room. The room is dark. I switched on the light. Didi is sleeping inside. For days, I haven't seen Didi sleeping so peacefully and so beautifully. I moved the hairs from over her face. Then I lay down beside her and buried my face inside her chest, between her withered breasts. There's still the smell of leftover milk in there. There's the metallic sound of a moving train inside her heart. I hushed inside her heart, then started running with the train. In whiskers, I went past hills and valleys, rivers, and forests. It turned from a train into a horse. I quickly ride the horse. The horse leaps into the sky. It starts flying. Is this a flying horse? There's boundless space around me, a wide sky. I forgot that I was lying buried in my Didi's chest. I keep flying in the darkness of the night sky dotted with stars twinkling like diamonds. The running horse suddenly turned to me. It looked like Ranjan uncle.

The next moment the horse stood up and, with a shrug, threw me down from his back, "You whore." I fell down trembling. There I keep falling down. I shouted in fear, "Ma-aa," I got thrown into darkness, and I kept falling. I shuddered in fear and Didi woke up. She never gets startled at my existence around her. She lovingly taps my head instead, "What is it, Sona? Are you thirsty?"

At once the city plunges into darkness before my eyes. Perhaps there's a power cut. The moonbeam leaps in through the window bar in striped silvery hue. The smell of dew blew in with it. Head resting on her lap I looked up to the ceiling and Alas! There's no ceiling now but a squarish sky above my head. There, to my utter surprise, I found all of my characters sailing in the white cloud. The characters from Shyaml uncle's story, Ranjan uncle's story, and my parents' story sailing there. The city is writing about all these characters and many more. I could see the letters. The characters whom I thought of expressing in letters, they themselves have drawn me in letters in exchange. I found my birth, my life, and my death all written in the sky, in their terms, in their letters. In each letter, I'm being born, I'm dying.

Suddenly, a sound alerts me. I found the bottle of poison that I left in my room came to me, whispering in a sad voice, "What happened? I'm waiting for you."

"I know. You go back. I will follow suit."

The bottle returns to its position.

I took a leave from Didi. Didi once again has fallen asleep. Unworried. Relaxed. I stood by the window. It's about to dawn. A cold breeze is blowing.

I move back to my room. I found the bottle standing like a head hanging low. I took it up like partners lovingly taking each other's arms. I put the mouth of the bottle inside my mouth like partners kiss each other's. I whisper, "Frankly speaking, you too are helpless. Calm down. Do you have anything left to say?"

The Tale of a Woman

I

At the beginning, none of the others noticed. Moni was the first in the group. "See the two dramatists! Such lewd, aren't they?" the four others left their play cards and joined hands, rather eyeballs, to look the way Moni gestured. There's a young couple there. The man in his early thirties, dressed in a reddish shirt and brown pants, was sitting with his legs raised on the seats. He has his pants rolled up to his knees, which shows his thin legs. There's a massive mole on his left heel, clearly visible. He has unbridled rough hairs, a contrasting neatly shaved albeit broken jawline and a brownish moustache. The woman with him is, at best, in her mid-twenties. She has a polished dark complexion and is dressed in a red and white saree paired with a matching red blouse. The saree appears new by its look. She is sitting on her knees and there are glimpses of her petticoat from under her saree. She looks pretty.

The man plays his fingers on the woman's right hand, tickling her from her palm to her shoulder. The woman rolls into laughter each time he completes his action. She is not moving away her hands either, seemingly enjoying the act. They're playing time-pass games, for sure.

Swallowing the couple's façade details with wide eyes at one go, Ila quickly reacted, "We shouldn't be watching like this; otherwise, they will start repeating their nuisance wilfully."

Anu twisted her lips in annoyance, "What a fuss of a drama!"

All in the group concentrated back on playing fish with their playing cards.

Their group goes by the name, Pancha Pandavi. Being a year older than the rest, Lakshmi is the leader of this group. The rest of the members are all around fifty years or so. Whenever they are called by their group name among acquaintances and relatives, the five ladies actually took pride in that. Anu and Ila are friends living in the same locality. The remaining of them became friends in the college. Lakshmi was already the General Secretary of the students' union at Bethune College by that time. During the college function, Durga's exceptional soiree of toppa songs, Anu's artistic sense of stage decoration, Moni's eloquent recitation, and Ila's friendly hype and spirited participation quickly attracted all five to each other. It resulted in an outing spree by bunking classes and fighting against the families to visit Shantiniketan during the Basanta Utsav. Anu's maternal uncle, who was an employee at the Viswa Bharati, arranged the girls' lodging. That was the start. Thereafter, these five college sweethearts made numerous rounds of Digha, Shantineketan, Puri, and Dooars. After completing college, however, Lakshmi was the first to get separated from others and married off to Siliguri. Then, one after another, friends got detached, spread far and wide from each other. Contacts were limited over the phone to "Hello! How are you doing?" But then, one day, the invitation of Lakshmi's younger son Arnab's rice ceremony reached everyone with a threat,

"Now, if you don't come, then never in this birth I ..."

The four seriously consulted and decided to go. However, Durga, being a schoolteacher, had a fear that she might not manage to sanction leave from school eventually. But it was actually accomplished. Then, after dealing with various embargoes from respective in-laws' places, they were finally able to break all shackles to meet each other on the pretext of the invitation. It was a couple of days of pure joy, rendezvous, and reliving the youth. It was then decided days ahead, they would start touring in groups at least once a year. And that year, they visited Gangtok.

A Kedarnath tour followed it, and then onwards till now, the girl group had at least made two dozen holiday trips through the length and breadth of the nation. In some of the trips, families too were included. There were also a few years in between when there were no outings for reasons ranging from personal health issues to daughter's exam to son's marriage. But nothing could harm the bondage between them, the affinity towards each other.

With age, their children grew up. First, Lakshmi's daughter and then both of Ila's daughters got married off. Then Durga lost her husband, and her elder son went off to the United States. Moni remained childless, though. Anu's only daughter is now taking training for JBT.

It's not that in this long period, they never had troubles between them, but that never put a question mark in the spirit of their group. They always co-existed with each other's problems.

This year, their tour destination was decided to be Puri. Actually, age caught them up, and their families were too concerned to leave five elderly women all by themselves on their own. But the group managed it by saying this was the last time they would be journeying together. They visited Puri a couple of times earlier, but the attraction of the sea in Puri is ubiquitous.

"So, guys, won't we have our meals? It's already half past eight," Moni reminded everyone.

"Wait, wait, none is hungry except you," Ila gave a mild snubbing.

Lakshmi was nostalgic, "Do you guys remember if we travelled by the same train last time we travelled to Puri?"

Moni replied, "Nah, then it was Puri Express."

Durga was immersed in a Bonful novel. Anu made a friendly banter, "My dear sis, aren't you eyeing the couple more than reading a book?"

"Stop it, will you!"

"Hi, Hi, Hi!"

Durga closed the book and looked out of the window. The pitch-black darkness makes one feel like blindfolded. A dot of light every now and then kept appearing and vanishing there in between. Keeping the playing cards aside, the five friends started gossiping among themselves.

In the S5 Sleeper coach of Jagannath Express, the group has reservations for seat numbers seventeen to twenty-one. Opposite to them, in the berths twenty-three and twenty-four, the couple were sitting. In the name of luggage, they only got a big shopper's bag, a fretted basket, and a sling bag. The man is carrying the sling bag on his back. He is now busy pressing tobacco in his palms.

Moni frowned, "Such a mess. Soon, he will start clapping tobacco dust that is polluting around."

The girl meanwhile took out food from the shopper's bag, a pound of bread and a bunch of bananas. There is also a little pack of sweets.

Lakshmi whispered her concern, "Untoasted slices of bread always harm you if taken in dinner. It's a direct invitation to indigestion problem."

Moni said, "Let's get our food out too."

Anu's repartee continued, "Sure, the ever-hungry friend of ours will have food in a lifetime, after all."

Roti, cabbage cooked sans onion, and a couple of kalakand sweets being served for dinner, Ila remarked while having food, "The couple must be newly married, possibly on their honeymoon trip."

Moni asked, "How could you make that out?"

"Why, look at the way she applied the vermilion on her forehead. Unskilled. The Shankha-pola pair, too, appears newly bought."

The group started observing closely. Indeed, the Shankha-pole pair is shining against her dark complexion.

Anu expressed her admiration, "Really it is. Lady Byomkesh. Or what else should I call you?"

Durga remarked, "Why? Byomkeshi!"

"Hi-Hi-Hi."

The role of laughter of the five ladies made the couple look upon them for once. Then, they concentrated back on their meal. Finishing their short meal, the couple drank water.

Lakshmi once again expressed her shock, "Water after untoasted bread! Indigestion will surely take their lives!"

"Ohh, stop your concerns. It won't harm people like them!"

After the nice dinner, they threw the plates out of the window, then after visiting the toilet, played another round of play cards and finally called it off for the day.

The couple were still in the middle of their deep conversations. But here, the ladies switched off the lights. So, only a dim blue light lit the surroundings. And in the middle of the night, in the half darkness, the woman's gigglings "Aye, don't... please... no" were often heard. God knows what immoral mischief was going on between those two! But they can hardly do anything about that. The ladies got lost in their slumber soon amidst the swaying train.

Lakshmi and Durga were in the two lower berths. It was beyond midnight when suddenly someone called, "Aunty, what will happen now, Aunty! Please wake up!"

A sudden push took Lakshmi aback in the middle of their sleep, and she screamed, "Who's it! Who's there?"

Her scream woke Durga up, too. She promptly switched on the lights. The girl was standing in front, looking scared and disoriented.

"What happened?" Lakshmi sounded irritated as she was forced to wake up in the middle of her sleep.

"What will happen now, Aunty? He didn't return to the train."

Durga asked back, "Who didn't return to the train?"

The girl hesitated a bit, "My husband, Dulal."

Possibly, the train had stopped for a while at some station. Now, though, it's running full speed. Durga felt curious, "Why did he at all get off in the middle of the night?"

"I don't know. He told me he has to bring drinking water."

"Oh, then worry not. He must be coming anytime. Maybe he had boarded some other coach. He can come through within the train."

"If he couldn't board at all?" the girl suddenly started weeping like a child.

This clearly moved Lakshmi, "Oh-ho, don't be so impatient. He is a young man; how can he miss boarding back? Sit and wait for some time, and you will see him back.

Finding the girl still stubbornly standing, Lakshmi switched off the light. In the blue light, the silhouette of the girl appeared to be from another world.

Lakshmi scolded her sternly, "I told you not to worry; go back to your seat."

This time, the girl listened. She returned to her seat.

Durga went back to her sleep. But Lakshmi was still awake. She could hear the girl weeping. She couldn't sleep in the middle of this nuisance. She stood up and went to the distressed girl.

"What happened? He still couldn't come?" Lakshmi put a hand on her head. The girl broke down completely.

Lakshmi sat beside her. "Don't be like a stupid child; there's nothing to cry. Do you know that so many times we have faced situations like this? All your worries are baseless."

The weeping girl grasped Lakshmi with her wet palms, and a neon light from a distance fell on both of their faces through the window glass. Lakshmi could see the girl's face in that light. Those tearful eyes looked extraordinary. Lakshmi told her, "Wait, let me call my friends."

She switched on the light and woke all of them. Everyone listened, but no one could give a rational solution. Everyone tried, though. They hardly remember now how much they were irked by the lewdness of the giggling girl and her mischievous partner all through the evening.

Anu sounded helpless in her question, "What will happen to her now?"

Moni said, "Can't understand how we should help. If he had at all boarded back by now, he should have reached here. But if he had boarded the General compartment, then of course he can't make it through up to this reserved coach."

Ila questioned the girl, "Where are you going to? Puri?"

"Hmm," the girl is trying hard to suppress her crying.

"What's your name?"

"Sandhya."

The conversation went on for the rest of the night. It's a story well known. Sandhya is a resident of Kacharipara in Bagnan, while Dulal is from Mecheda. Both are flower sellers at the Jagannath Ghat. They used to sit side by side, selling their spread. Therefore, as commonly happens in such cases, they met, talked and finally fell for each other. Dulal is from a well-off family compared to Sandhya. His family, Gope by cast, have got their own flower garden. Sandhya's family is lower both in terms of caste and wealth. Dulal was about to back off from the relationship when his family didn't agree, but somehow, a crying Sandhya melted his heart down, and they both got married at Kalighat after eloping. They boarded at one of Dulal's friend's places till boarding a train today for a honeymoon trip to Puri.

While listening to Sandhya's life story, Byomkeshi detective Ila was the first to express suspicion to Anu beside her, whispering her doubts, "Listen, do you think the boy may flee? I mean, such things are quite common nowadays."

II

At ten in the morning, sitting in the first-floor room of Sindhu Lodge located at Swargdwar, Lakshmi and Anu were busy calculating the tour expenditures. Moni was busy applying cream on her face, standing before the mirror in the room. Durga is reading a book, sitting on a chair. Ila is lying lazily on the bed.

Yesterday, after reaching Puri, they searched for Dulal a lot on the platform. Failing to find him, they went to the police station. The inspector assured them he would do everything permitted under the law to help them out and would immediately communicate anything he could hear about Dulal.

Meanwhile, Sandhya came out of the bathroom and declared, "Let's go. I'm ready."

Durga lowered her book and wondered, "So fast. Only a while ago, you went for a bath."

Wiping the towel over her wet hair, Sandhya confirmed, "Sure. I finished bathing."

"Did you use the soap?"

"Nah."

"You dirty, good-for-nothing girl," Durga rose from her seat and came closer to Sandhya; she checked her shoulder and showed her how dirt had accumulated on her uncleaned neckline. Durga dragged her back to the bathroom, "Come in, wash this with soap. Otherwise, don't sleep with us in bed. Lay on the floor."

Sandhya obliged. Durga made the girl sit on the floor of the bathroom and, sitting behind her, started cleaning her back, shoulder and neck with scrub and lather herself. There is too much dirt to clean, and the water soon turns soil coloured.

Durga lightly scolded her, "For how long you haven't used the soap?

"No, of course I did it."

"Ohh, really... which year you did so?"

Her remarks made others roll in laughter.

After a thorough cleaning, Sandhya's dusky back started glittering like a silvery hilsa in the sun. One can't fail to notice two folds of puppy fat by her waist. Durga got lost in her thoughts momentarily. Suddenly, her thoughts broke when she discovered scar marks of scratches on the back of Sandhya's neck. Those are blood-red marks. Durga could well understand those are marks from last night. She lightly touched those scars. Smiling, she pointed those to Moni. Moni came closer to observe. At first, she couldn't notice, and instead, she kept staring at Sandhya's bare young back—youthful skin, rounded arms, and a head full of hair. Sandhya was kneeling on her knees.

But after finding those scar marks on Durga's insistence, Moni just threw back a half mile. It's more out of indolence. Hence, it seems lifeless.

"O aunty, have you finished?"

"Wait, my dear," Durga started applying shampoo on her head. Moni backed off and got busy with herself before the mirror. The mirror shows her aged image where the skin at the corner of her eyes has visibly grown older, and the skin around the navel, too, feels like a lump of fatness wrapped in rough skin. This really hurts the woman inside Moni.

Meanwhile, the bathroom door closed as Sandhya got back to bathing. While washing her hands in the washbasin outside the toilet, Durga remarked, "Listen, Lakshmi, I'm sure the boy actually fled."

Ila agreed, "Ditto. I feel the same."

Anu resonates, "Let it be. Let her live with us for a couple of days. After that, however, it will all depend upon her destiny..."

But within only a day time, the young girl moved closer at heart to all the five elderly ladies. They are freely mixing with her. They have made her believe that Dulal must have failed to board the train and instead returned home. So, after a couple of days, when they will return, Sandhya can return to her in-law's place. The simple girl as she is, Sandhya had believed them.

Moni suddenly raised her voice from amongst all, "Listen, don't take it otherwise, but you all are doing quite in excess with this girl."

Anu protested, "What's the excesses you found?"

"What else then? Cleaning her with soap and shampoo, letting her sleep by your side, Lakshmi is treating her almost like her own daughter."

Lakshmi got hurt listening and observed, "Don't be so rude, Moni; you should have understood it too if you yourself had one..."

Upon hearing this, Moni's face went dark. The atmosphere quickly turned heavy in the room, and emotions flew high around. Everyone went silent. Meanwhile, Sandhya appeared in the room from the bathroom with a bang on the door and declared, "I am ready now, really ready."

The group of six women are walking along the Gourbat Shahi road towards the Jagannath temple. While Ila, Durga, Anu and Sandhya are walking ahead, listening to Durga telling tales from the Puranic history of Nilachal Puri, Moni and Lakshmi have slightly fallen back. Durga's voice is audible to them, too, and both are walking quietly, the morning incident understandably still playing in their mind. Suddenly, Lakshmi holds Moni's hand, "Moni, dear, please don't keep it in mind; I never meant to hurt you."

Moni looked up to her friend and replied with a smile, "But there's nothing wrong in your words."

"Please, Moni, I'm really feeling bad about it. It was a sudden emotional outburst. Actually, within a day's time, I had grown so fond of this girl that I couldn't resist myself."

Moni pressed her hands back caressingly; Lakshmi laughed a relieved laughter. Moni joined her.

On the other end, Durga kept commentating, "You have to understand this: Jagannath is the body hair of the Puranic Nil Madhav..."

Everyone kept listening to her. Sandhya's mouth remained open in awe. She kept tripping on the road all the way because she was too bogged down listening to Durga's tale about the temple. The group reached the Arun Stambh before the Lion's Gate. After resting for a while, the motley group of women entered the temple. Before the divine trinity, Sandhya folded her hands and prayed for long. Then, coming out of the sanctum sanctorum, they made rounds of the temple courtyard.

Standing by the eternal banyan tree there, the Akshay bat, Durga explained to Sandhya, "See, this is a hope tree, the wood formation of the Lord Anantdev. People submit their hidden desires, the most cherished dreams before Him." There, one could see the desires posted in the branches of the tree in the form of small chips of bricks tied in knots.

Sandhya ran closer to the tree and bent down before it with folded hands, murmuring all her prayers, submissions, despair, etc.

Moni asked her, "Everywhere, on each doorstep, what do you keep praying for?"

Sandhya blushed in reply, "What else can I pray for?"

"Why? Why don't you pray for Dulal in your life once again? How about pressing God for your precious love?"

Sandhya smiled a fading smile, "That's what I prayed about. I prayed for his safe reaching home."

Ila gave her an affectionate snubbing, "That's enough of smartness; you don't have to pray for a grown-up man's safe travel back home. That he can do even without your prayers."

After making rounds of the temple, everyone came and sat beside the Khajadwar out of tiredness. Lakshmi announced, "O God, I just can't move even a bit. Enough of walking for the day." Sandhya still chose not to sit; rather, she kept roaming around when Anu called her to them, "Watch it, girl, don't go far from us. Otherwise, you too may get lost in the crowd."

The ladies started gossiping again. Nobody noticed that Ila suddenly stood up and went to a corner of the Khajadwar in search of something. Anu was the first to notice and asked,

"Hey, Ila, what are you up to?"

Ila came back silently.

"I believe you're searching for something."

"I'm sure I did it there somewhere, you know."

"What?"

"After a couple of years of our marriage, I came here with my husband and scratched a line with a key ring. But couldn't find it now." It surprised everyone. Ila is searching for a twenty-year-old memory.

Lakshmi pacified her, "Are you crazy! Can a scratched line exist for so long?"

While returning to their lodge, Moni dragged Ila by her and asked, "So, are you planning to return here again with Arun?"

Ila looked at her and tried smiling, "What ru-bb-ish."

III

Two more days went off touring maths, temples, and seabeach. Time flew by. The day before return, the weather turned bad, and the sky darkened in the afternoon.

Around half past one in the day, when they were going out to have lunch, Moni expressed anxiety, "It's too dark outside. Possibly, it will rain hard."

Anu joyously reacted, "It would be fun then. I have never witnessed the sea in the rain."

It happened just as they thought. It started raining even before evening amidst complete darkness around much before sunset. Their lodge is near to the sea, and the sea beach can be seen in the rain from the balcony. Ila, Moni and Durga started watching the heavy shower from there. The sea is rough and roaring as if a thousand angry tigers are howling inside. Through the darkness of the sky hanging above them, lightning kept cracking down, creating a frightening vista. High waves continued breaking on the sand. All of them felt both scared and thrilled. They forgot everything else in the world.

"Oh... why are you all still standing outside? Come back in the room."

The three got back to their sense upon the call from Lakshmi.

Anu invited, "Let's all sit together."

Sandhya is flying around like a small bird.

Lakshmi requested Durga to sing something, "Hey Durga, why don't you sing? It's been really long since we heard you last."

Durga expressed disbelief in being cajoled to sing, "Oh, I can't anymore."

"Don't be stubborn. Sing."

"Aunty, please sing." Sandhya took Durga's hand in her hands.

Durga started, a Ramkumar toppa,

"Vidhi dile jadi bichched jatana... O Destiny, if you have at all been given the pain of separation, "

The next song was *"Kishorir ki shorir holo...* The maid is made of a figure..."

She faltered on the high note, but nobody complained.

Ila was fascinated, "What a voice you've got."

Moni requested, "Can you sing the song ... *Je raatey mor duarguli bhanglo...* On the stormy night when my doors fell apart."

"Hmm... but perhaps I forgot some of the lyrics."

"It's okay. You start, and I will prompt you."

Durga started from *"Shob je hoye gelo kalo...* The world went dark..."

The strong winds from outside entered the room; it blew the bedsheets, the grey hairs of the middle-aged women, the end of their sarees and all. The atmosphere inside remained silent, meditative. The melody floats,

"...Ondhokarey roinu porey swopon maani... I lay in the dark as if in a dream..."

Durga suddenly surrendered, "I can't continue anymore."

Her face reddened; she was panting for breadth. Everyone consoled her, "Okay, okay, it's enough." Suddenly, Sandhya talked between them, "Aunty, can I sing?"

"You? Can you sing? Which song?"

"Rabindranath."

"What? Where have you learned?"

"At our school. It was our prayer song."

"Okay. Sing."

Sandhya started closing her eyes, "Aguner paroshmoni chhoao prane... *Purify my life with the purging touch of fire, With your blessings of searing pain...*"

"Oh! What a nice voice you have got!"

Sandhya continues, "Byatha mor uthbe joley urdhyapane... *Let my pain be ablaze and rise above despair...*"

Suddenly, Durga stood up and went to the balcony; Anu followed her.

"What happened, Durga? Why do you leave?"

"Just like that."

"What a voice you have kept till now. You shouldn't have left singing."

Durga looked at her friend for once and then moved her sight towards the sea. She sounded husky in her replies, "I didn't leave anyone. Everyone left me."

There, a peer's hand covered the hand of a fifty-five-year-old elderly woman with a friend's support. The world's getting washed by the torrential rain, meanwhile.

IV

There's the return train tonight. But eleven in the morning, the five of them were sitting on the beach. Sandhya keeps sprinting past them, to and fro, from the sea. Sometimes, she joins them in their talking. The very next moment, she is playing on the waves. The morning remains cloudy.

Ila lamented, "This is the last time we're travelling. Hope you all will continue to be in touch,"

Anu said, "Look at this girl, so straight, so pure, but see her fortune!"

Durga rued, "I'm really feeling bad about it. If the man doesn't accept her, what will happen to this helpless girl!"

Ila shows confidence, "Even if she doesn't find a shelter anywhere in this world, still nothing will happen to her. Rather, I pray she doesn't go back to being such a bad person. She's young. She will surely forget, forgive and move forward in life. See how she had already managed to overlook her grief."

Lakshmi pointed out, "After all, at her age, you used to be the same." They both laughed.

Sandhya sprinted back to them, panting; she sat beside them. The wet end of her saree moved, and her heavy breasts peaked out from between her neckline. A few girls from a distance were watching in surprise. Moni quickly alerts her, "Are you out of your mind? Fix your dress."

Sandhya obliged and tied the end of her saree at her waist.

Durga asked, "So, are you thinking of coming here again to accompany your husband?"

"Nah... No."

"Oh! But why?"

"Again, if he gets lost," finishing her words, Sandhya again ran to the sea.

Ila remarked, "Sandhya has got a figure similar to Anu's younger days, isn't it Lakshmi?"

Anu says, "Why, you were no less, remember?"

"Aye, stop it."

Again, a roll of laughter.

Laughingly, the ladies looked towards the sea. They keep staring. Sandhya is bathing. Jumping with the waves, diving deep, floating. It is a fantastic scene to watch. Moni spoke, "We grew old, didn't we?" perhaps she was merely thinking aloud.

Nobody responded. In the decaying light, each of them found their younger selves out there in the sea in place of Sandhya. From the known past, out of the memoirs, desires, dreams and untold tales.

Manifestation of Eyes

I

"So? How's it?"

"Brilliant. Wow... Awe… ssoooo... urgh! Ahh... (*cough*)!

Before she could even finish her words of appreciation, Shatabdi started coughing in excitement.

And as a concerned Barun quickly swung into action, patting and tapping her lovingly back into routine, Shatabdi, his wife, hugged him tight in her salon-curated body, probably after a long, long time. Barun could smell a sweet, light aroma from her thirty-seven-year-old body. Again, after sailing around the two bedrooms, kitchen and toilet a bit, caressing the smoothness of their walls, Shatabdi planted an unthinkable kiss on Barun's face.

Wow! Barun thought so he was no longer smelling foul in his mouth. Meanwhile, wiping her lips in a handkerchief, his wife asked, "How much advance has to be paid?"

Barun tenderly replied, "That's something you should never insist me to reveal; it's a request."

A substantial amount of half a lakh rupee he had to pay in advance to acquire this flat in rent adjacent to Dum Dum Metro station. On the fourth floor of this five-story building, there are large windows in the southwest and even an *oh-so-lovely* balcony. Six hundred and fifty square feet. Sanjay, his office colleague, tipped him about the property. The owner is among Sanjay's acquaintances. Thereafter, behind his wife's back, Barun continued a long bargain over this property for the last month. Whereas the owner demanded seventy thousand rupees in advance and three thousand rupees monthly rent, but Barun successfully lowered it to two and a half thousand monthly rent and fifty thousand advance amounts. Sanjay's support was a big help all through. Barun was assured that this would be definitely likened by Shatabdi considering its proximity to the metro station. Therefrom,

Esplanade is a zip away, and Shatabdi's school, where she teaches, is a mere five to seven minutes' walk. Barun, though, had to take a bus to reach Minto Park after getting off at the Exide metro station, but that's something sheer insignificant in comparison to what they are experiencing presently.

Barun is an accountant at an automobile company. Shatabdi teaches history at a renowned English medium school in the city and earns a couple of thousands more than Barun. Shedding all his past habits and hobbies, Barun now only watches television at home as a pastime. On the contrary, Shatabdi is quite determined to pursue her dreams. So, she reads a lot, and there are piles of books at their home, from philosophy, prose, and poems to fine arts, psychology, and many more. It amazes Barun how a person can read so much in a life. An arranged marriage took place between Barun and Shatabdi. Her earnings were lesser then.

"There is a children's park nearby, too; Neel won't have a problem."

"Do you think he will get time to play? I am rather concerned about his school and his tuition classes."

"Those, too, have been taken care of." Barun sounds content. "I have been informed that his school bus ply from BT Road."

"Oh! How come you transformed overnight into such a responsible..." Shatabdi's face was seemingly gleaming in admiration, the way it used to shine in those early days of their marriage. Barun had a faint hope of receiving a second kiss, but it was in vain. Instead, she put her hand on his shoulder and got busy strapping back her shoes.

Neel is the only son of Barun and Shatabdi. Neel's real name is Agnidev, and he is about six years old and studies at the third standard in a prominent school in Srirampur. It's not that Barun's real name is just Barun, either. Basudev, Barun's father, actually named his son Barundev, but after growing up, Barun likes to introduce himself as Barun Chatterjee. It's also not that Barun doesn't have a home, and so there's no such need to rent a home for themselves. Because Basudev built a house in the peri-urban Bagpara of Rishra over eight cottahs of land long ago in 1964, and his son Barundev was born there. There, one can still find paddy fields only walking a few metres from the house where, in his childhood days, scores of times, Barun lost his ways while playing with his friends amidst the thick green of the crop plants and was forced to take help of the locals to return home late in the evening. His mother often reprimanded him, but that never could stop the simple and mischievous country lad he used to be. In their teenage days, he hung around and smoked bidis with friends in those crop fields. And then, with the passage of time, job, marriage, birth of his son, son's education, etc., took his place and changed him. But what has not changed are his mofussil schedules. Because Barun still rides his bicycle from his home to Rishra rail station, he keeps it in the garage and takes a train to Howrah and afterwards a bus to his office. For the past fifteen years, this remained his unchanged routine. Barun starts from his home at nine in the morning, while Shatabdi had to start an hour earlier by cycle rickshaw or an autorickshaw, whichever stops first on her call. Every day, Barun had to continue with a laborious journey pressing with the commuting crowd on the train, fighting for six inches of a seat upon getting a chance with a "Dada, can you push a little, O dada, here I'm talking to you, listen please" cry and thereafter keep adjusting for the rest of the journey. Everyday.

During his earlier working days, Barun tried to concentrate on wearing clothes properly ironed and shoes meticulously polished, but the regular struggle in the streets soon taught him the hollowness of all these. Because after fighting the long war of a daily passenger's life each day when Barun used to discover himself finally in the mirror of his office toilet, he felt like crying in shock watching his wrinkled, sobbing clothing and clay-laden dirty shoes. Shatabdi's condition was no lesser. Though comparatively less crowded ladies' compartments of local trains used to give an ignorant Barun a different idea till he discussed that with her. She explained,

"Do you know, women passengers behave the worst with each other?" and then she enlightened Barun on the wide varieties of subjects under the sun which ladies raise in rail compartments to carry on with their daily quarrels.

So both of them were wearing out day by day, fighting with life. Initially, there were less earnings, but then age was on their side, and both managed somehow. Now, Shatabdi has put on weight while getting to know more about life. Barun, too, is forced to hook his trousers under his tummy, losing his youth to age. The untenable life and their ageing were becoming difficult, and both were searching for some respite. It was then that one day, Shatabdi raised the issue and proposed searching for a home in Kolkata. Barun was startled upon hearing this at first. Their Rishra house is a large one, shaped like the 'L' letter, with rooms lining up with a running red floor veranda by their side. A basil pod, now dead, in front of the house, announces the quintessential middle-class prayer for prosperity and peace at home. There are nine rooms, one after another. And, of course, all are not built in one go. Five rooms were built before Barun was born, while four more came up before his eyes. Barun learnt from his mother that his father once used to live in a rented house in Paikpara, in the suburbs, and always dreamt of having a house of his own in the city. But his meagre salary didn't allow him to realise his dream in the city itself, and thus, after days of compromises, he could finally make it in Bagpara of Rishra, where his dream castle took shape for his only son, Barun. Barun remembers how a truckload of construction materials used to arrive before their house, during winters after winters of his childhood. Cement, sand, pebbles. His father used to stand, supervise and even try his hands himself in the building works, constructions, and re-constructions, taking leave from his office for days together. His father knew every brick and mortar of the house. Nevertheless, this house was constructed on a low land, and water logging always disturbed them there, monsoon after monsoon. So, landfilling became an equally important duty to his father. But it was a losing fight as water logging took a toll on the root piling of the building. The lintels started bearing cracks, and repairs slowly failed to be the real answer to the problem. The building admittedly ate the lion's share of his father's earnings, and still, the bricks continued to become muggier, soaked in dampness, lime and mortar cracked, and cement and plasters flaked away.

"Consider your house as Maa Lakshmi, the goddess of prosperity. Always believe that any spending behind a house never fails your wealth."

It was the last piece of advice from his father, given a few days before his death, that Barun can remember. The toxicity of bone cancer had already overpowered his resistance by then. The huge expenses behind his treatment had devastated Barun and Shatabdi's savings, too. Meanwhile, amidst this continuous attack on fortune and fate, Barun's father one day called him and instructed, "Listen, dampness ate the basement of the front room, the oldest of all, and the muggy bricks and mortar there are flaking out. The room needs a fresh coat of cement. Look into that." Barun tries his best to reason that it will be a fruitless act since age has caught up with the house, and this won't stop the walls and ceiling from falling. But to this, his father argued with child-like immaturity, "How can you call this fruitless? What you do to your favourite clothing that accidentally gets torn is what you need to do with your house, too." Barun had no answer to his father's emotional contention. Neither did he have enough capital to fulfil his father's demand. Even one day, his mother interfered, "You should consider your father's request; who knows, maybe this could be his last wish..."

But Barun stuck to his point, "It's a sheer frivolous demand. There is already enough spending daily that I have to take care of, so..." Barun didn't finish his sentence, and neither did his mother wait to argue like his father. His father, too, fell silent eventually. He actually stopped all types of conversations with Barun. Then, in a few months' time, the old man departed in his silence. The man who taught Barun the nitty-gritty of house construction—such as emphasizing the waterproofing of the roof, treating masons with sweets on the day of roof casting, and soaking the newly constructed floor with ankle-deep water, among many other things—departed in silence.

"Have you informed your mother?"

"No. Not yet."

"Why?"

"I will tell her later. Let's go."

"Can't we stay a bit longer?" Shatabdi pours all the sweetness of the world in her voice.

"Wait for some more days, dear, and you can stay here forever. So, without wasting time, let's go for now because otherwise, Neel will get angry with us." Barun showed concern, but he sounded confident and proud.

Today is the Navami day of the Durga puja, and they have made commitments to Neel for pandal hopping later today. Nobody knows why they went there, as Barun only told his mother that they were going out to sort out a small task and would quickly return. They didn't bring Neel with the fear that he might disclose everything to his granny before Barun divulged it in a planned way to his mother. Barun fears his mother might protest or get angry and jeopardise the whole plan. Such emotional nonsense will kill the fun of this long puja vacation.

"You'll be surprised when you'll see how I decorate this house."

"I don't doubt that." Barun laughed with contentment.

"Your house appears to have been part of the ruins of the Harappan civilisation."

The phrase "your house" made Barun feel bad as he learned once again that even after fifteen years of marriage, Shatabdi still couldn't make her in-laws' place her own. It pains him.

II

Ekadashi, the eleventh day of the Durga puja festival, arrived. Today, Barun woke up late. His head felt heavy and was spinning. Yesterday was a long night as there was a private Dussera party among six old friends in the local club with loads of mutton washed down by a couple of standard bottles of Blue Label. Drowsily, he could barely manage to walk back home yesterday but threw up everything being inexperienced in drinking.

Shatabdi's rebukes were mild, though, and her behaviour was still quite generous to his midnight nuisance. She even spared Barun and cleaned his vomit on her own. Barun understood that she was going to bear his vices for her self-interest. Barun thanked his luck. He plans to bunk the office today out of laziness. After all, one more extra leave next to an extended vacation won't be treated seriously in the office.

"Wake up. Listen to what your son's telling." Shatabdi entered with a cup of tea.

"What tale arose up this early in the morning?"

"Our kiddo won't budge from this house. His peers here are the best he has got to play with. Also, he has learnt that there's a children's park coming up on the ground in the north. I don't know where he has learned all these, but I suspect your mother is behind it all."

Barun's temper shoots north too, "There was no need for you to speak about these so early. You could have waited for my signal."

"You? Huh! A whole year would have passed then. Don't I know how you still shiver before your mother's scolding?"

"What nonsense! Now, call Neel to me, would you?"

Shatabdi exits. Barun started thinking over her points. She's right. Barun's mother was always strict. Instead, his father was friendly. Scoldings, beatings, disciplining, tutoring, everything was his mother's forte. Father only used to hand over his salary once a month, and mother used to take over from thereon. So, in the house, Barun has always seen his mother as the real patriarch. Even after marriage, this continued. Shatabdi, however, never interfered in this, as she had to stay away from home for long hours for work. In fact, she shares the same bitter-sweet relationship with her mother-in-law, which is common in most households. For example, "I don't know why your mother is so high-handed!" or else "I wonder what this lady thinks of herself" are some of the limited remarks Barun mostly had to hear from his wife till now. But after his father's demise, Barun's mother gradually retired into a shell. Other than her grandson Neel, she started avoiding talking to Barun and Shatabdi. She even restricted her movement between her bedroom and the meditation chamber. Barun hired a cook at home long ago, so she has been relieved from kitchen duties since then.

Neel rushed to Barun and announced, "I won't go anywhere." It was a desperate protest of a kid from the third standard. Barun never scolded his son in the manner he had seen his own father. And like him, he left the duties of disciplining their ward to Neel's mother. However, Neel does not deserve scolding; summarily, he is a good boy, albeit a bit stubborn. But that's something like most kids today.

Barun lovingly dragged his son, "Come to me, kiddo. Sit closer."

Neel was watching him with gazing eyes and then slowly asked, "Why did you vomit last night?"

Barun was stumped, "Who told you that? Your mother, I guess?"

"Nobody. I watched you myself."

"Oh! I see. So, you woke up?"

"Hmm. Will you vomit again?"

"No. No." Barun smiled.

"Do you know Bittu's father does that every night?"

"Ahh... Really! Who told you that?"

"Bittu. Himself."

Neel's friend Bittu's father, Ayan Mukherjee, is the CTO of a company. He had a trophy wife. The man is a bribe taker, and that's a known fact. But that he's a drunkard is news. Barun started having a strange good feeling inside upon hearing it.

Barun suddenly asked, "What else do you know?" but then quickly resisted himself and turned the direction of his question, "What has your mother told you?"

"She said we will leave this house and shift to Kolkata. But I won't go, I have my group of friends here. I can't leave them. Then there's a children's park coming up in the northern ground..."

"Listen, son, where we have planned to move, there are many friends waiting for you; I met them already. Each of them is a good boy. I have talked with them. Also, there's a beautiful children's park nearby with half a dozen swings. There's a swimming pool too.

After uttering loads of lies to his six-year-old boy early in the morning, Barun stopped to watch the result from the corner of his eyes. This is Barun's style of facing ludicrous situations. Shatabdi condemned this style in the past as that of an escapist. Possibly, she won't call him by that name anymore now until he hurts his self-interest in the future.

"But what will happen to the mango and guava trees that we sowed?"

"Those may die..." Barun has to stop, as he can't lie anymore. The plants were sowed by his father when he was in college, and they still bear fruits regularly.

"But then we're not going completely," Barun was searching for words.

"Then?"

"O Lord! So, your mother hasn't told you everything?"

"No. What's that?" The kid's eyes broadened with hope.

Finding a way out finally to contend with the boy, Barun added to the child's hope, "We are not leaving the house completely. We will be coming here in the weekends to stay a couple of days."

"Really?"

"Yes. Then you can meet your old friends too."

"But baba..."

"Now what?"

"Granny's crying." This irritates Barun because he does not have any solution to this.

"Why is she crying?"

"After hearing that, we will be leaving her here."

"Okay. Then go and explain it to her."

Neel leapt from the bed to run to his granny when Barun called him back, "Listen, listen."

"What is it?"

"Don't reveal everything now. Reveal it later."

"Why?"

"Just like that. Okay. Go."

The tea by his bedside was already cold, so he finished it in one gulp and left the bed. He felt discomfort because he couldn't clear his stomach since yesterday night's torture on his digestive system. Still, he went to the toilet. He was not feeling well.

Earlier, he thought of buying mutton for today's meal. But then he abandoned the idea and bought chicken instead. His stomach is not feeling right. Neel rushed to him as soon as he entered his room. The cook bunked the work, and Shatabdi had to take up the responsibility of cooking today. However, she does not look sad; instead, she appears visibly excited. Barun noticed that she was preparing a vegetarian dish for his mother. Perhaps the non-vegetarian items will be prepared later. Barun's mother is not very strict about touching non-vegetarian dishes, though. However, Barun is unsure whether Shatabdi's generosity is out of compulsion.

"Baba, I won't go if Granny doesn't."

Barun has felt fed up tackling the same issue repeatedly since this morning. "Why? What happened now?"

"Granny denies taking your offer. She won't be going."

"But why?"

Having said that, what Barun fell short of telling is that someone who has inhaled barrels of soot and smoke daily, while traveling from their house to Kolkata's Strand Road and enduring the drudgery of a demanding job, would never dare to refuse such an offer.

"Can you go and call her for me? Or okay, leave that to me. Go back to your room instead."

"What will I do there?"

"Go and draw something."

"Can I do wall painting?"

To this, Barun pauses before agreeing, "Okay, do as you wish." His son has this peculiar habit of drawing huge features on the floor and walls of the rooms instead of doing those on paper. The walls and floors of his own room are under layers of crayon colours, while other rooms were not spared either. Earlier, Barun's father used to scold him for this, but now there's nothing to stop him. Shatabdi, instead, boasts of her son's odd habit, announcing to everyone that he must have been a mural artist in his previous birth. She admitted him to an art school, and the kid has undeniably honed his skills. His murals of man, hills, trees and rivers on the peeling walls of the old house herald his good sense of art.

Barun entered his mother's room with watchful steps. His mother was busy cleaning cobwebs in her room.

"Maa."

Barun's mother turned hesitantly to his call. She wore a distressed look, complete with a pair of reddish, swollen eyes. She clenched her broom firmly.

Barun cleared his throat before offering his own reasons, "I heard from Neel that you're crying, but why Maa?" Barun tried hard to act casual and ignorant.

His mother promptly turned away, shouting back, "Nothing that you've to worry about, son."

Barun couldn't hold himself anymore and pleaded, "Maa, please listen; all these had happened in quick succession in the last couple of days. I was about to tell you everything. Then, nothing has been finalised.

"When are *you* planning to move?" Her voice clearly sounded unconcerned and banal.

"Maa, you're coming with us too."

"Not at all. Spare me." Barun's mother spat fire in her shout after a long, long time.

Barun tried to gather himself back and begged, "How can you be spared? How can you be left on your own in a big old ruinous house? And apart from this..."

"And apart from this...?" there's a great deal of rage in Barun's mother's voice now, "Have you sold the house already?"

"Ufff, Maa, are you out of your mind! Why should I do that...?"

Barun tried to be brave, though behind everyone's back, he had already tried his hand at that too, but failed to get a good quote. The promoter once came and had a look at this dilapidated building from the outside, and the offer he gave was miserably low. In fact, it was so low that Barun calculated it wouldn't pay back Barun's and Shatabdi's annual travel fare.

The promoter, however, reasoned, "Brother, the location of your house is reasonably far from the rail station, which means building a new apartment here won't be much profitable. Apart from this, your house is ruinous and doesn't carry any value; only the land carries some value. But then, how much land value can you get in a remote location like this? Therefore, whatever I'm offering you should be a profitable proposition. Think about it." Barun noticed an unmistakable wry smile on the promoter's face that day.

Initially, Barun was hoping that if he could earn good money by selling the house, then he could adjust his home loan accordingly and acquire a modern apartment closer to the city. But his hope met with utter disappointment. Thankfully, Barun hasn't told anyone about this news yet. Otherwise, Shatabdi would have taunted him against his father's choice of such a faraway place to build a house. It would have felt bad to hear something against Father. Somewhere deep inside, Barun respects his father for building something of his own, on his own. He has achieved his dream, at least with as desperate an attempt as it could take. Now, how many men can achieve that?

"Listen, Maa; please listen..." Barun continued with his act, "Look at me, please."

Barun dragged her mother's chin towards him when his already weeping mother couldn't hold back her tears any more. It was after a considerably long period that Barun's mother broke down in his arms. The last time she did that was when she opened Barun's father's wardrobe after his demise.

Holding her weeping mother in his arms, Barun had a weird good feeling. He gently ran his fingers through his sobbing mother's hair and rested his case, "Maa, please understand our problem; the pain of daily travel that we both have to take up is taking a heavy toll on our health and with that, I doubt that we can live beyond sixty."

To that, his weeping mother still argued, "Why? Your father did the same thing all through his age."

"Maa, days have changed. Nowadays, the number of passengers commuting by train has increased, making local trains in the morning unbearably crowded. Even reaching the boarding area of the train arriving at the platform at Howrah during peak hours is nothing short of a Herculean task. Crowd pressure often seems to break the ribcage. Daily commuting by train is becoming an inhuman effort with growing ages. Since, by God's grace, both of our incomes have reached a handsome amount presently, my question is, couldn't we earn a better lifestyle for all of us? Couldn't we fancy a new home to our liking?"

Having said that, Barun reckoned deep inside that his mother would definitely contend this by saying, "Why don't you try rebuilding your ancestral house?" And so, he quickly made up his explanation, "and then, the condition of this house hardly gives us that opportunity, as years of reconstruction work and thousands of rupees spent have yielded zero outcome. Imagine the annual maintenance charge behind this big house. Look at your room, ceiling seeping, walls cracking; it is becoming risky even to live here. You can't even buy good furniture for such rooms. Don't you feel that?"

His helpless mother before her determined son, falling short of words, continues weeping and shivering, perhaps blaming him silently. Barun could feel somewhere Neel is hiding and watching them both. Then silently the kid moved back to his room and closed the doors. The doors bear a photo of the comic hero phantom, drawn by Neel himself. Barun does not know if his son too will be weeping behind the closed door, blaming his father for everything.

Barun uttered a very feeble statement to his mother, "Stop crying please, I have planned to return here every weekend." Although Barun has proposed this solution now, but both Barun and his rational mother know that this is one very irrational proposition.

"What's the plan for shifting?"

"Let's see. But before anything, let the Lakshmi puja day pass. Why don't you discuss with the priest about an auspicious day for shifting? And please don't keep crying, okay?"

Finishing a mountainous job while he was returning to his room, Barun's wife peeked from the kitchen inquisitively, "Could you make her agree?"

Barun couldn't respond. He chose to remain silent.

Lakshmi puja celebration has been done with much pomp and glory in the house since Barun's childhood. His father used to pick the best available idol from the local market, spending at least 3-4 hours in the selection, making little Barun grow impatient every time. Buying of the idols is followed by an elaborate shopping of different religious items, fruits, and vegetables. Barun understood that his otherwise thrifty father always spent generously for Lakshmi puja. And this is where he himself used to perform the priestship. The whole house was always lit with decorated lights to welcome the goddess of prosperity amidst brightness and illumination. His father believed that the goddess lived in the house, and Barun once heard him telling that to his mother in bed at night.

What Barun's father had felt all through his life, Barun failed to. To him, the ruinous house always remains devoid of any prosperity. However, though during the year of his father's passing, the puja couldn't be celebrated, but Barun too had always tried to keep the scale of this puja celebration, the same. Starting from buying the best idol, to shopping elaborately for the puja items, fruits, sweets, and everything, Barun had tried doing it all. This day too, when he arrived with his ornate stock riding a rickshaw in the evening, Barun was caught with surprise watching the old house lit up. It's not that he doesn't know it, as he himself had instructed the electrician to light up the house. But then it reminded him of the day when he had himself adorned his bedridden father in the best of clothing just for sake of his pleasure. The rickety old man was really looking odd in some splendid piece of clothing that day much similar to the house now in the glorious cover of chains of fairy lights.

"Please pay my fare."

Barun came back to his sense with this call of the rickshaw puller.

Barun entered the puja room with his shopped items after paying the fare. His mother and his son were busy cleaning the photographs there. There was a small photograph of his father's too in the crowd of those. They kept it like that. It was because, once his father had told him, in his happier days, "after my demise do not hang me on the walls, it's quite painful to remain hanging there." Barun kept his words. His mother offers sandalwood and flowers to it every day. Shatabdi was busy in doing household chores.

"Maa, do you like the idol?"

"Yes. Put it on the altar. Wait, let me blow the conch while you do so."

After installation of the new idol over the red cloth on the altar, Barun's mother fell crying.

"What happened now? Why are you crying?"

"Granny, Granny!" Neel too was concerned.

"Nothing."

"Please tell us. Neel, can you go from here for some time, let me talk with my mother."

"Today if this man were alive, could you even think of shifting?" Barun's mother is shivering.

"Oh Maa, now how many times I have to explain you that, we're not leaving this house permanently."

Today everyone in the house is busy arranging for Lakshmi puja. Barun's mother is there in the puja room. Barun's wife is there in the kitchen. Barun's son Neel is busy drawing alpana with rice-powder paste and cotton balls. Barun, too is running errands to shops though most of the time sitting idle. He doesn't want to sit idle as that reminds him the fact that this is going to be his last Lakshmi puja in this house. He tried his best to make the puja look wholesome and memorable though. Quite a few times he made rounds of his mother's room. This room is one of the oldest, where in the black polished tall cot Barun spent his childhood with his parents. Now, it belongs to his mother. There is a creaseless bedsheet spread over it. The walls are muggy. Flaking mortars have drawn on it, maned lion, Rabindranath and many more. In spite of his mother's physical presence, Barun can still feel his father's invisible presence in the room. The feeling makes him grow impatient, and that pushes him out of the room. He has to fast today since he will be performing the puja himself. Fasting is tough for him. He took out the *Purohit Darpan* and started revising the process of performing Lakshmi puja. Then he switched on the television set. After a light lunch of sagu he took a short nap.

The evening rolled in. Barun, decked up in his father's white puja attire, sat for puja. Satabdi meanwhile finished cooking, took a bath, changed into a beautiful saree, and joined him. Barun felt impressed looking at his beautiful wife. Neel too is there in the room, sticking closer to his granny. Barun felt surprise to find his little son first time in the puja room. But he didn't show it, silently starting the puja instead. Obeisance, sanctification, invocation, offerings, seeking blessings one after another. Shatabdi keeps blowing the conch as per the demand of the rituals. Sounds of conch from neighbouring houses are also blowing inside the room every now and then. His mother is sitting in a corner like a statue. Barun kept staying, "O Goddess, Holy Mother, may you come to us, may you stay with us." After invocation of life in the idol, the next step is manifestation of eyesight. Neel is watching the puja rituals for the first time in his life and was bombarding her mother with questions and enquiries.

Barun tried saving her, "Don't talk during the puja ritual, watch it now and ask me later."

For manifestation of eyes, the ritual includes preparing kohl from the soot of the oil lamp holding the ghee-soaked trident leaves of *bael* over it. It's a test of patience and Barun had always watched her mother performing this job with elan since his childhood. He therefore gestured his mother for the job while chanting mantra. Meanwhile Barun was feeling that his father was gazing at him from the photograph installed at the altar. He started feeling uncomfortable. Despite the best of attempts therefore, he couldn't concentrate up on the puja rituals. His mother meanwhile gathered some kohl on the *bael* leaves and raised it before his face. Now, the ritual is to hold kohl smeared leaves one at a time on the eyes of the idol and chant the mantra to manifest the eyesight upon the goddess. But the way his mother held the trident leaves before his face, a scream came out of Barun, "Give it in my hand, why have you raised it before my eyes? Are you intending to touch it on my eyes instead?" he quickly followed it up with a lighthearted warm smile, but his momentary yell was still echoing in the large house.

Barun was not feeling well. He laid back on the sofa after the puja under the speeding fan. He tried watching the television and tried to lighten his own mood. Meanwhile, Shatabdi came and sat beside him.

"Oh! Why you're playing the television so loud, lower the sound," saying that Shatabdi quickly muted the blaring TV.

Neel ran to him with an enquiry, "Baba why granny burnt those *bael* leaves?" Sick and tired Barun helplessly looked at his wife for some respite.

Shatabdi came to his husband's rescue, "Kiddo, it's a process to manifest eyesight on the goddess." Having said that, the next moment she turned to her husband with a newly found enthusiasm, "Do you know there's a santhal tribal scroll painting called eyesight manifesting painting."

Neel quickly asked back, "What's a Santhal scroll painting?"

"Those are special paintings done by the Santhal tribes."

Explaining to his son like a professional teacher, Shatabdi turned back to her husband, "Do you know their process of manifestation of eyes is a really interesting one. I read about it in a book on folk arts. Are you listening?... Uff, even I was working all through the day, but was not as weakened as you."

"Na... Nah, I'm listening. You keep saying..."

"When someone dies in a Santhal family, their artisans make a scroll painting of the deceased and go to the deceased's house to seek alms. They draw a symbolic figure, devoid of the eyeballs. With that, the artisans seek alms from the deceased person's family to complete the figure by adding the eyeballs, as it's believed that without them, the soul remains blind and roams aimlessly in distress in the other world. Just imagine the peculiar art of earning!" Shatabdi laughed.

Barun only responded with a monosyllabic, "Hmm."

Neel listened to the whole story with wondering eyes and then rushed away from the room.

After supper Barun retired to his bed with a world of utopian thoughts bugging his head. Shatabdi was still in the bathroom when Neel entered calling, "Baba."

"What?"

"Can you come to my room for a moment please?"

"Why?"

"Please come once."

"Tomorrow."

"No, you have to come now."

Barun thought for a moment. His son is a stubborn child and ignoring him will only increase his insistence. Hence, Barun gave in and accompanied him to his room. There was a new figure on the wall of Neel's room. An arrow beside the drawing indicated that it was Neel's grandfather. On a second look, Barun discovered that the figure contains eyes with no eyeballs.

"O baba, grandpa is in distress there in the heaven. Give me what I want, and grandpa will get his eyes back and will be happy again."

Barun suddenly became furious at his son and couldn't hold himself back from scolding, "What's all these nonsenses? Stop this. Immediately go to your bed."

"Baba give me your words that you will never leave this house. I promise that I'll draw grandpa's eyeballs but you have to promise me too. Should I draw the eyeballs? Do you promise to stay back?"

"You little brat! What have you all thought of? You'll corner me as a villain in the house..." Barun stopped as suddenly as he started shouting in rage.

As his stubborn son's hand was raised to the wall to draw those eyeballs, Barun wrapped himself in a shell like a worm.

"Don't draw, don't put back the eyeballs, Neel, please, I can't do it, I can't do it!" After saying this, Barun couldn't stand there anymore and hobbled outside in shambles, panting in search of fresh air. The moonlit night was painted in the silver moonbeams of Kojagori. And one could see Neel's alpana glowing in the moonlight where white impressions of Goddess Lakshmi's feet ran from the veranda to the inside of the old house. Before losing his senses, Barun clearly saw the goddess of prosperity enter the house.

The Winged One

I

Drenched in sweat while scrambling through the uphill trek from Manebhanjan to Chitre, tackling the final couple of kilometres with our heavy rucksacks strapped to our back, Bhanu couldn't resist anymore but asked our friend, Chandrasekhar.

"Swear by this; don't you want a life like ours?"

We are childhood friends, and meeting each other after fifteen years. *We* include me, Bhanu, Gour and Chandrasekhar. All now profusely perspiring even in the nasty cold of the mountains, exhaling heavily, getting rid of our jackets and woollens. Chandrasekhar is better off, though, and less tired, as he is used to all of these. His life has been that of a vagabond till now.

Devaleena, Gour's wife, proposed the trekking trip. And we all accepted promptly. After all, it's an opportunity for an adventure after a long time. Bhanu though hesitated, "Really! Trekking! With a physique like mine!"

The hesitation is completely understandable, though. The way he's swelling day by day by consuming liquors all sourced in bribery and he would surely commit suicide if someone showed him his past photographs. However, Bhanu's wife Anjali stepped in to boost the confidence of his hesitant husband at that point, "When septuagenarians can make it in this route, why can't you?"

This discussion occurred when we gathered at Gour's home last time to ponder over a suitable vacation place after the Durga Puja. After striking out the regular list of Digha, Dooar's, Ajodhya Hills etc. the Sandakphu trek was finalised.

"Won't you invite your other friend?" the inquiry came up from my wife, Leena.

"Friend? Which friend?"

"Of course, Chandrasekhar."

The conversation made others go silent for some moments until Gour broke it and said meekly, "Alright, let me ask him. He will refuse me for sure."

At night, when we rolled into bed after dinner, I asked Leena, "How did you suddenly come up with Chandra's name?"

Leena shot back with a sting, "Because I know you three very well. Wherever you go, the three of you start with your drinking spree. So, if this man comes along, at least we'll get company when travelling."

Her reasoning surprised me, for such a trivial matter like that, how my wife could cause me such an embarrassment before my friends. And that too for a man whom she had met years ago! Astonishing! But then Gour's words rang in and believing firmly to hear a rejection from Chandrasekhar soon, I fell asleep.

Unbelievably when the invitation to the trip was sent to Chandrasekhar in his village home at Beliatore, he accepted it. Gour murmured in shock, "What an untrusted gink he is that he agrees to come with us!"

Now that his participation appears so odd and astonishing, there was a time when I, Bhanu, Gour and Chandrasekhar were not only childhood friends from the same village but were more than that. Since our schooldays in Bankura's little hamlet Beliatore, we grew up hand in hand. Then it got extended to our college days in the City College's night classes when we hung around in the same residential mess in Bowbazar and even had tuition from the same places. Chandra got himself admitted to the Commerce faculty of the college in fear of losing us, his dear friends, though Commerce was not at all to his liking. We pressed him, and he gave in. We started flapping our wings more with stepping into the city. Coffee House to Nandan, Kumartuli to Bansberia, and everywhere we flew together and flocked together. Amidst our deep conversations, there often dropped-in personalities from Sartre to Borges, Picasso, and Bergman to Bade Ghulam, all of them. And of course, not only were our discussions always laced with gossip and debate on others, but our life also often used to get imbibed in impromptu musical gigs while orchestrating my flute with Bhanu's Rabindrasangeet and Gour reciting in his deep baritone voice. Chandrasekhar was always the silent spectator among us. He used to watch us, listen to us, read a lot and speak only occasionally. Probably, deep inside Chandra was a poet. But none of us ever found him writing verses. But in his occasional speeches, he sometimes spoke about unbelievable stories. For, in the middle of a conversation on modern medical science, he suddenly added – that twenty thousand years ago in the stone age, cavemen committed brain surgeries with stone tools. In another such instance, when we were discussing Rabindranath's opinion on death and the afterlife, Chandra informed primitive people used to spread red flowers as a symbol of life over the graves of their near and dear ones. We don't know what enjoyment he drew from these pieces of the past history of thousands and thousands of years. His eyes used to glow though while mentioning such stories. Saliva accumulates in the corners of his mouth out of excitement. I now wonder if Chandra was a history buff or an ancient history lover! Though unsure of that, I always believed he was one of us; he was someone like us. All four of us secretly bore this common dream that our lives would not be of struggle; they would be a bed of roses. We will take birth anew each day over and over again, afresh, and live out our dreams till the last drop of wishes we had.

After that, I was the first to acquire a job in a government bank. Bhanu followed suit. He made it to the Sales Tax department. Gour was fortunate to find employment at a renowned MNC. Only Chandra relented back with folded hands ignoring our innumerable poking and forcing. He embraced the private tuition job much like the door-to-door job of a village priest. Perhaps he didn't wish more. Jobs in hand, we settled in Kolkata while Chandrasekhar returned to our native place.

With the passage of time, life took its natural course progressing into prosperity, marriage, and more prosperity for the three of us, barring Chandrasekhar. So, we had a new team comprising of the three of us in the city, with Chandra occasionally appearing like a wild card entry from his village house. So, it only touches lighter topics in conversations whenever he is around. To speak the truth, none of us felt the past warmth in each other's presence. But this man wrapped in history from head to toe, although he lost touch with us, never lost his attraction among our family of wives and children. They increasingly keep soaking in the comfort of each other's company. We, the older three companions of Chandra, might have sometimes frowned at that helplessly. The last time we met him was probably some eight months ago when he suddenly appeared at Gour's place without notifying any of us. We found him in poor health at that time, complexion burnt in the sun, shoulders dropping under the weight of age, unkept brownish beard and moustache, hairs thinning. Actually, nothing but those two dreamy eyes were the same. It didn't feel good. Though, when I asked him why he was deteriorating, he laughed it off, saying it was all because of his recent three-month-long excursions in the Jhargram among the native Mig tribe there. What a lunacy! While we had updated our attitude with time, Chandra had fallen back to our outdated college days' philosophy of flapping wings alone amidst outcast imaginations. Only lunatics and inert objects live like that! We sure have raced miles ahead of him in the walks of life, but did he at all understand that? I wondered why he agreed to join us on the trip despite all the distance grown between us.

However, whatever the ideological difference between us be, presently, the four of us are together after a considerably long time. And there are three more women, our wives. And two children, in addition, comprising my son, Neel, who studies in the fourth standard and Bhanu's daughter, who is in the third standard. Gour's daughter Jhimli, also a third-standard kid, couldn't be part of the team as her school opened just after the vacation, and she had to leave for her hostel.

During our journey by train, while the three of us were discussing the nitty-gritty of the share market, nooks and corners of the domains of sales tax and the lady secretary to Gour's office boss, Chandra was observing us all through as if watching three aliens. His way of looking gave a precise amount of discomfort to all of us. Bhanu, unable to take that anymore, tried to divert him, "Hey Chandra, why don't you take this opportunity to narrate the Mig's story to our wives and children?"

While our families should have retorted in response with "No History now, please", they instead leapt at the offer in chorus, "Yes. Yes. Chandra-da, please say something about them."

Good lord, what an unreliable, ungrateful family we have.

Chandra started with a big smile, "In which words can I explain their story? After all, they don't even have their own language."

"What do you mean?"

"Yes. They have a limited vocabulary. Apart from perhaps half a dozen adjectives that offer significant descriptions and a few syllables to convey emergencies, they do not possess many words in their lexicon.

Leena expressed disbelief, "Sweet God, is that even possible! Such an interesting fact! Tell us more."

Then Chandrasekhar recounted the story of the Mig tribe. A bizarre account, a laughing stock it was. A tribe which has a spoken language composed of only a few countable words. The rest of their expressions depended on mere sign language. While Clapping stands for praise and happiness, blaming and dislikes are expressed by holding one's forehead. Discontent stands for walking straight. Peace and prosperity in life stand for a stroll. And so on. Unbelievable, ain't it!

Bhanu quipped, "What a mess, brother! Then how do they express 'I love you' to each other?"

Chandra replied, "With silence."

Bhanu felt a strong punch in the face for his crude joke. He could find no more words.

Chandra looked at me, "Achintya, the funny part is although they are short in their vocabulary compared to any civilised modern language, they're surprisingly honest and poised. They don't steal, fight or cheat even living below the poverty line."

I couldn't understand what Chandra was pointing to. I started feeling uncomfortable and suddenly fell short of words. It was only when Neel spoke to him, I was saved.

"Chandra uncle, I wish to hear from you about cavemen of the primitive age."

Potu echoed, "Yes, uncle, you have to tell that story."

I thought Chandra had turned into an unexplainably unbearable person. One who deals with all the obsolete subjects of the world. I could remember Bhanu once concluded that those who couldn't do much in life embraces righteousness, sinks in the depth history to find a way out, in search of solace.

Now, while the rest of us were walking together, the children were walking ahead holding Chandra's hand. And it was then Bhanu suddenly gestured to me and Gour caught pace with Chandra. We followed. Bhanu quickly reached Chandra's side and scolded the children, "Children don't rush and run in the hills. Stay by your moms."

The children felt sad but had no choice but to return to their mothers. Chandra looked up to guess what we were up to. He quickly deduced that Bhanu must have a plan to tell him something. And making his prediction accurate, Bhanu then asked our friend Chandrasekhar,

"Swear by this, don't you want a life like ours?"

Chandra replied with a light smile, "I don't want a life, pal."

"Oh, you don't want life! Then, what do you want?"

"I want something more soulful. Life is a crude algorithm of habits. And that's why it's sheerly meaningless to me."

Gour tossed his question, "So you think there's a soul missing in our life?"

II

Our itinerary included one night at Tonglu and the next day at Kalipokhri. From Kalipokhri, we reached Sandakhpu around one in the afternoon the day after. Honestly speaking, we nearly felt lifeless after the hard trek. And collectively, we felt we could have rather avoided the risk of this heavy trekking. It was oppressively heavy. Bhanu's knees had poorly swelled, and he's inconsolable, repeatedly applying pain killer spray and cursing the rest of us for his condition. Actually, while at Tonglu, we briefly planned to rent a trekker jeep to get us ferried up here. But Chandrasekhar, the gink he is, climbed uphill almost as quickly as a Himalayan goat, much to the awe of our families. As a result, we had to cancel our plan of renting cars and instead resorted to walking behind him.

Otherwise, we feared getting taunted by our own people. But this had actually raised our anger. On one side, there was a fear of losing to Chandra, and on the other, the anger of still losing in front of him despite our best efforts. When we tried our level best to be heroes before our family, but to our utter disgust, they still chose Chandra as their winner. This made us wonder how Chandra could be so ungrateful to us when it was only due to our consideration that he could be part of our trip. He should have accepted that he is at our mercy. But no, there's almost no sign of that, and instead, our children became his fans and started moving like shadows around him. Our repeated efforts of resistance bore no fruit. Bhanu was even rebuffed by his wife once for trying to resist his daughter Putu from sticking with Chandra on every footstep. And my! Her words were strong, "Let her be when she's not biting your pie!" Good Lord! We thought about how our very own families were behaving like unknowns to us in presence of this man. Only he's to be blamed for all this!

Two rooms were reserved for us at Hotel Sunrise with the best of arrangements. And dead tired, we leapt onto the bed after reaching there. In this health condition, all of our air balloons of excitement and enthusiasm for exploring a new place had already burst. The untold wish now is to spend the remaining two days here in the comfort of the bed, in sleep and leisure. Gour almost took an oath, "Give a damn to the itinerary; I swear I would not walk anymore in this life."

Anjali taunted, "What a shameful condition you three are in! What we women had done with smiles had turned you men into tears!"

To this, our little Putu jokingly added, "Even we children had made it easily! Baba, you only act like an old haggard!" She continued laughing, and even a strong snubbing from Gour couldn't douse the laughter riot. Thus, Bhanu too had to shout in support, "Shut up, you laughing fellows!" to calm them down.

Meanwhile, Chandra was indifferently meddling with stocks inside his rucksack and innocently asked me, "Hey can you spare your toothpaste? Actually, I spent mine."

But his request, as innocent as it may be, gave me a chance to throw a little gibe at him, "What! Spent so quickly! How? That means you must have got some extra teeth!" Bhanu chipped in; he didn't want to sit back and waste the opportunity either, "Do you eat toothpaste?"

But Leena protested to this eye-soring banters at Chandrasekhar, "Behave yourself, can you!"

Putu lovingly requested, "Chandra uncle, can we be there at that hill? It's so beautiful."

Chandra eyed the hill to the east through the glass pane of the hotel windows, "Tomorrow we'll go there for sure."

Gour quickly interfered, "But Putu, I will never let you go anywhere without my permission."

Meanwhile with the vanishing of the devastating fatigue from the body, the bitter cold weather of the afternoon completely overpowered us. We quickly huddled inside the blankets together. With the day growing older, we crouched in the eight beds allotted, in the warmth of the thick quilts. Putu was with her mother.

After some moments of silence, Devaleena stated from under her cosy cover, "My stomach's rumbling, I'm hungry."

My wife supported her, "True. Blame it on our long walks. This has surely increased our appetite."

I couldn't agree more, "Not at all impossible. After all it's not our usual iron-laden drinking water back home, which forces us to fast at night after a hearty meal during the day."

While none of us was ready to leave our positions and challenge the freezing temperature of the afternoon, Chandra quickly got up, "You people keep resting. Let me see if I can be of any help."

I resonated, "Yes brother, please see if you can help. I'm too tired with you now."

Leena joked with a laugh, "Lazy bone."

Bhanu supported me, "Why, you're no less either."

The food that arrived afterward was something I would have gladly tossed out of the window had it been served to me at home. Syrupy khichdi, paper thin omelette, served with an ounce of pickle was what was dished out in the name of lunch. But alas! Did somebody call it Ambrosia! Why? Because the magic was not anywhere but hidden in the greatness of the place. I was hell bent for a siesta after lunch but failed to fulfil my wish, thanks to my family and friends. As a result, we walked through the bends of the road which trundled from Sandakphu ahead up to Phalut and then sat down in the open space in the middle of nowhere. The late-day sun now cast softer rays, while the cold wind brushed across a landscape painted in pastel greens and blues, where lush green hills stood in striking contrast to the serene blue sky.

Leena was mesmerised, "I will never forget this experience of a lifetime."

Putu remarked to his father, "Baba, can you imagine we're now the toppers of West Bengal."

Bhanu couldn't understand his daughter, shrugged, and frowned, "What nonsense!"

Putu answered, "Why? Don't you know that we're now standing at the topmost place of our State, the highest point."

Chandra was smiling. I understood this 'topper' word had been invented by him to preach a new concept of 'being a topper means reaching a new high.' Our team got busy in a friendly conversation. I was enjoying that too until I noticed that the children were getting cosier with Chandrasekhar. In a flash of a second, I was stunned, shocked, and flabbergasted all at the same time. I shouted at Neel for reasons unknown, "No, don't go to the edge of the cliff, come back to me." Neel's look in return was peeving! A kid is peeved at his own father! I felt nervous before my son's rebellious eyes.

Chandra meanwhile raised a point, "We have come here at a very nice time of the year."

"Why?"

"You'll find it. Wait for the night."

Gour mocked, "Nice things already had been meted out by you, dear. No more needed."

But then Devaleena's taunt was equally stinging, "Now stop behaving like an old haggard." She then told Chandra, "Why don't we walk up the road a bit?"

The other wives in the team agreed to her proposal in chorus. But we, the men, didn't even buzz from our seats. Chandra didn't either. I was surprised by that as I never expected such courtesy from a half-literate countryman like our friend.

"Chandra uncle, please come with us," there was an unmissable earnestness in the children's voices, too.

"Nah. Today, you carry on by yourself. I will join you tomorrow."

So, our overenthusiastic gang of wives and children continued walking on the bends of the hilly roads. Soon, the team vanished from our eyes on the faraway bend, and an eerie silence embraced us in this lifeless land. The silence was spooking us, and Bhanu could bear that no longer.

"Oh Lord, this killing quietness will now burst my ear drums."

I couldn't agree more. I never thought a calm and quiet place could be so unnerving. It was extensively uncomfortable.

I searched for words to speak to break the silence and asked, "Hey Chandra, are you still tutoring there in the village?"

"Yes", there was a noticeable smile through his thick beard.

"Did you open any coaching institute there?"

"Nah, I go to houses to teach students."

"Good Lord, what a waste of opportunity! Open an institute. It's quite a profitable job nowadays."

But Chandra only met the business idea with a smile.

"This is why you achieved no success in your life because you laugh at the opportunities that come your way." The conversations were heating up gradually and then suddenly Gour remarked, "Watch out, guys. It's getting dark, and our families are still stranded in this unfamiliar land."

Bhanu, too, poured concern in his voice, "Right. We didn't notice that. Shouldn't we walk ahead and look out for them?"

But Chandra showed no concern and casually remarked while adjusting the wrap of his shawl, "Don't worry. They'll be back soon."

But that couldn't stop Bhanu, "Huh! Now that's the callousness of a bachelor who doesn't know the value of a family – wives and children." He was growing impatient.

The rest of us were nervously thinking of a move while we heard the familiar chatter of known voices from the invisible bend of the road ahead. We felt content and thankful as we knew that our families were returning to us.

The clock went half-past-eight when we had already finished our heartfelt supper containing roti and cabbage curry and rolled under the warmth and comfort of our blankets. It was then Chandra rushed inside and hurriedly said in excitement, "Quickly come with me; I will show you something."

"Oh! Where?"

"Outside. Of course."

"At this hour of the night. Have you lost your mind?"

"No, but if you come along, you will surely lose yours."

Neel was clinging to her mother under the blanket, and he was the first to show interest, "What is it, Chandra uncle?"

"The Moon," Chandra's voice oozed excitement.

To this, Bhanu replied with utmost disregard, "Oh! The Moon. Good. You keep looking today. We'll try seeing it tomorrow morning instead."

"What are you saying, my friend? The reason for which you came here, you want to lose that?"

"Okay. We didn't deny that either, but you're being told that we'll take a look at it tomorrow," Gour's voice was more pacifying.

"Don't push your luck! Maybe tomorrow it will rain heavily, or someway there will be no visibility to enjoy such a view in the mountains."

Devaleena pushed us, "Let's go. If we could make up to here, then why can't we go outside?"

We men had to yield to our wives' cajoling, reluctantly leaving the comfort and warmth of our beds, wrapping blankets around us as we followed suit.

And outside what we witnessed had let me question myself about the greatest of the poems I had ever read about the moon! I couldn't remember who was the first person on the earth to write a line or two in the praise of the moon. I was trying to find the right expressions and the right words to describe the beauty I observed. But I found none.

It was literally a mercurial night soaked in silver, and on the depth of a dark blue sea above my head, there was a round maiden floating, spreading pearly aura. There were some glistening clouds, too, deep down the valley, who were looking up to us like white cotton from our quilts. Within seconds, we were out of words and dumbfounded. There was only one thing prevailing: our bewitchment before this fascinating beauty. And then Putu's sudden remarks felt just so befitting, "Uff! What a beauty!"

Chandra whispered, "*Kojagor*!"

Suddenly, from out of nowhere, a freezing, bone-chilling wind blew, which scared our hearts out. Bhanu sped back to the room with the frightening scream, "O God! Save me."

Chandra was indifferent and uttered words surely laced with lunacy, "Look down in the deep. I feel like jumping."

I laughed, "Go ahead. Jump."

But my wife was the more serious one among us and sternly stated, "Ahh! What kind of an answer is that? Chandra da, why are you moving closer to the cliff? Come back quick."

Chandra quickly followed with a smile through his thick beard. His teeth sparkled whiteness in the mercurial night.

III

Bhanu was furious when all of us returned, and he targeted his anger at Chandrasekhar, "This is too much of lunacy, Chandra. You're all grownups, and I couldn't object to your going out, but why are you persuading the children to follow you?" Chandrasekhar was caught unguarded by this sudden outburst and started fumbling, "Really... I didn't mean to... the beauty caught up with me so much that I..."

"To hell with your *beauty*. Who will be responsible if our children catch a cold or sickness?"

Anjali protested, "Why are you blaming him alone? We all went out together!"

"Why are you taking his side? Did he pay you for that!"

"Mind your language!"

"Don't ask a concerned father to mind his language because I can't get a doctor for my kid here in this hamlet in case of a medical exigency."

"Ahh! Don't fake your concern for Putu all of a sudden now. Never have you shown that in your whole life." Anjali's voice choked as she broke into tears.

"Wow! Really! So she's growing up on her own without her father?"

"Urgh! Bhanu! Now stop. What a mess you're creating at such an early hour of the morning!" Gour was forced to raise his voice now that the scene was about to go out of bounds.

Bhanu walked out in rage.

"Such a vile man he is; he has ruined my whole life," Anjali wept inconsolably.

"Anjali, please, calm down," my wife Leena said, holding her by her arms.

"Leena, you don't know what I'm going through..."

"Okay, okay, let bygone be bygone, Anjali."

Anjali threw herself in the bed, burying her face in pillows to hide her tears and pain.

The whole schedule got awry as the morning started in the worst of moods. Actually, we all went out early in the morning to witness the sunrise. Even the kids accompanied. But Bhanu didn't. In fact, we couldn't wake him up despite our best efforts. Now, when we returned, this was how Bhanu reacted.

So we stood there like idiots, not knowing how to react for some time till Devaleena gestured for us to move out from there. We couldn't agree more and took the opportunity. Gour remarked, "Curse my luck! What a mess of a situation! This laggard will neither go himself nor let us go."

Chandrasekhar was silent all through but now whispered, "We shouldn't have taken the children with us; otherwise, it wouldn't have been like this."

I was already upset with Chandra, and now his words sounded like unwanted meddling to my ears. I shot back, "If you had understood that…! Now at least shut your mouth."

Chandra went silent and distanced himself to a corner far from where we were standing.

Gour again commented in disgust, "It was a big mistake to invite Chandra with us."

The whole of our schedule was spoiled, and Anjali didn't agree to wake up from bed. We pursued Bhanu to go to her, but he was driven away, too. Under the burden of his wife's angry refusal, Bhanu proposed, "Let her be alone. There's no point in requesting her, so let's enjoy ourselves."

But none of our wives agreed to his proposal. I thought they resisted themselves in order to show support to the girl gang they had. The children took the side of their mothers and stayed back. So, the three of us roamed around a bit. In the afternoon, while returning, Gour pointed out, "Where's Chandra?" I admit, none of us marked his absence meanwhile and asked, "Hope he has decided not to return out of anger."

But Bhanu's mood was still hot, and he angrily remarked, "If that happens, that'll surely happen for good. I don't even want to see his face again. But that'll not happen. I bait, we will see him gossiping with our family back in the hotel."

And Bhanu was right because the moment we returned there, our moods flared. Because we could see Devaleena, Chandra and Leena were sitting on the floor immersed in some deep conversation while our kids were glued to him, busy playing. Anjali was no longer in tears and was talking fairly well while half laying in the bed. Her face still held a smiling expression while we entered as she tried vainly to hide her mood.

"Papa do you know who were the people who started to mummify their dead ones much before the Egyptians?"

Now I was in no mood to answer such questions and therefore gave back a stern, "No. Not at all."

Meanwhile, I was instead analysing whether Leena's sitting posture is too closer to Chandra's to raise my doubt on her character.

"Now where did you all go? Couldn't find you."

"Really? You tried looking for us? Which way?" I couldn't stand his pleading of innocence and ignorance anymore.

Coming out of the room Bhanu shouted in fury, "Chandra is sheerly playing with us."

Gour interfered, "Leave it. Tomorrow is the final day here. Let's have a drinking party tonight."

Bhanu made face, "And Chandra needs to be forced into it."

I raised doubt, "I don't think he will agree."

"Of course he will. After all, since it will be free for him, he will not lose the chance."

The truth is, none of us knows the real reason behind our repugnance about Chandrasekhar although there is no hiding about that feeling of rage or some similar unspecified feeling that we, the highflying friends hold against our poor childhood buddy. Among us, Bhanu is a ruthless CTO in the Sales Tax department, an alcoholic, and a notorious bribe-taker. On the other hand, Gour is a Regional Manager to his company. He possesses a beautiful private secretary who escorts him to pleasure trips twice every month citing office tours. While my other two friends have got such longer and stronger wings already spread over the world of vices, I had to remain content in a smaller world within the limit of a fixed government salary. However, that gives birth to a befitting sense of jealousy against my high-flying friends, but the fact is all three of us still flap much stronger wings in comparison to Chandra. We have always believed that we were considerate and kind-hearted every time we kept him with us. In return, we expected him to be grateful for our support. But somehow, we don't understand why our families can't see that our vagabond friend is no match for us. Is there some magic about him that we failed to notice, which is captivating our families despite all our desperate attempts to insult, demean, and abuse him? I sometimes feel guilty for mistreating him, yet he continues to stand by us shamelessly. In response to every cruel word we speak, he offers nothing but dignified silence, revealing a magnanimous side of himself that seems to defy the rich, successful image we hold dear. Why is he disregarding our position of power? Why does he challenge our egos? What more of us does he choose to ignore?

IV

Chandra politely refused the third peg.

We friends were bemused, "We know a Chandrasekhar who was a binge drunkard. What happened to that?"

"I couldn't digest anymore."

"What's that you couldn't digest anymore? Liquor? Or us?" Gour's voice sounds unmistakably candid while he keeps filling Chandra's glass with liquor.

Chandra smiled his silent smile. And this smile shook me every time with disgust.

Bhanu says, "Listen Chandra, you must understand that you can't run your life this way. Change yourself. Because you're only living a parasite's life, and trying to dramatize that life like that of a hero before our wives and children."

I felt alarmed at Bhanu's ruthless words, he must have been drunk by now after the three large pegs he had gulped. He was light with his words even a few moments ago, but what he's throwing now in the name of opinions are absolute threats.

Chandra remained silent.

"Why are you not speaking? Mince some words."

"I never intended to disturb you or interfere in your lives."

Hearing his words now, a sudden flash from the past appeared before my eyes: my wife, Leena, sitting close to him, talking and laughing together. With that, I couldn't hold back. Sipping and gulping a fiery dose from my glass, my lips got distorted, "Then what were your intentions?"

To this, Chandra's answer was utter innocence, "I didn't want to lose the chance of catching up with you all after a long time."

Gour mocked, "Us? That includes our family too?"

Chandra beamed, "Yes, the children, Putu and Neel, they're like flowers."

Bhanu, the vicious one he is, laughed out cruelly, "Huh! Flowers, are they? See Chandra, I am sorry to say that I clearly understood your hidden intention to come with us. But I must tell you that you've failed to succeed in your heinous intention since I will never let, neither my wife nor my daughter, to go any closer to you. They're still living on my money and I continue to possess them till we return home."

Bhanu has picked up his speed. My head was spinning, too, and in my tipsy condition, admittedly, I enjoyed all of his words. After all, there's no denying that he's speaking on behalf of all three of us. We felt the same deep inside us.

Chandra finally broke his silence, "Please don't talk like this, Bhanu."

So, finally, the words had hit him. Ah, and that's such a good feeling.

Gour shouted, "Then how should we have said it? You swine! How could you even think of demeaning and hating us? Do you even have the standard to do so?

"I never hate you, people."

"Then? Sympathy? Is it? You think you mercy upon us? Huh?" Bhanu is madly pissed off in his voice, "I pee on your mercy. Don't talk rubbish in front of me."

Chandra didn't utter anything else. He silently left the place.

But there's no stopping of Bhanu and he carried on screaming, "Why are you fleeing? Come back!" and then he started talking to himself, "And why blame outsiders when my own people are cheating upon me, bloody betrayers!"

Gour, tipsy as he was, but more content in his words, poured Bhanu another drink, "Leave it, forget it."

"Forget it? How? In what way we're lesser than him?"

Meanwhile before my eyes Leena's getting closer to Chandra, they're so close that Chandra's heated breaths are touching her shoulder, neck and deeper. The moment a hiccup arose deep down my throat, it opened the channel upto my stomach. I couldn't resist myself, puked, and spewed the last drop of liquid inside me. I felt like a complete blackout. My whole body went numb. I barely managed to drag myself to a corner and succeeded to sit with my back against the wall. And with my eyes wide shut I saw Chandra is walking away from me holding hands of my son, Neel. I couldn't bear anymore!

Suddenly Bhanu's voice came in between, "Look what you have done, littered the whole room!"

"I had drunk beyond the limit. I shouldn't have done it," my voice felt weak while responding.

"Then why did you have it?" Bhanu's voice smacked of disgust but I'm too feeble now to even react.

Meanwhile, I heard Gour murmuring, "But where's Chandra; where has he gone?"

"Where's the scumbug gone?"

The thought hit me, too. Really, he's nowhere to be seen.

"Must be enjoying life sitting on one of our wives' laps."

Bhanu raged, "The swine he is, I won't let this go on, I will not allow him to play around anymore."

So, mustering the remaining strength in our tipsy feet, the three of us stood up. As the three of us, barely-in-sense drunkards, managed to stumble out of the ground-floor dining room of the hotel, we found Chandra standing at a distance by a cliffside. And there was the mighty Kanchenjunga, too, standing still in the moonlit night much like a lump of cloud. Ahh... suddenly, I got goosebumps out of some unknown thrills I thought I was about to get. We, the three vicious souls, almost cruised through our way silently behind Chandra. Chandra didn't notice our presence. He was standing still.

"Chandra"

Chandra looked back hearing Bhanu's call. The amount of calmness in his eyes is intolerable.

"Look, you should be sentenced for your deed," Gour's voice sounded awfully drunk, but he managed to carry on somehow, "Undoubtedly, you're a worthless fellow, but… but, you somehow think of yourself as a great soul. You think you will cast your spell on everyone. But you're simply worthless. You're a failure in your life. You're jealous of us. So, there's no place for you in this world. So, so..." We were slowly moving towards Chandra with feeble steps.

Chandra was standing close too the cliff. The corner of Chandra's shawl was flying in the strong wind rising from the depth of the valley, flapping like white wings. I could see he has the longest and strongest of wings among the four of us.

Bhanu screamed in wild rage, "You go away forever, get lost," and pushed him towards the cliff end. Chandra looked surprisingly still. His eyes sans fear. I started having a peculiar feeling inside. The three of us together started pushing the old friend of ours from the cliff.

Gour yelled, "We're throwing you off the mountain, have some fear Chandra, please feel afraid, please cry for your dear life!"

Finally, by the cliffside, it was Bhanu who gave him the final push, "You go away, Chandra, Just go away." We joined hands with Bhanu in pushing Chandra but we watched in awe that Chandra was gliding through the deep gorge, his two wings resembling lumps of white clouds floating in the vast expanse. After some time, he melted amongst those white clouds flapping and fluttering. I felt like puking again.

"So, finally, it ends." Bhanu was laughing uncontrollably and loudly like a lunatic. Soon, the roll of laughter turned into a scream of crying. All of us did. But I can swear, we only meant to laugh. And laugh intensely for succeeding.

At that very moment, our children, Putu and Neel, arrived at the door of the dining room with a call. But the poor fellows were horrified to find their fathers and uncles vomiting all over the floor, covered in their own mess, laughing and crying hysterically, pushing against the walls, and rolling on the floor like madmen.